LEAGUE

of

AMERICAN
TRAITORS

LEAGUE

of

AMERICAN
TRAITORS

MATTHEW LANDIS

Sky Pony Press
New York

First Edition

This is a work of fiction. Names, characters, places, and incidents are from the author's imagination, and used fictitiously.

Sky Pony Press books may be purchased in bulk at special discounts for sales promotion, corporate gifts, fund-raising, or educational purposes. Special editions can also be created to specifications. For details, contact the Special Sales Department, Sky Pony Press, 307 West 36th Street, 11th Floor, New York, NY 10018 or info@skyhorsepublishing.com.

Sky Pony® is a registered trademark of Skyhorse Publishing, Inc.®, a Delaware corporation.

Visit our website at www.skyponypress.com
Books, authors, and more at www.skyponypressblog.com

www.matthew-landis.com

10 9 8 7 6 5 4 3 2 1

Library of Congress Cataloging-in-Publication Data available on file.

Jacket image: iStock
Jacket design by Sammy Yuen

Hardcover ISBN: 978-1-5107-0735-1
E-book ISBN: 978-1-5107-0738-2

Printed in the United States of America

To my students, who rule.
And to traitors everywhere, who suck.

"Traitors are the growth of every country, and in a revolution of the present nature it is more to be wondered at that the catalogue is so small than that there have been found a few."

— George Washington, September 27, 1780

———————————

CHAPTER ONE

Jasper flinched as his dad's casket hit bottom. The sound was cold and final, like a giant safe locking in place. There was also some creaking involved because the coffin was dirt cheap. It was the only one Jasper could afford. He was actually surprised it didn't splinter on impact.

"Would you like to say anything?" the funeral director asked. His name was Bill or Tony or something short. Jasper had been having trouble keeping details straight lately.

"I'm not really sure what to say," Jasper said.

"Some share fond memories of the deceased."

"Anything else?"

"People sometimes pray."

"For who?"

"Those the deceased left behind."

Jasper looked around the empty cemetery. "So, pray for myself."

"I suppose."

Jasper shivered in the late-September morning air. The paper-thin suit had felt like a wool jacket during his mom's funeral three months ago. That casket had been closed, too, on account of the tractor-trailer that had pulverized her car.

"Can I say something to . . . him?"

"Of course."

1

Jasper boiled it down to basics. He spoke from the gut. "You were my dad, but I never felt like your son."

Bill or Tony or something coughed.

"And I want to know why you didn't like us." He was pissed now, and it felt great. "Actually, I want to know what you liked instead of us, besides alcohol. You loved that. Couldn't wait to get your drink on."

Was it wrong to mock a dead person?

Who cared.

"You sucked as a dad and husband and she should have left you so—"

Rot in hell came to mind, but it wasn't genuine. Jasper's anger faded because the truth was actually way worse: he'd always wanted a dad. A real one who didn't just come around for awkward birthday dinners. Who wasn't an alcoholic.

You can't fix that now. Because you're dead.

"Thanks for being a horrible person."

A minute went by.

"Anything else?" the funeral director asked.

"No. I think that covers it."

Jasper kicked some dirt into the hole and walked to his car. The '86 Volvo would probably be the next thing in his life to die.

Two weeks ago, he'd gotten home from taking the SATs to find a detective in his driveway. The cop couldn't explain why Jasper's dad had been at a hotel in Charlottesville, Virginia, or how he'd drowned in a nearby pond. He'd been drunk (shocker), and after searching his hotel room, local police had settled on accidental drowning. His wallet and credit cards were still on him, so the cops didn't suspect foul play.

Jasper put his head on the steering wheel. Did hating his dad require knowing why the man had been such a complete mystery?

Didn't matter.

It was over.

I hate you.

"Excuse me, Mr. Mansfield." Somebody was knocking on the car window. "May I have a word?"

Jasper rolled down the window. "If this is about the house, I have another week."

"It's not." The man was a well-dressed statue: tall, lean, face like a granite slab. He had cold blue eyes that made you feel like a wolf's prey.

"What do you want?"

"There's something I need to discuss with you."

Jasper detected a slight British accent that the man was trying to hide. "Are you . . . a relative or something?" It was a long shot.

"No."

"And you want me to just come with you."

"Yes."

"You could be a serial killer."

"I give you my word that I'm not."

Jasper thought about that for a moment. Better play this one safe.

"Bye," Jasper said, slowing cranking the manual window up.

The man set his jaw. "What I have to discuss concerns your father's will. It won't take much of your time, but it is essential."

Jasper stopped cranking. "Essential for what?"

"For your future."

"Did he leave me any money? I could really use it for the house if he did."

"Unfortunately, he did not," the man said.

Of course he didn't. "Then, Mr. Not-A-Serial-Killer, I'm not interested."

"How do you know that when I haven't told you anything?"

Jasper turned the key in the ignition and willed the engine to catch. It choked twice before settling into a rackety hum. "My dad was never around. He didn't care about anybody but himself. I can basically guarantee you that his will reflects that."

The man tugged on the bottoms of his black leather gloves. For a second, Jasper wondered if he was going to strangle him. "*Nil desperandum*, Mr. Mansfield. I assume you're familiar with that phrase?"

Jasper blinked, pretending that he wasn't. "I have no idea what you're talking about."

The man made a scraping sound in the back of his throat. He handed Jasper a black business card through the gap in the window. "Try to not be such a brat the next time we meet."

A beat-up Crown Victoria that looked like a fake cop car pulled up and the guy moved to get in, then hesitated, and turned back to Jasper. "Cheer up," he said. "After all, you're not the one who's dead."

CHAPTER TWO

Jasper woke up shivering on the living-room floor. He'd rolled off the mattress again; the night terrors were getting worse. He climbed back on and pulled the covers to his neck. Her portrait stared down at him from above the fireplace. He wouldn't let the bank take it. He'd murder anyone who tried.

Somebody banged at the door. Jasper zipped his hoodie and peeked out a window. A big lady in khakis paced around the secluded gravel driveway.

"The bank notice said I don't have to be out for a couple more days," he called through the window.

"Hello? Are you Jasper Mansfield?"

"Yeah. What do you want?"

"Oh, hi. I'm Janine Tallison, your court-assigned guardian."

"I didn't ask for one."

"That's not how it works."

"How does it work?"

"When a minor enters the system, I help with the transition."

"What does that mean?"

"I place you with a foster family."

Jasper's stomach lurched. "Janine, I can tell you with a hundred-percent certainty, that's not going to happen."

"I realize this is hard, Jasper."

"Do you?"

"I've helped many kids transition—"

He gripped the windowsill. If she said "transition" one more time, he was going to throw a lamp at her. "Leave, please."

"Jasper—"

"Seriously, get out of here."

He slammed the window shut.

Janine paced around the driveway for another ten minutes, made a phone call, then left.

★★★★

Jasper's high school guidance counselor called the landline an hour later. Jasper let it go to voicemail, then deleted the message without listening to it. The guy called back at eleven, so Jasper ripped the phone from the wall. A couple kids from school texted, but he didn't respond. He ate ten pancakes and watched half a season of *Law and Order* before passing out. He dreamed somebody was after him, and woke up screaming around midnight.

The cable cut out the next day. Jasper figured that was probably because somewhere in the three-month mountain of mail was the cable bill he had no money for and no idea *how* to pay. The electricity went next. After the cable, that wasn't so bad. He'd been rereading his mom's guilty pleasure collection of Danielle Steel, anyway. It was the natural gas being cut off that led to the transformation of his home into a legit hermit's den.

Jasper spent that morning chopping wood and the afternoon worrying about what to eat. He'd cleaned out the perishables weeks ago and was working his way through the mountain of whole-wheat pasta that his mom had hoarded in the storage closet. Boiling water over an open flame in the fireplace was actually really hard/super dangerous, but he made it work. It was all he had left.

One week after Jasper buried his dad, the agent from the bank finally showed up to repossess the property. Or, at least, Jasper guessed it had been a week. The days had started running together since Janine stopped coming; Jasper had parked the Volvo behind the shed in an attempt to convince her that he'd taken off. The living room was a rat's nest cluttered with books, clothes, and heavy blankets, and Jasper smelled like a bum. He'd also grown pretty comfortable with the outdoor toilet situation, which was exactly where he was—whizzing in the high weeds beside the driveway—when the guy arrived.

"Brisk day," said Richard Corker. Jasper hadn't seen him since his mom's funeral, where the bank's agent had gone over the finer points of a sheriff sale in annoying detail. Jasper had forgotten how much the man looked like a pig. "Should we go inside and wait for Ms. Tallison?"

"Who?"

"Janine Tallison—your guardian. She'll be meeting us here to sign the papers on your behalf."

Jasper zipped his fly. He eyed the distance to the front door. He could definitely outrun the guy and lock him out. "What if I don't leave?"

"How do you mean?"

"Like, what if I just stay? What can you do?"

Mr. Corker scrunched up his pig face. "The police would escort you out—but that won't be necessary. Ms. Tallison said that she would be taking you to your foster family today."

Jasper caught sight of the gazebo in the backyard, and the pond behind it. The thought of another family using it brought on a familiar gag reflex. Or maybe it was hearing the phrase "foster family."

"I need another week," Jasper said. He had no idea where he was going with this, just that he needed to stall. Big time.

"Why?" Mr. Corker asked.

"Because . . ." he said, floundering for something—anything. "Because I am emotionally unstable. Any paperwork signed on my behalf wouldn't be admissible in a court of law."

Thank you *Law and Order* for that one.

"I don't think that's how it works," Mr. Corker said.

"Listen, Richard—can I call you Richard?

"It's Dick, actually."

Yes it was.

"Listen, Dick," Jasper said. The plan was forming now—he could see it taking shape as his brain came back online. Money . . . he'd need money. But first he had to get this guy to leave. "I am on the edge of a breakdown, okay? I am not leaving this house today. That's just a fact. Now, you can call the cops, in which case I will totally freak out and make a scene—lots of screaming and yelling and cursing, at you—and you and Janine will feel like horrible people—"

Dick's cell phone went off. He fumbled for it and answered, "Hello. Ah—yes. Hello, Janine." He listened for a while. "I see. Ah ha. Well, that's bound to happen in your line of work." Dick nodded. Looked at his watch. "No, that won't work, my afternoon is booked. No—tomorrow, too. What about Friday? Same time? Okay. Good. Yes, yes, I'll see you then."

Jasper was trying to do the math in his head. *Friday.* Three days. That should be enough time.

Dick put the phone back in his pocket. "It seems Ms. Tallison got held up in court, but is available this Friday. Is that agreeable to you?"

Jasper nodded.

"Friday, then." Dick got back into his car. "We'll be back Friday, October 5th."

Jasper sucked in a lungful of cold air. "Right. Okay—thanks."

Richard Corker did a five-point turn and drove away.

Jasper charged his cell phone in the Volvo's ancient cigarette lighter port and then took pictures of every item in his house. He walked to the far corner of the property and found an unsecured Wi-Fi signal, and posted the images on Craigslist. By dinner, he had twenty interested buyers. Anything he wanted to keep he shoved into the Volvo, starting with his mom's portrait.

Jasper didn't have an exact destination, so he packed a suitcase for each season; everything else went on Craigslist. When he came across the black suit he'd worn to both his parents' funerals, he wadded it into a ball and threw it in the fire.

A card fluttered out as the clothes went up in flames.

CYRUS BARNES
ATTORNEY-AT-LAW

Jasper turned it over and saw faint lettering on the back.

THE LEAGUE

He wondered if it had anything to do with the Latin phrase tattooed on his dad's left forearm—*Nil Desperandum*. Jasper thought about Googling it, then remembered that he didn't actually care. His dad was dead, and his secrets could rot with him.

★★★★

By Thursday night, every couch, bureau, desk, lamp, and table was sold. The back porch swing went, too, so Jasper counted his money on the cold stone patio. He'd netted almost six grand—more than enough to keep the Volvo gassed up for wherever he wanted to go.

The wind shifted and blew the gazebo screen door open. Jasper had avoided it because going in probably would induce an all-out breakdown. Definitely would. The tiny building had been their temple. His mom had written all her books there, Jasper curled up on the squeaky couch near her desk, lost in some fantasy book that was way better than his real life.

Jasper walked across the yard and stepped inside. He sat in her worn chair and ran his fingers over the writing desk. He could easily have gotten eight hundred for it, but the thought had never even crossed his mind. He opened the drawer and found a copy of her first novel. The heroine died at the end; he'd always hated that.

Underneath the book was an envelope. *To Jasper, Happy Birthday.*

He swallowed. She'd died a week before his seventeenth birthday. This was a message from the grave.

> *My dearest son,*
>
> *You will not always be a young man. A day is coming when you will be asked to act much older than you are, and I want you to be ready. Do not shy away from difficult tasks, for anything worth doing in this life will be difficult; do not give in to your emotions, lest they lead you astray. Do not fear the unknown, but make it known.*
>
> *Above all, remember who you are: my son.*
>
> > *All my love,*
> > *Your mother*

Jasper reread it three times, then tucked it inside the book and left.

That night, he cried himself to sleep.

CHAPTER THREE

Jasper walked out of his house on Friday, October 5th. He was shaking with nervous excitement. He didn't have a freaking clue where he was headed—he'd figure it out on the way. Jasper left the house key in the door. Court-assigned guardian Janine Tallison could choke on it.

The Volvo moved slower than normal because he'd stuffed it to the ceiling. People kept honking and passing him, so he turned down a side road that dropped toward the Delaware River. The road got steeper, and he pumped the brake.

Nothing.

He shoved his foot to the floor.

The Volvo went faster.

Jasper's stomach lurched. He yanked on the emergency brake, and the car slid sideways onto loose gravel. He cut hard to the right and straightened out, still gaining speed. Spotting the T-intersection ahead, he white-knuckled the wheel.

HONNNNNNNK.

He narrowly missed a two-ton gravel truck as the Volvo rocketed through the intersection and caught enough air to sail clear over the guardrail and into the river.

Jasper's vision splintered as he slammed into the steering wheel. Frigid water spilled in, reaching his waist in seconds. He couldn't feel his legs.

A morbid peace suffocated him: maybe death was just easier. Was there really anything left for him to live for? Wandering the Northeast until he ran out of money seemed super depressing. He should just surrender. It would be so easy.

The water reached his neck, and he whimpered. He could hold his breath for a while, but why? Better get it over with. He closed his eyes and prepared to inhale, praying the coroner wouldn't find traces of urine in the car.

Then water sloshed in his nose, and he started choking. He clawed at the seatbelt—what was he thinking?—but it was stuck. He kicked out, but his feet were lead.

Then, suddenly, he was free—somebody had set him free. A hand fumbled around his waist. Jasper gasped at the pocket of air near the roof as somebody grabbed his ankle and pulled him under. He surfaced seconds later, thrashing like an idiot.

"Stop." Her voice was iron, like her grip.

Jasper let himself be dragged to land, water flooding in his ears the whole way. His feet banged against the stony riverbed and he stumbled ashore.

"You might be the luckiest person on this planet," the woman said, panting.

Jasper was on all fours, coughing up water. He squinted at the soaked EMT: twenty-something, pretty, and obviously in way better shape than he was. Brown hair turned almost black from the water brushed her shoulders.

"Never had someone drive off the road right in front of our ambulance before," she said, less iron in her voice this time. "Didn't even have to turn the sirens on."

Jasper just sat there sucking in air. He was glad she'd saved him from an embarrassing death. What was he thinking, giving up like that?

"Is he stable?" shouted a guy from the road. The woman gave him a thumbs-up. Another EMT was diverting traffic.

She checked his pulse. "Can you remember what happened?"

"The . . . brakes." Jasper saw his stuff pop to the surface and float downstream. His clothes. The portrait. Gone. He had a hundred bucks in his pocket, but he'd stashed the rest in the glove compartment. "They wouldn't work. I kept pressing them . . . but nothing happened. I couldn't stop."

"That, I saw." She moved a penlight in front of his eyes. "Brake lines in those older cars go all the time. The good news is you're not still in it."

"Am I in shock?"

"Definitely."

That made sense. The world seemed weirdly calm, even though everything had just gone straight to hell. "I feel like I'm floating."

"Probably concussed, too. We need to get you to a hospital."

She helped him climb the slope to the ambulance, her hand firmly on his bicep. Some cars slowed to watch, but the ambulance driver waved them on. He seemed angry. Jasper climbed in the back and lay down on the gurney. The guy fumbled with the straps like it was his first time. The ambulance started moving.

A hard shiver jolted Jasper. The shock must've been wearing off. *"Idon't h-haveinsurance."*

The woman put an IV in his arm. "Not a problem."

Jasper thought he saw the EMTs trade looks. Then, again, he was shaking like an earthquake. *"Oralotof m-money."*

"Don't worry about it," the guy said. He flicked a syringe.

"Whatisthat?"

"To help you focus."

The man emptied the syringe into Jasper's IV.

A warm sensation spread across his chest and quickly escalated to burning. Jasper's heart rate doubled.

"Jasper, I'm going to ask you some questions, and you're going to answer them." The woman got two inches from his face. All iron again. "Did Cyrus Barnes give you anything at your father's funeral?"

"What?"

13

She slapped him, hard. "The lawyer. Did he give you anything at the funeral?"

Panic clawed at Jasper's throat. How did this random lady know his dad was dead and that Cyrus Barnes had been at the burial?

"Who are you?"

She pulled his T-shirt up. The other EMT unpacked a defibrillator kit and pressed the shock pads to Jasper's chest. A high-pitched whine started, then grew louder.

"Answer the question."

Jasper gaped stupidly.

"Hit 'im."

Jasper screamed. The charge felt like a grenade going off inside his chest cavity.

"Did Cyrus Barnes give you something at your father's funeral?" the woman yelled.

"No!" Was that him wailing? Jasper's mind spun. Were these people after Cyrus—and now *him*? What did Jasper have to do with *any* of this?

She slapped him again. *"Liar!"*

"His card . . . *just* his card."

Her eyes narrowed, and he knew she didn't believe him.

The next shock lifted him off the gurney.

"The *research*!" she screamed. "Where is it?"

"What are you *talking* about?"

"We've got company," the driver yelled.

The woman peered out the back window and cursed. "Increase the voltage."

"He can't take much more," the guy said.

"Do it!"

"Hold onto something," the driver shouted. The ambulance bucked to the right. Both medics fell as supplies rained down from the shelving units.

"Time's up," the guy said.

14

The woman groped her way back to Jasper's side. "I'm not done with this traitor yet."

Both EMTs flew into the bulkhead as the ambulance slid to a stop. Jasper kicked against his restraints and wriggled free. He ripped the IV from his arm and scrambled for the door. His fingers were on the latch when he started choking.

"WHERE IS IT?" The woman had wrapped the IV cord around his neck and wrestled him to the ambulance floor. "When I let go, you're going to tell me."

Jasper's vision narrowed. He clawed at her hands. It all seemed so incredibly stupid.

My father's research?

IT?

He was going to die in a state of total confusion.

The ambulance doors swung open. A man with a shaved head and muscles everywhere pointed a silver pistol at the woman's skull. "Let him go."

She tightened the cord. "You wouldn't dare."

He pistol-whipped her across the face. As she went limp, the cord loosened from around Jasper's neck.

The gunman dragged Jasper to the fake cop car from the funeral. A guy in the back seat with silver hair was staring out at him. Jasper strained his vision to make out the figure. Was that . . . the lawyer? Cyrus . . . Barnes.

Cyrus cleared his throat. "I assume you are ready to discuss your father's will, now?"

CHAPTER FOUR

J asper shoved himself up to sitting. He tried to say "yeah" but it came out all croaky.

"Very good," Cyrus said. He rolled down the window and whistled.

The bald, retired-UFC-looking dude checked the woman's pulse, then shot a hole in the ambulance tire. A tall black guy in jeans and a leather jacket Jasper hadn't seen before held the EMTs at gunpoint as he backed slowly toward the Crown Vic and slid into the backseat. UFC took the wheel and reversed down the dirt road at a clip, cutting a sharp angle that sent the car into a one-eighty. Without taking his foot off the gas, he corrected the turn and tore down the winding road.

"Assessment, Byron," Cyrus said.

The gunman took Jasper's pulse and checked his pupils, just like the woman with iron hands and voice had. "He'll live."

Around three minutes later, Jasper started crying.

It was embarrassing to have a meltdown in front of these special-forces dudes, but whatever. He'd just almost been murdered.

Byron handed Jasper a water bottle and went back to scanning the countryside.

"You were following me," Jasper said to Cyrus.

"When I want something, I go after it no matter the cost. Your father and I had that in common."

"Really?"

"There is much you don't know about him—information that may give your relationship context."

"Context?" The bottle crinkled as Jasper clenched his fist around it. "My dad pretended that my mom and I didn't exist for seventeen years. The context of our relationship is that I hate him."

"And you might still feel that way when we're finished. But at least you'll have the full picture."

Jasper thought of the iron woman—how she'd called him a traitor. And how she'd wanted his dad's . . . research? Is that what Cyrus meant?

Jasper recognized the on-ramp to I-95; his mom used to go this way to see her publisher in the city. "Where are we going?"

"Philadelphia. My firm is headquartered in Center City." Cyrus looked out his window. "Black van, Larkin. Four o'clock."

Byron shoved Jasper's head down and drew his weapon. Jasper heard the soft click of the safety sliding off. His heart pounded. Larkin changed lanes and punched the gas.

"Not following us," Byron said, letting Jasper up.

Thirty minutes later, Larkin exited toward I-676 and central Philly. He cut through the city, avoiding intersections that put them in standstill traffic for too long. At every light, Byron readied his pistol. *Who wants me dead?* Jasper thought. He wondered if Cyrus and the gunmen—whoever they were—had the wrong kid. It would be really awkward if all this were a giant mistake.

But they'd obviously been following him for a while. And Cyrus didn't seem like the kind of guy who made mistakes.

Context.

Logic said there was more to the story.

It's not like Jasper had a choice anyway.

Near City Hall, Larkin turned into an underground parking garage and drove to a freight elevator. Byron did a sweep of the area and signaled the all-clear. Jasper followed Cyrus and Larkin inside. Byron shut the outer wooden slats before the elevator doors closed, and headed back to the car.

Twenty floors up, the doors opened onto a large foyer. No big signs or marble counters, just a desk and lots of people buzzing around dressed in professional clothes. It was like a really nice law firm had once been here, but they'd moved out and left these people behind.

"Counselor." A woman in heels and a high-waisted skirt met them at the doors. Amber hair twisted in a tight bun. Jasper pegged her for thirty and way out of anybody's league. "All go as planned?"

"With a slight variation," Cyrus said.

"Lunch is ready."

"Jasper will take his in the conference room. I have some calls to make."

She pressed a finger to her Bluetooth headset. "Send lunch to the conference room. Forward the Counselor's calls to me."

"Jasper, this is Sybil," Cyrus said. "She is my paralegal. I consider her an extension of myself, as can you."

"Anything else, Counselor?" Sybil asked.

"Please escort Jasper to the restroom. He requires a change of clothes."

Jasper followed her down a wing to a giant bathroom. He emptied his bladder and smelled himself. It wasn't good.

There was a knock at the door and Jasper poked his head out.

"Shower," Byron said, shoving a towel and clothes at Jasper through the opening.

Jasper stripped down and looked in the mirror: bloodshot eyes, burn marks on his chest, a red stripe across his neck. A hunch that shrunk him below his normal six feet. Ribs poking out where they shouldn't. He must have lost twenty pounds since his mom died. His blondish-brown hair was months overdue for a cut, the ends curling near his eyes.

In the shower, he scraped off layers of river sludge and sweat. He took his time getting clean. Who was he that people wanted him alive, showered, and dressed? *Traitor.* Jasper shivered under the hot water.

Where did the iron woman fit into this? And his father's research, whatever that was?

Unsure what to do with his dirty clothes, he shoved them in the corner, then put on a white dress shirt and dark skinny slacks. Apparently Cyrus wanted him to blend in with the employees. He slipped on the dress shoes but left the vest and tie on the rack.

Outside, Sybil set a quick pace back down the hall Byron trailing behind them. "Much better, apart from the hair. A little long, isn't it?"

"Yeah." Jasper's chest ached. His mom had always cut his hair to save money.

Sybil left Jasper in a conference room with floor-to-ceiling windows. If they were open, he could have pissed on City Hall. He ate a grilled-something sandwich and slurped down some soup, seated at a giant oval table, wondering if it'd be rude not to offer Byron any. Body-guarding had to be hard work.

Sybil returned twenty minutes later. They snaked back toward the bathroom and then turned down a hallway that dead-ended outside of Cyrus's office. The lawyer waved Jasper into a hilariously huge space—a studio apartment, really. It was mostly empty except for a desk, a bookshelf, and a few leather chairs, probably leftovers from the rich firm days.

"Please, sit," Cyrus said.

Jasper settled on a chair edge. His knee bounced rapidly. The soup and grilled-something sandwich fought each other in his gut. He should have eaten slower.

Cyrus sat opposite him. "This morning was rather traumatic for you. The last few months have been as well, I'm sure."

"I think that's an epic understatement." Then it hit Jasper. "My dad was in the mafia, wasn't he?" It was logical—the long absences, the drinking. "And you're the mafia lawyers. And that lady was with another mob family. They wanted to whack me because my dad ratted somebody out."

"No."

"You're sure?"

"Positive."

It had been worth a shot.

"Jasper, did you go to public school?" Cyrus asked.

"Private."

"Did you have many friends?"

Jasper shrugged. "Sure."

"They came over to the house. Stayed the night?"

"I usually went to their places."

"Why?"

"My dad was weird about people coming over."

"What else was he weird about?"

"Me having a phone. Social media. Getting my license."

"Your father was against all of these?"

"Yeah."

"Did you find that strange?"

"I found it ironic. The only part of parenting he wanted was the not-letting-me-do-stuff bit."

"Did your mother ever tell you why he acted that way?"

"His job, or something. All the sleazy people he met selling medical supplies."

"I see."

Jasper didn't like that answer—too leading. "What's that supposed to mean?"

"I'm trying to point out that your father went to great lengths to keep you secluded."

"Him being a weirdo doesn't explain why some random lady just tortured the crap out of me."

"True enough." Cyrus stood up and got a folder from his desk, then handed it to Jasper. "Her name is Elsbeth Reed."

Jasper examined a grainy picture. She looked different without the EMT gear, but the photo had captured the same pyscho, dead-eyed stare. "So obviously you know who she is."

"Elsbeth is the fifth-generation descendant of Joseph Reed—George Washington's right-hand man during the American Revolution. She hates you because your ancestor betrayed hers."

"Which ancestor?"

Cyrus adjusted his frameless glasses. "Benedict Arnold."

CHAPTER FIVE

Jasper had a flashback to AP US History. "The guy who switched sides to help the British?"

"Yes."

"The traitor."

"The same."

"I'm related to him."

"You are his sole surviving heir."

Jasper waited for more. The lawyer said nothing. "That's kind of a letdown."

"Is it?"

"Are you *sure* you're not in the mafia?"

Cyrus did that throat-clearing thing. "Quite."

"I'm just saying the mafia makes a lot more sense than all this happening because I'm related to some guy who betrayed America two hundred years ago."

"Two-hundred and thirty-seven years."

"Right. . . . See, this is my point. The Revolution is ancient history. There is no way that anybody cares about what some guy did that long ago. Aren't we best friends with England now? I mean, we joke about their teeth but you can get fish and chips anywhere."

"Arnold's treason still enrages the True Sons of Liberty—the descendants of America's Revolutionary generation," Cyrus said. "To them, his treachery lives on through you."

Jasper rubbed his temples. *Arnold's treason. True Sons of Liberty.* Somewhere, Nicholas Cage was having the last laugh.

"You have to get how stupid this sounds. I'm not trying to be difficult—you saved my life. And you gave me these really nice clothes. But, come on."

"Three months ago, your father informed me that he believed he was being followed. I had Larkin tail him." Cyrus motioned to the folder.

Jasper pulled out a still from a security camera. People stood in line at a desk with luggage stacked in front of it.

"These pictures are from the lobby of your father's hotel, taken the night he drowned. Please note the figure ducking into the stairwell."

Jasper squinted.

And then he shivered so hard it must have looked like a muscle spasm.

The iron woman.

"Are you saying—" The room tilted for a second. "What *are* you saying?"

"I believe she murdered your father because she didn't get what she wanted. Then she tried to claim it from you."

"The research?" Jasper raised a hand to his neck again. "*It?* But I don't know what *it* is."

Cyrus went to his desk and paged Sybil. "We are about to find out."

A minute later, Larkin and Byron wheeled in a slate-colored safe that came up to Jasper's chest when he stood up to examine it. It was old and heavy—the kind you needed explosives to break into. For this one, maybe a rocket launcher.

"What's in it?"

Cyrus handed Jasper a leather-bound folder. "Your inheritance."

Jasper stumbled through the first paragraph of the single page—all clauses and compounded references to the Testator (his dad) and the Executor (Cyrus).

"Article three," Cyrus said.

Jasper moved down the page:

I devise, bequeath, and give to my son, Jasper Mansfield, all my research contained within the safe residing in the basement vault of the League of American Traitors headquarters.

"What's the League of American Traitors?"

"A collection of families whose ancestors ended up on the wrong side of American history. Revolutionary traitors such as Arnold."

"And my dad was a part of it?" Jasper asked.

"He was."

Context. "So he when he was away . . . he wasn't selling medical supplies."

"Not exactly."

"What was he doing, then?"

"That is the question." Cyrus let his statement hang for a moment. "You must first understand that the True Sons of Liberty follow a strict honor code that prohibits naked aggression. Your father's murder and your abduction are unusual."

"A code?"

"*The* Code. Under it, violence is strictly limited to duels. The Oligarchs—the True Son's ruling elites—consider it Scripture."

Things were sliding back toward the ridiculous. "As in 'I challenge you to a duel.' Glove-whipping. Swords."

"Pistols are preferred." Cyrus said it casually, which freaked Jasper out. Like it was totally normal to face someone and blow them/get blown away. "Breaking the Code is dishonorable, and the True Sons of Liberty value honor above all else. Thus, I suspect that whatever your father was looking for, that thing threatens their organization uniquely."

Don't ask. Just walk out. These people are delusional.

But Elsbeth Reed—she wasn't nothing. She'd attacked him. That had happened.

And the will, the safe—they were right here. Okay, so the explanation for this whole thing was completely insane, but it was evidence of *something*.

This wasn't the mafia.

"What was my dad working on?" Jasper asked.

"I have no earthly idea."

"If you had to guess?"

Cyrus let the silence stretch out for a moment. "A way out. If I had to guess."

"Out? Of what?"

"Out of your duel."

Jasper had that floating feeling again—blood diving from his head to his toes. His lungs were working really hard, but also seemed to not be working. "No . . . I'm not . . . into guns. I'm good."

"Jasper, your ancestor is the most hated man in American history. When you turn eighteen, this office will receive hundreds of official requests challenging you to a duel. You will only have to accept one, but the Code demands that you accept."

"I'll run away, then. I don't care." The office felt weirdly small. Was that wall moving toward him? "This is *insane*."

"You can choose to hide, like your father—many do—and the League will help you. But you will be in violation of the Code, and the True Sons of Liberty will hunt you down, take your property, harass you, make your life impossible—barely a life at all. However, if you choose to duel, and if you survive, you are free to live in peace—no one will bother you again. That is the Code."

Jasper swallowed some bile. "So I can run—and maybe die—or stay, and definitely die. Or become a murderer."

"Perhaps you should sit."

"I'm good."

Jasper swayed and grabbed the edge of the safe.

Then he puked.

CHAPTER SIX

S orry," Jasper said to the janitor.

The man grunted as he rinsed out his mop.

"Would you like anything else to eat?" Sybil asked.

"No. Thanks."

"I ask because most of your lunch is on the floor."

"Yeah. No, I'm fine."

She pointed to a spot the janitor had missed. Jasper's blast radius had been impressive.

Byron came in with a clean shirt. He also had a thick, black coat that would reach Jasper's knees.

"Join me on the roof," Cyrus said. It wasn't a request.

Gray clouds hung low over the city. The wind cut like glass at this height. Jasper watched people jaywalk around City Hall and wondered how they'd react if he told them the descendants of the Founding Fathers wanted him dead because he was related to Benedict Arnold. Would they care? Would they even believe him?

Insane. All of this is insane.

"You are not the first to react so dramatically," Cyrus said. "Learning of one's lineage can be difficult."

"Lots of people have puked in your office?"

"Most cry. Your father did."

Something shifted in Jasper's chest. "My dad cried?"

"Your father learned of his past as you did, through his father's will. He took it very hard. According to the notes of my predecessor, he wept."

"When was this?"

"Just before your first birthday."

Jasper leaned on the cement wall. A pigeon landed nearby and eyeballed him. *Context.* "Why didn't he tell me?"

"I can't answer that. And it doesn't matter."

"His whole life being one epic lie kind of matters to me."

"Why?"

"You're serious?"

"Would you feel better if he was an honest man?"

"For starters. Or if he'd just been present. I would have settled for that."

"The best guard dogs do not stay inside the fold while wolves gather," Cyrus said. "They prowl outside, searching out danger."

So his dad was trying to help him? But hold on.

"Do the guard dogs also come to your birthday parties drunk? Or bolt from their wives' funerals, leaving their sons to navigate sheriff sales of their houses alone? Is that normal guard-dog behavior? If you're about to tell me that I shouldn't care about any of that because he did all of this for me, I'll probably puke. Again."

Cyrus stared the pigeon down, and it flew away. "I did not promise you a better father, Jasper. Only a fuller picture of the one you had. You are free to hate him, but do not let that hatred cloud your judgment."

Jasper's mom had said that in her birthday message. "Did she know, my mom?"

"I imagine so."

Maybe that's what her letter had meant—she'd been trying to tell him the truth.

A wave of nausea washed over him. "Her car accident . . ."

"A tragedy, but unrelated. I investigated it myself."

Jasper's stomach felt calmer. There was no way he could handle her dying because of this mess. "It feels like I'm in that movie, *The Matrix*," he said. "Blue pill, red pill situation."

"I'm not familiar with that film."

Big surprise there. "There's no going back, is there?"

"If there were, would you want to?"

Jasper saw himself in the car with court-assigned guardian Janine Tallison, driving to a foster home. Or shivering in the parking lot of a McDonald's, counting how much money he had left. "I guess not. But I don't really want to go forward, either. Dying wasn't really in my immediate plans."

"We all die, Jasper. The question is, what will we die pursuing, and is that cause worthy of our lives?"

A beam pierced the gray canopy, and then another. Jasper watched a hole open up as two clouds drifted apart. Sunlight poured onto City Hall. "His research—this way out. You want me to pick up where he left off? Try and figure it out?"

"Fight or hide—those are the only choices League members have. But you have been offered a middle path, and ten months to plot a course through it."

"Are you gonna help me?"

"I have already enlisted several students at our academic institution to do just that."

"You guys have a school? In Philly?"

"Northern Vermont. It's remote and well-guarded."

So . . . Hogwarts. And plenty of bad stuff happened to Harry there. "And what happens if I can't find anything? My dad was working on this most of my life and I've got less than a year to figure it all out or die."

"Like all League members, you will learn to use a gun in the event you choose to duel. I leave the choice of whether you'll accept your challenge to you and your instructor."

28

The clouds drifted back together, sealing out the light again. Jasper could smell rain coming.

Run.

Die.

Kill.

These weren't choices. They were sentences.

Insane. All of it.

But did that make it any less real? People wanted him dead—that was one hundred percent true. Jasper had no money, no home, or a foster home future, all of which utterly depressed him. Also true.

"You should really watch *The Matrix*," he finally said. "People will get the analogy. It would help with the transition."

"Have you decided, then?"

"I wouldn't call it a decision. I have nowhere else to go."

Cyrus turned to face Jasper. "*Nil desperandum.* Do you know the translation?"

Jasper shook his head.

"Never despair. It has been the Arnold family motto for three centuries—your father had it tattooed on his arm, inscribed it on his flesh. Now you must carry the mantra. There is no one else."

A raindrop hit Jasper's face. The storm was here.

"All right," he said. "I'm in."

CHAPTER SEVEN

Byron and Larkin didn't care that 30th Street Station was a ghost town. The gunmen stood so close to Jasper they were basically on top of him. Cyrus bought two tickets and the four descended to the tracks below to wait for the 5:07 AM train to Springfield, Massachusetts.

"Byron will deliver you to an escort in Springfield," Cyrus said. "The escort will drive you north to Juniper Hill Academy, our school in northern Vermont. You'll arrive by early afternoon if there are no incidents."

Jasper tugged on the handle of his suitcase. Byron had packed it at some point while Jasper had tossed and turned on the couch in Cyrus's office. Other than the safe and a prepaid phone, the case was the only thing Jasper had left in the world. "*Incidents*. Like another ambush?"

"Our escorts can handle themselves. Don't worry," Cyrus said. "Your safe will be delivered to you in a few days. By then, you'll have met your research team and settled in. I'll visit periodically to evaluate your progress and offer whatever support is needed. Do you have any questions?"

"So there're other kids at this school whose ancestors did other bad stuff in American history."

"Correct."

"Saying it out loud makes it sound even more insane, you know."

"That's to be expected."

"I still don't get why I even have to go to school," Jasper said. "I mean, I have ten months to live."

"The headmistress is not in the habit of bending rules, in spite of your circumstances." Cyrus waited a beat. "But I'd have you attend classes anyway to maintain appearances."

Jasper heard the train whooshing into the station. "Appearances?"

"I cannot prove it," Cyrus said, lowering his voice, "but I believe the True Sons have somehow wormed their way into our organization. That would explain how they knew where to find your father. And you."

"So, you think people from their secret organization are spying on your secret organization."

"I do."

"Sounds a little paranoid," Jasper said. Actually it sounded completely paranoid and totally ridiculous.

Sort of a theme lately.

"Maybe," Cyrus said, "but we must protect against the possibility that they have informants within the League. That is why you must carry on as a normal senior, and that means attending classes. The safe—the entire project—must be kept secret."

The train came to a stop. A few people spilled out looking like they wished they had jobs that didn't require a 5:07 AM train. Byron walked into the car and scoped things out.

"Thanks . . . for watching out for me," Jasper said.

Cyrus shook Jasper's hand, hard—a man's handshake. Probably the first Jasper had ever had.

★★★★

Jasper fell asleep before the train pulled away, one of those deep, black canvas of nothing, too deep for dreams, sleeps. It was probably the first real rest he'd had since his mom died.

He woke at ten and followed Byron to the dining car. The body-guard bought them each two sausage biscuits and a bottle of orange juice, which Jasper drained on the walk back to their seats.

"So," Jasper said after inhaling a biscuit. "You're in the League, too?"

Byron just kept staring straight ahead down the aisle.

"Right. Stupid question." It was gonna be a long ride. "Thanks, by the way. For yesterday."

"You're welcome."

That was an improvement.

"So, did you ever duel?" Jasper asked.

Byron might've growled.

"Is that rude to ask? Sorry. It's my second day."

He drummed his fingers and watched the countryside whizz by. Woods. Fields. Towns. Highways. Most of the Northeast really looked the same.

"What about asking people about their past? Is that rude?"

"Depends on the person."

Jasper couldn't help himself. "What did your ancestor do?"

Byron made a sucking sound with his teeth.

"Sorry. Never mind."

"He fought in the king's army during the Revolution," Byron said.

"Like my ancestor."

"No." It was hard to tell if Byron was angry because he always wore that stone-cold killer mask. "Mine left his patriot master because the king promised land in Canada to all runaways."

It took Jasper four seconds to get it.

Master.

Runaways.

Slavery.

"That sucks," Jasper said. His face burned hot. *That sucks?* Obviously it sucked. Understatement of the era. "Sorry—"

"There was no land." Byron's jaw muscles rippled.

Jasper raised the orange juice bottle. "To getting screwed by the past."

Instead of returning the toast, Byron took out a hardcover book and shoved it into Jasper's hands. "Biography of Arnold. Counselor said you'll want to get a head start."

"Okay." It beat trying to make conversation.

An hour later, the train pulled into Springfield. Jasper trailed Byron through the small station to a massive, dual-cab black pickup truck jacked up high over mud tires. A lanky man around fifty climbed down and shook Byron's hand. He had tanned skin and salt-and-pepper hair that brushed his shirt collar. His jeans and work boots gave off a mountain vibe. A kid dressed pretty much the same way tossed Jasper's black suitcase in the rear cab.

"Colton Donelson." He had long hair like the man, but a wider grin. He was probably a little older than Jasper. "That's my daddy, Rufus. Nice to meet you."

"Jasper."

"I know who you are." The last two words slurred together. *Yar.* "Back seat's yours."

Jasper figured Byron wasn't the type to go in for a hug, so Jasper thanked him with a nod. Byron returned the gesture.

"Welcome to New England," Rufus said. The truck rumbled to life and pulled onto the highway heading north. "First time?"

"Yeah."

"We ain't natives neither—from Tennessee, originally." Rufus drove with one hand on the wheel, like he was joyriding.

Jasper didn't see any guns. Was this really a security detail? He wished Byron had come along.

A walkie-talkie crackled next to Rufus. He grabbed it and said, "I see ya."

Jasper turned and spotted another truck rolling up behind them. He let out a breath.

"Chilly rolled out the red carpet for you," Colton said.

"Manners," Rufus told his son.

"Who?" Jasper asked.

"Headmistress Chillingsworth," Colton replied.

Rufus took an exit and wound along a back road to an industrial yard. Twenty guys with pump-action shotguns stood around a third pickup. They broke into three groups and hopped into the truck beds. One of them banged on the cab and Rufus took off toward a shadowy set of hills way off in the distance.

Now we're talking.

Colton pulled a sawed-off shotgun from under his seat. Jasper couldn't not stare.

"Pretty good looking, ain't she?"

"Yeah."

Colton half-turned and slung a big arm over the back seat. "Lacy."

"What?"

"That's her name."

"You named your gun *Lacy*."

"Kind of a tradition where we come from to name a weapon after the women who broke our hearts. Metaphorical, and all. Couple of my brothers and cousins—them boys in the back—some of them use their mamas' names, but that's always risky on account of them finding out. Point is, I'd start thinking of one before Kingsley gets ahold of you."

"Who's Kingsley?"

"He's the weapons instructor at Juniper Hill. You'll meet him soon enough, and then wish you hadn't. But he's the best shot this side of the Mississippi, my daddy notwithstanding. He'll be the one to train you. You ever held a gun before?"

"No."

"Keep that to yourself or Kingsley'll blow a gasket. He's Irish, and all, so when he cusses it's hard for me to tell exactly what he's saying, but I'd just as assume it was all profanity, being that it usually is."

Jasper's gut was knotting harder by the second. "Okay."

"Real sorry to hear about your parents."

"Yeah." Jasper liked the way Colton said it—straight-faced. No pity. "Thanks."

"Now Old Hickory—he being our ancestor—was fourteen when he was orphaned. Already fought in a war, too. Hard times makes you harder is what I'm saying."

Another AP flashback. *Old Hickory.* "You're related to Andrew Jackson?"

"Not by blood, on account of him not having any kids. But yeah, we trickled down from his adopted kin."

"But—" Better just state the obvious and see where it went. "Jackson wasn't on the wrong side of American history. He was a pretty popular president. He's on the twenty-dollar bill."

Colton flashed white teeth. "We ain't in the League officially. More like hired help. See, them Libertines never did like us on account of Jackson's low class and all—"

"What're Libertines?"

"True Sons of Liberty, same difference. Got your Washingtons, your Jeffersons, your Reeds—them three Oligarch families run the whole thing—and some other names you'd probably know."

Jasper's hand went to his neck. *Reed.*

"You all right?" Colton asked.

"Everything's just sinking in."

"How'd you get them marks on your neck?"

"Leave it," Rufus said.

Jasper caught his eye in the rearview mirror. Had Cyrus told them about the ambush? *Trust no one.* "You guys used to be a part of the . . . Libertines?"

"I wouldn't call us participants exactly," Colton said, "but yeah, we was members till a couple years ago."

"What happened?"

Colton looked at his dad.

"Libertines never did think we had enough bite," said Rufus.

"Our kin don't duel," Colton said. "Ironic as it is, being that Jackson was pretty famous for that sorta thing."

"So the True Sons—" Jasper started.

"Libertines."

"Right—Libertines—they make all their members duel?"

"More or less," Rufus said. "Part of their honor culture."

"Did you guys?" Jasper asked.

"Jackson did enough damage—his Native American policies, and all," Colton said. "My daddy and his brothers figured why spill more blood? No honor in that, 'specially not in killing somebody's grand-baby that we ain't ever even met."

Jasper bobbed his head. "That's what I told Cyrus. This whole thing is insane."

"One man's crazy is another man's justified," Rufus said. "They got guns, and they got their Code. Plenty of resources to hunt down your kind when y'all run away, too." He let out a big sigh. "When them True Sons pushed us out, seemed only natural to lend a hand and even the field."

They crossed into Vermont and the shadowy hills turned to moun-tains—the Green Mountains, Colton said. Nothing like his Great Smokies apparently, but tall enough. The forest got thicker and blazed fall orange. The trucks climbed steep switchbacks that could barely be called roads—potholes, mostly, with asphalt and dirt. Jasper kept wait-ing for Colton to say, "Be there soon" but then the trucks descended a ridgeline and started climbing again. Jasper could have sworn they were going in circles.

Three hours in, Rufus almost rear-ended the lead truck when it skidded to a halt. Jasper held his breath as men fanned out in a giant oval around the trucks, scanning the mountainside.

"Downed tree," the walkie crackled.

Rufus got out and supervised the removal.

"Easy now," Colton said. "Never seen a Libertine this close to campus. Even they ain't that stupid."

Jasper noticed Colton still held Lacy ready.

An hour later, the caravan crested a ridge. The road turned straight as an arrow and smooth underneath. Ahead, Jasper spotted an old iron gate with ten-foot brick walls fanning into the forest on either side. A faded placard on the brick read Juniper Hill Academy, Est. 1935. Ten guys in jeans and flannel shirts opened the gate and let the trucks through. A couple carried assault rifles. Two held back barking German shepherds.

Trees lined the lane like a colonnade, half of them dead or dying. The front and rear trucks peeled off toward some crumbling cottages, but Rufus stayed straight, aiming for a big, square building at the end. Jasper counted twenty dormers jutting out along the second story, most missing shutters. The white stucco had black streaks like it had barely survived a fire. Overgrown walkways cut through overrun hedges, all of it covered by a foot of dead leaves. The place looked abandoned, like fifty years ago the school had closed and let the forest take over.

Rufus pulled around the front loop and shut off the truck. A girl with brown, curly hair and a billion freckles waited on the walkway dressed in jeans and a faded hoodie. Not skinny or fat, and pretty in the kind of way you'd say your sister was.

Colton stowed his shotgun and jumped out. "Hey Lace—"

She walked right past him and threw her arms around Jasper.

CHAPTER EIGHT

The hug lasted long enough to get awkward. Jasper kind of just stood there holding his suitcase. The girl was almost his height.

"Uh . . ."

She pulled back and looked him over.

Then she hugged him again.

"I'm glad you're here," she said.

"Okay."

"I'm Lacy."

"Jasper."

She laughed. "Yeah, I know."

Colton glared. Jasper coughed awkwardly. He was definitely in the middle of something here.

"The headmistress sent me to get you," Lacy said. "Let's go."

Jasper waved to Colton and Rufus. "Thanks."

Colton got back in the truck and slammed the door. He continued glaring at Jasper as the truck pulled away.

"How was the drive?" Lacy asked.

"Good, I guess."

"Did you meet her?"

"Who?"

"Lacy. His shotgun."

"Yeah."

The girl rolled her eyes. "It was one date. And he took me deer hunting. Seriously."

Lacy led Jasper into a dingy foyer that smelled like a retirement home. Furniture from another century dotted the waiting area. Lacy pressed a call box near the door marked *Administration*. "He's here, Headmistress."

"Send him in," the box squawked back.

"I'll take you to your room when she's done with the induction stuff. Dinner's at five thirty." Jasper thought Lacy might hug him again. "Everyone's really excited to meet you."

And then Jasper endured another hug that he still wasn't quite sure how to return since he'd known this girl for all of three minutes.

Jasper walked into a tiny office. It was dark and empty.

"In here, Mr. Mansfield."

Jasper pushed open a door that connected to a larger office. The headmistress stood ramrod straight by the window reading some papers, glasses perched on her nose. Her short, frosted hair matched her voice exactly. Her gray pantsuit told Jasper she was one hundred percent business.

"Sit." She pointed to a chair in front of her desk. Jasper did as he was told.

She continued reading by the window.

Finally, she settled down in her chair and stared at him across the desk. "I am Miriam Chillingsworth, headmistress of this school. You will address me as Headmistress, or Headmistress Chillingsworth. Any variation or supposedly clever pun will result in a demerit. Accrue five demerits, and you will find yourself in the adjacent office working as my secretary after class. Is that clear?"

"Yes."

"Yes, what?"

"Yes, Headmistress."

"Here is your schedule." She handed him a sheet of paper. "I have reviewed your grades from your previous school and find them adequate."

Jasper scanned the list. The classes were pretty much identical to his old school, except one.

Dueling, Advanced. He wondered if Chillingsworth could hear him swallow.

"We do not usually admit students after the start of the semester, so consider yourself lucky." Her gray eyes bored into him. Jasper felt like confessing something just so she'd let up. "Counselor Barnes requested more than half my security detail to escort you from the train station. When I did not approve it, he went over my head to the League's Directors."

Jasper wasn't sure if that was a question, so he just nodded.

"You will not receive any more special treatment, Mr. Mansfield; I have more than a hundred students under my charge. I do not care about your past or your current circumstances. Only your future is my concern. You will follow *my* rules, you will keep your grades *up,* and you will learn to *defend* yourself. Is that clear?"

Jasper took a second too long to reply, "Yes, Headmistress."

"Is there a problem?"

"My schedule says I'm in advanced dueling."

"And?"

"I've never even seen a real gun until yesterday."

"Then I hope you're a fast learner."

The headmistress threw more paperwork at him—class syllabi, dorm rules, cafeteria hours, student lounge policies—and then had him sign a contract saying he would follow all of them, or else. Most of the punishments involved being her personal assistant for a varying numbers of hours, based on the infraction.

"Do you have any questions?"

Jasper shook his head no.

"Verbal questions require verbal answers."

"No, Headmistress."

"Then you may go."

When Jasper reached the door she said, "This is my school, Mr. Mansfield. Do not forget that."

Jasper looked her dead in the eye. *Trust no one.* "Yes, Headmistress."

CHAPTER NINE

Lacy put a finger to her lips.

She guided Jasper down the hall, side-stepping a patch of torn carpet. The overhead light flickered. "I can't prove it, but I think she keeps the com open to eavesdrop on us," Lacy said. "How was it?"

"She's kind of intense."

"That's one word for it."

"Does she really make kids who break her rules work as her secretary?"

"Chilligraphy."

"What?"

"She makes you handwrite all her teacher memos in cursive, and then deliver them. Chilligraphy. It's really painful because who learns cursive anymore? It ends up being hours and hours of writing, your hand cramping, until she decides your handwriting's good enough to copy her memos."

They hit a stairwell and went up to the second floor to another long hallway with a sign that said No Females Allowed.

"Don't worry about it," Lacy said. "I'm on her good side. My dad's a Director."

"That's cool." Jasper's suitcase wheel caught a patch of torn carpet and flipped over. "Actually I don't know if that's cool. I'm just tired of asking questions that make me sound like an idiot."

"My dad's one of the League's five board members. Permanent 'Get Out of Chilligraphy Free' card."

Lacy stopped at a door opened halfway. The room was small with a ceiling that slanted toward a single window on the back wall. A narrow bed was pushed against each side wall, and closets were built in on either side of the door. Clothes were tossed everywhere.

"I told him to clean up," Lacy said.

"It's fine."

"They moved everybody out of the singles last year when the pipes burst in the east wing, so it's a little cramped."

Jasper picked the bed that looked least slept in and put his suitcase on it. "My other house was actually my car, so really, this is great."

Footsteps pounded outside. A short, thick kid with buzzed hair shoved Lacy out of the way. "You." He pointed at Jasper. "You!"

"Uh—"

"Are about to get bear hugged. Don't fight it." The kid wrapped his arms around Jasper and picked him up off the ground. "We're airborne, people."

"This is Sheldon," Lacy said. "Your roommate."

"One-handed." Sheldon spun Jasper around and waved his free hand. "I am Atlas. Bow before me."

Another kid lurked in the door. He had wild red hair and some acne, was tallish and lumpy, and was rocking a tuxedo T-shirt. A giant pair of headphones were slung around his neck.

"Tucker, this is Jasper," Lacy said.

"Hello." Deadpan voice, almost robotic. He was mostly staring at his phone, which was one of those giant ones that was basically a tablet.

"Dude, you weigh like a hundred pounds," Sheldon said. "Tuck, feel how light he is."

Tucker didn't look up from his giant phone.

"Body slam." Sheldon threw Jasper on a pile of sweatshirts. Some pretzels crackled underneath. Sheldon pulled him up, again. "Broseph." He pointed to Jasper's neck. "Elsbeth jacked you up pretty

43

good. Please tell me Larkin punched her in the face. I'm begging you to say Larkin punched that witch in the face."

"How do you—how do you know about that?" Jasper asked.

"Cyrus gave us the rundown," Lacy replied.

"So now, give us the face-punching details," Sheldon said.

Three people, Jasper thought. Not much of a team.

But better than none.

"He pistol-whipped her," Jasper said.

"*Whaaaaaaaaaaaaaaaaaaaa—*"

Sheldon went on like that for a while.

"When the angel of death is busy, God gives the assignment to Larkin, and the earth trembles," he finally said, after he'd got himself together.

"He bromances hard and fast," Lacy told Jasper. "Just a heads up."

Sheldon moved Jasper's suitcase to the other bed. "Okay, so the heater on that side is broken. You can have my bed. I generate a ton of heat on my own. That's why I sleep naked. Are you cool with that?"

"Uh . . . yeah." Jasper nodded slowly.

"I'm messing with you," Sheldon said.

Tucker reached a hand into his pocket and threw Jasper some orange earplugs. "You're gonna want these."

"I live heavy and I sleep heavy," Sheldon said. "Sue me."

"He sounds like a tractor-trailer changing gears," Tucker said.

Lacy kicked an empty soda bottle. "I told you to clean up before Jasper got here."

Sheldon looked around. "I did."

"Study lounge," Tucker said. He walked out without waiting for anyone to object.

On the main floor, they headed down another wing with bare patches of floor where the carpet was just gone. Lacy cut through an abandoned classroom that turned out to be a side entrance to the library. Half the shelves were empty. They climbed a wrought iron circular staircase near the back and filed into one of the dozen study rooms along the catwalk. The space was triple the size of Jasper's dorm room and definitely smelled better.

"Welcome to the least crappy place in this total craphole." Sheldon shoved Jasper onto the couch and then sat next to him. "Red Hot Chilly Pepper has an annual budget of zero dollars for anything but security, so we have to bring in our own stuff."

Lacy grabbed a notebook and pulled over a chair from one of the two computer cubbies. Tucker sat crisscross on the floor and sipped a soda. He was still glued to his phone.

"I call this meeting to order," Lacy said.

Sheldon bounced up and down. "Let the record show I am ready to piss myself from excitement."

"Stricken," Lacy said.

"And let the record show Jasper looks like he just got back from a wedding."

"Also stricken." She peeked up from her notes at Jasper. "But if you need clothes, Sheldon and Tucker can help."

"All of my sweatpants are now your sweatpants," Sheldon said.

"I don't wash my clothes a lot," said Tucker. "But you can have whatever you want. Except my Whitesnake T-shirt."

"Thanks." Jasper waited a beat. "What's Whitesnake?"

Tucker looked up—straight at Jasper—and stared at him for a full five seconds. "The greatest metal band of the 1980s."

"Oh. Right."

"Tucker's favorite thing—other than Whitesnake," Sheldon interrupted, "is knowing weird stuff and then making you feel like a total idiot for not knowing it, too."

"The correct order of planets in our solar system isn't weird," Tucker said.

"Yeah, but you know the hydrogen levels of their atmospheres, too. Bro, that is weird."

Lacy was actually writing this down. "Okay. In attendance are: Lacy Church, Tucker Paine, Sheldon Burr, and Jasper Arnold."

"It's Mansfield," Jasper said.

"Everybody goes by the ancestor who put him here," Sheldon explained. "It just makes things easier."

Jasper didn't like that at all. It felt like he was legitimizing all this insanity—saying that it was okay.

"Note that Jasper's obviously weirded out by this policy," Sheldon told Lacy.

"Noted. Introductions. Go."

"Sheldon Burr." He flexed. "As in Aaron Burr, the guy who shot Hamilton in a duel. You know about the musical. Also, of the maybe-plot to create an independent nation in Mexico. Charged with treason, found not guilty. Still ruined his career. Which the killing Hamilton thing kind of already had."

"Tuck."

"Thomas Paine was born in Norfolk, England in—"

"Cut it down, man," Sheldon said.

Tucker sighed and put down his phone. "You probably know Paine because he wrote *Common Sense*, an essay that convinced British colonists in America to declare independence from England."

"Yeah," Jasper said. "He was—he was like the *man*, wasn't he?"

"Before and during the Revolutionary War, yeah," Tucker said. "But a couple years later he wrote an essay that accused Washington, who was president then, of being a power-hungry dictator and military fraud. *That* turned America against him."

Tucker went back to his phone.

Lacy finished drawing a bullet point. "And I'm a descendant of Dr. Benjamin Church, the Boston physician caught trading secrets to the British. The only actual traitor in this group, until you showed up."

"The White Whale." Sheldon mimed reeling in a fish. "You're up."

"Right," Jasper said. "Okay. So, according to what I remember from AP American, plus what I glanced over on the train ride up here, Benedict Arnold switched sides during the Revolutionary War. He tried to sell West Point, this military fort in New York, to the British, but the deal went south."

Sheldon patted Jasper's shoulder. "It's a safe room. Let it out."

"I think that's it."

"Not even close," said Tucker. "Arnold became a British officer and led attacks against the Patriots. Like when he raided the port city of New London, Connecticut, just a couple miles from where he was born."

"Probably killed some childhood friends," Sheldon said. "Cold-blooded mofo."

Jasper let that soak in. "No wonder that Reed woman hates me so much."

"She probably hates you so much because her ancestor called Arnold out for being a Loyalist lover, which he *definitely* turned out to be," Lacy said. "And that brings us to your dad's research."

"Right," Jasper said. "I haven't gone through it yet, but Cyrus thinks my dad was really upset about me having to make this decision about hiding or dueling—"

Tucker pulled on a pair of giant headphones.

"Okay. Yeah, so Cyrus thinks my dad . . . Is he okay?" Jasper asked, nodding to Tucker.

Lacy looked up from her notes. "Tucker doesn't really like talking about dueling. . . ."

"He thinks it's beneath him," Sheldon said. "Like, his brain is too important to the world to risk taking a bullet. Kind of a snob about it. Now, keep going."

Jasper nodded. "So, apparently my dad was working on a way out for me, so I wouldn't have to live in hiding or fight."

Sheldon and Lacy traded a this-is-what-we've-been-waiting-for look.

"Okay—that." Jasper pointed between them. "What's that about—the fanboy routine. Why are you guys so invested in helping me get out of this duel? You don't even know me."

"We'll all be challenged," Lacy said. "Me, this summer. Sheldon and Tucker, next year. But you could escape. And that's a win for us all."

"Not if you're dead," Jasper said. "Or in some witness protection thing. I don't get it."

"Think about it, dude," Sheldon said. "Arnold's descendant strutting around in the world, nothing the Libertines can do about it. Big giant middle finger to their whole jacked-up Code."

"Or they might just send Elsbeth after me again."

Lacy pulled a leg underneath her. Shook her head. "The Directors would never let that happen."

"Donelsons would go SEAL Team Six on her," Sheldon said. He held his arms up like a machine gun. "*Pop-pop-pop.* You get me?"

"Yeah." Jasper looked over at Tucker. Headphones on. "Are you guys . . . you know. Gonna duel?"

"Burrs don't hide." Sheldon said it hard and slow, like a creed.

"So, you'd be okay . . . killing someone?"

"Self-defense, yo."

"But you could just avoid it by not fighting."

"Burrs. Don't. Hide."

"Right, but—"

Lacy put a hand up. Her meaning was clear: *STOP TALKING!*

Jasper pressed his lips together.

"Dueling is complicated," she said. "Most of us go into hiding because we don't want to die, obviously. Libertine kids train longer and harder. But some kids duel because winning means a normal life. Or"—Lacy tilted her chin at Sheldon—"because it's just what their families have always done."

"Seven generations," Sheldon said.

Jasper caught Tucker looking at Sheldon, almost like he'd heard him. Then Tucker got up and threw himself in a beanbag chair, back to them.

Lacy pulled one of her brown curls taut. Jasper couldn't help thinking it looked like it hurt. "Killing someone, even in self-defense . . . it changes you," she said. "We've all seen it. The question isn't really should you run or fight—it's can you live with yourselves if you win."

Run.

Die.

Kill.

Jasper would have to make that choice, too, if he couldn't find his dad's way out.

And he had no idea what he would do.

"I move we adjourn this meeting so Jasper doesn't have to climb in the dark and maybe break his neck," Sheldon said. He threw a pillow at Tucker to get his attention, and the boy took off his headphones. "Initiation time."

Tucker pulled something out of his pocket and did a quick, rehearsed flicking motion with his wrist. Light glinted off the metal, but it still took Jasper a couple seconds to figure out that Tucker was wielding a six-inch butterfly knife.

CHAPTER TEN

Behind the manor house, they crossed a field where the grass came up to Jasper's knees. Rusted goal posts were collapsing in on themselves at either end.

Jasper kept an eye on Tucker's knife.

They passed a cinderblock gymnasium with a sign that read GUN RANGE, and followed a dirt path into the woods. Jasper spotted a decaying brick building that Tucker explained was the old headmaster's house. They reached a clearing and walked to the base of a giant tree where nooses hung from the branches; a number of severed ones lay on the ground.

"What," Jasper said, "is this?"

"This is a super old cottonwood tree with a bunch of nooses on it," Sheldon said.

"It's a metaphor. . . ." Tucker handed Jasper the knife.

"It's also tradition," Lacy said. "Seventh graders come here their first week. You climb up, carve your initials into the tree, and then cut down a noose. Think of it as a reminder that no matter what the Libertines say, we are not our ancestors, and we don't deserve their crap."

"Don't use the ropes," Sheldon said. "They might snap, and you could fall and maybe die. The irony would literally kill me."

Jasper climbed slowly. It was getting dark, but as he ascended, he could make out initials carved into the trunk. Twenty feet up, the etchings were easier to read. Jasper scanned the trunk for space, but there wasn't a free square inch.

"Higher," Sheldon called up.

So Jasper kept climbing. Soon, he could see the manor house, the gym, and the faint outline of the gateway in the distance. There was plenty of open real estate up here.

The blade sliced through the bark easily. Jasper was done in five minutes, and he had to admit, it didn't totally suck. Nearby he saw the letters *NBB* carved into the wood. They looked like a work of art. That kid had serious skill.

Or maybe he'd just practiced. As Jasper continued examining the trunk, he saw that *NBB* had been carved into the tree at least twenty times.

Jasper thought about the tattoo on his dad's arm. *Nil Desperandum. Never despair.* Except his dad had completely despaired. He'd been a freaking alcoholic.

Context.

"You're not off the hook," Jasper said to the air. It was no different than talking to a corpse in a box. "You could've been a dad and tried to fix things. Your secret quest doesn't change how awful you were."

Jasper wasn't sure he'd ever be able to let go of his anger, even if he did find a way out of dueling. And he wasn't sure if he wanted to. That version of his dad was still too raw to be washed away by this surprise explanation.

But what twisted his stomach was the other thing: what if he still failed? Then his dad had been awful for nothing. Jasper wondered if that would break him. If he'd become a drunk, too. Maybe that's how the story ended.

Maybe he was more like his dad than he wanted to believe.

A breeze whipped through the branches, setting the nooses swaying. Jasper grabbed the nearest one and started slashing at the rope. When it was loose, he held the loop out for a second, took a deep breath, then let it fall.

★★★★

"I wouldn't eat that," Sheldon said. "Or that. Or pretty much anything on this side of the buffet—it'll all give you diarrhea."

Jasper studied a bowl of taco meat. "How about that?"

"Definitely not that," Tucker said. He shoved past Jasper—no *excuse me* or *sorry*—and piled spaghetti onto his plate. No sauce.

"Nuggets are the safest bet," Sheldon said as they continued down the line. "Bacteria cannot survive a deep fryer."

Jasper piled some on his plate next to a quivering pile of neon orange macaroni. They got fountain sodas and joined Lacy at a round table.

"Let's talk workflow," Lacy said. "We can meet in the study room by three thirty on weekdays. If you can't make it, text somebody so we're not all waiting around."

"Like, if maybe you're going deer hunting," Sheldon said. "And you'll be gone for hours in the woods. With Colton. Hunting deer."

Lacy winged a nugget at Sheldon, but missed and hit Tucker in the arm. The kid barely noticed—he was back on his phone.

"Jasper, do you know when the safe's coming?" Lacy asked.

"Cyrus said a couple days."

"Is that enough time for you to finish the network?" she asked Sheldon.

He gave her a thumbs-up. "Totally separate from the campus Wi-Fi. A no-joke firewall. Chilly P will never find it."

"Nobody looks up anything related to this project on any computer but the study room ones," Lacy said. "We don't talk about details outside the room, either. We pretend this project doesn't exist. Got it?"

"Got it," replied everybody but Sheldon. He was staring at a pack of straight-haired brunettes walking by them.

"'Sup ladies—"

The girls blew right by him.

"'Sup ladies' is not working for you," Lacy said. "And we all agreed that the World War girls were out of your league."

Sheldon watched them get in line. "Stone-cold foxes, every one of them."

"So, is that how it works?" Jasper asked, pointing to the girls. "People hang with their eras? Like cliques."

"Pretty much. Shared history, and whatever." Sheldon started pointing to tables. "Got your Revolutionaries—mostly Loyalists. World Wars, we've been over them. Then there's the early 1800s crew—the guy who tried to kill Andrew Jackson is the only legit traitor there. The Cold War kids are mostly descendants of spies and, ironically, keep to themselves."

"What about them?" Jasper nodded to a goth convention happening at a corner table. Black clothes, gauges, piercings, all of them brooding like somebody died.

"Civil War," Lacy said. She was doing that hair-pulling thing again. "Most of them had ancestors in the Confederate government."

"Why do they dress like that?"

"Same reason they won't duel," Sheldon said. "See that girl in the middle, short hair? Nose ring and a scowl that could melt your soul? That's Nora Booth. No, don't stare—"

Jasper caught the girl's eye for a second. *Hollow* seemed like a good word. "What's her deal?"

Tucker pulled his headphones on. Lacy was seriously going to pull that curl out.

"She dueled two summers ago," Sheldon said. "Now she's on a crusade to end dueling. Won't even pick up a gun at the range. None of her friends will, either."

"I thought you had to be eighteen to fight," Jasper said.

"You can challenge early with parental permission."

Jasper looked over again, and was rewarded with a nasty glare from Nora. "I need some more soda."

He got up and refilled his cup, scoping out some stale brownies on the dessert table. He kept accidentally staring at the goths.

"Fresh batch." A cook held out a plate of chocolate squares.

"Thanks."

The guy watched as Jasper took a giant bite. He ate one, too. Then a second—*Was he crying?*—then turned and went back to the kitchen.

"Sharing is caring," Sheldon said when Jasper settled back in his seat. "Hook a brother up."

All Jasper could taste was salty metal. "They're not that good."

"Obviously—"

A hand grabbed Jasper's wrist. He smelled smoke.

"Drop it."

Nora Booth.

"Drop. It." Her voice was more of a hiss actually. The brownie landed on Jasper's tray and crumbled. "Lace, get Colton in here. Now."

Jasper's stomach cramped hard. He lurched forward and groaned.

"Lacy!"

Jasper thought his ribs might break. The floor suddenly seemed like a good idea. He slinked down to the dirty linoleum.

"Sheldon, get me some water," Nora said.

"Wha—"

"Shutupandgetit."

Jasper pressed his face onto the tile. It was so hot. Somebody sat him up.

And then Nora was dumping salt water into his mouth and he started coughing and she drained another glass down his throat, cursing at Colton to go into the kitchen. Jasper was puking and puking and his eyes watered and everything he'd eaten since birth just came out. And feet—there were feet everywhere as kids watched, and now he was shaking and cold and staring at his puke and he couldn't stop shaking and he just wanted to sleep . . . so he lay down in his puke and shivered because every part of him was freezing except for the hand on his back.

CHAPTER ELEVEN

Jasper woke up on a plastic cot.

An IV bag was hanging next to him. He traced the cord to a needle in his right arm. Another one ran into his crotch. Things felt weird down there.

A dark shadow in the corner turned into Byron.

"Where am I?" Jasper asked.

Byron leaned out the door. "He's awake."

Cyrus walked in, followed by a balding guy wearing a stethoscope. The doctor ran a penlight across Jasper's eyes, checked his pulse, and consulted a clipboard.

"He needs to be in a hospital."

"Your opinion has been noted several times," Cyrus said. "How is he?"

"No organ damage, from what I can tell. He needs to be monitored around the clock—heart rate, urine and stool samples, hydration levels."

"Were you able to determine the poison?"

"If I took him to a hospital, I could run labs."

"He stays here," Cyrus said. "Will there be long-term complications?"

"I won't answer that without a full battery of tests—at a *hospital*. But you should thank that girl who pulled the saltwater stunt. She probably saved his liver and kidneys."

Jasper realized he was wearing sweatpants. "How long have I been here?" he rasped.

"Two days," the doctor said. "And you'll stay for another three until I come back."

The doctor put on latex gloves and removed Jasper's catheter. He checked the IV bags and complained about the room being filthy before Cyrus walked him out.

"I gotta piss," Jasper said.

Byron held Jasper upright as he went. The bodyguard was probably mocking their for-sure-size difference down there. Jasper spotted blood in the toilet bowl.

"Your kidneys are filtering out the toxin," Byron said. "Doctor said it will last a few days."

Jasper limped back to the cot and chewed on sawdust toast. "Did they find the cook who gave me the brownies?"

"He locked himself in the freezer."

"He's dead?"

"Yes."

An hour later, Lacy, Tucker, and Sheldon filed in behind Cyrus—all wrinkled clothes and bloodshot eyes.

"We messed up," Lacy said.

"It's not your fault."

"It is mostly their fault," Cyrus said. "They were ordered to watch out for you." He glared at each of them. "The cook's name was Thomas Malcolm, a Loyalist descendant. The headmistress hired him six years ago after he graduated." Cyrus lowered his voice. "His attempt on Jasper's life is proof that the True Sons have infiltrated our organization, as I previously suspected."

"Whoa," Sheldon said. "That's kind of a reach, isn't it?"

Cyrus stared daggers at him. "And what explanation would you give?"

Sheldon opened his mouth to say something, but thought better of it and lowered his head again.

"If that's really what you think, we should tell my dad," Lacy said. "The Directors could look into it."

Cyrus looked over his shoulder, and then he actually looked up at the ceiling—like one of those paranoid people who think the government is listening in on every conversation through tiny recording devices. "We tell no one until I know for sure who we can trust."

"But Jasper—" Lacy protested.

"Jasper is alive, no thanks to any of you." Cyrus opened the door and motioned somebody to come in. Jasper heard the hard *clunk* of combat boots on tile.

Nora Booth.

She looked tougher up close, tattoo murals on both arms and black bangs diving hard over one eye. Smaller, too. Her black jeans and tank could've fit a twelve-year-old.

Cyrus shut the door behind her. "Ms. Booth saw danger where no one else did. Our success may depend upon it again. I've asked her to join us."

Lacy was trying to disappear into a corner. Sheldon and Tucker studied the tile.

"Nora's class schedule has been rearranged; she will be with Jasper at all times during the day. A contingent of Donelsons will also shadow him and stand guard over his dorm room at night. Do not interfere with any of them. Do I make myself clear?"

Three nods.

"The safe has been moved to your study room. When Jasper recovers, you will commence the project. Now, back to class."

The trio filed out like prisoners.

Nora didn't budge.

CHAPTER TWELVE

The headmistress dropped off textbooks and syllabi from the classes Jasper was missing. Nora refused to let her in the room.

"Young lady—"

Nora shut the door in her face.

"You don't trust her?" Jasper asked.

"I don't like her."

Time felt like it was blurring. Jasper would wake up to find Nora sitting or standing or pacing the room. She'd make him eat stale toast and guzzle water and then stand behind him as he pissed.

"I've got this," he'd say.

She wouldn't move a muscle.

Colton came back the next morning with eggs and orange juice. Nora chatted with the Donelson guards outside.

"How y'all doing in here?" Colton asked.

"Still alive."

"Lacy and them taking it hard?"

"It's not their fault." Jasper drained the container of OJ. "So, you took her deer hunting?"

"Rained most of the time. . . . Saw a couple, but nothing worth shooting."

"So, then, what did you do? Just sit in the woods?"

"Ain't a whole lot to do around here."

"Maybe coffee or something like that would have been better."

"I guess." Colton looked over his shoulder at Nora. "Ain't right, her being here."

"Why?"

"You heard what happened?"

"Yeah, she dueled."

"The other thing, with Lace—"

Nora came back in holding coats. "We're going for a walk."

★★★★

The courtyard sun blinded Jasper. Dead shrubs lined broken pathways that made a big X across the space.

Nora settled down on a cement bench and lit a cigarette.

"How did you know the brownie was poisoned?" Jasper asked her.

"They never bring desserts out after lunch. And the cooks never talk to anyone."

Jasper shoved his hands in his coat pockets. Winter was on the way. "The doctor said making me throw up like that probably saved my life."

"Saw it in a movie. Didn't know if it would work."

"Worked pretty good."

Nora inhaled half her cigarette in one pull. "What'd your fan club say about me?"

"Nothing."

She blew smoke in his face.

Jasper coughed. "They said you dueled two summers ago, but now you won't pick up a gun."

"And they told you about the pills."

"Pills?"

"Chillingsworth brought in a shrink to fix me. He gave me some pills."

"They didn't tell me about that."

"I downed the whole bottle. They had to pump my stomach. Put me in the same room you're in now."

"Okay . . ."

"Now you can stop talking shit behind my back."

Jasper didn't know how to respond.

Nora flicked ash at him. "You need a haircut."

"So people keep telling me."

She offered him the cigarette. He took a pull, and then spent five minutes trying to not die of a collapsed lung.

"I won't tell anyone that happened," Nora said.

★★★★

The doctor came back two days later. He did a lot of complaining about Jasper not being in a hospital, but told Chillingsworth he could return to classes the next day *"if you continue to closely monitor him."* Nora escorted Jasper to his room, then left him under the protection of the guards standing there. Jasper guessed she was going off to smoke. Two Donelsons walked him to the showers, then back to his room. Tucker had laid out a pair of jeans and a T-shirt with a giant snake on the front.

He'd also left a note:

Sorry we almost got you killed. Here is my Whitesnake shirt.
— Tucker

In the study room, Jasper tried to catch up on the work he'd missed, but mostly stared at the safe and the clock, waiting for the others to get out of class.

Nora brought him a grilled cheese sandwich and six bottles of water. Her hair was wet and she smelled like lavender and smoke. She made him drink a whole bottle, then kicked her combat boots up on the table and started reading a giant, worn book titled *Poetry*.

At exactly three thirty, everybody crowded into the study room.

"Dude." Sheldon threw his arms around Jasper and squeezed him hard.

Lacy walked in a ten-foot circle to avoid Nora. "We're really sorry."

Tucker examined Jasper's T-shirt. "You're wearing it," he said. "Good."

After reassuring everyone that he was fine and they could stop apologizing, and promising Tucker that he would eventually get around to listening to some Whitesnake, Jasper kneeled down in front of the safe. He messed up the combination twice before he felt the lock give with a *click*. He cautiously pulled the door open.

Stacks of books, composition notebooks, and accordion folders tumbled out. Half a forest, really.

"Holy crap," Sheldon said. "Your dad was busy."

"This is gonna take forever," Jasper said.

"Please." Tucker grabbed three notebooks and went to the beanbag chair, already reading.

"Dude speed-reads," Sheldon said. "Photographic memory, too."

By midnight they'd skimmed most of the folders—nerdy articles on Arnold, his life, and his treason. A handful were filled with documents on Joseph Reed's role as governor of Pennsylvania during the war, and Washington's Culper spy ring led by some guy named Benjamin Tallmadge who was apparently really good at messing up British battle plans. Tucker devoured five of the thirty composition notebooks, which turned out to be notes on the stack of biographies. The pattern continued there: most were about Arnold, then Reed, and a few on Washington. Lacy catalogued everything in a super-encrypted spreadsheet on Sheldon's super-encrypted server. Nora read poetry, though Jasper caught her now and then peeking over the book to listen when somebody shared a finding.

Everyone forgot about eating.

"Now what," Jasper said, "is this?"

He'd pulled out a piece of string with four index cards taped to it from inside one of the accordion folders. It was a mobile, like something he'd made in elementary school. His dad had written a name on each card, top to bottom.

Washington.

Reed.

Arnold.

Boswell.

"Boswell?" Sheldon said. "Who the balls is that?"

"Don't know."

"Google-me." Sheldon hopped on the computer and ran a search. "Nothing on the first page. That's never a good sign."

"Maybe this is Boswell," Tucker said. He held up a photograph of a kid sitting on the end of a dock.

"No, that's me." Jasper reached over and took the picture. "Where did you get it?"

"It was in this notebook."

Jasper turned the picture over. On the back, someone had written *Nil desperandum.* He put it in his pocket. His chest felt hot, and he didn't like it. "I'm pretty tired. Let's call it a night."

They returned all the contents to the safe. He closed and locked the door, and they filed back to the dorms, Nora and the Donelsons trailing behind them the whole way.

Jasper waited until Sheldon started snoring to take the picture out. He couldn't get the note out of his head.

Never despair.

If his dad had really loved him, why hadn't he ever said it—even just once? Yeah, so he'd apparently cared, but what did it mean now? If the man who held on to that photo was the real James Mansfield, could this version repair all the damage the other one did?

Jasper stuffed the picture under his mattress. He'd lie if anybody asked, but deep down, he realized maybe he was releasing the death-grip he held on his hatred of his dad. He'd fight the sensation every inch of the way, but it was happening.

Pretending was starting to feel like too much work.

CHAPTER THIRTEEN

Jasper woke up at seven to Sheldon digging for sweatpants. Naked.

"If you got it, flaunt it, bro," Sheldon said.

Apparently breakfast meats were even more likely to give you explosive diarrhea, so Jasper grabbed a mini cereal box in the cafeteria and followed the others to the south wing. Pretty much every student gave him looks because: A) they'd probably heard about him almost dying; B) Nora marched in front like a gargoyle; and C) a pair of six-foot-plus Donelsons were trailing him. It was the new kid's worst nightmare, but it was also the price of not dying.

The Juniper Hill classrooms were big, and lots of the auditorium-style seats were broken. In calculus, Jasper's entourage stood in the aisle like event staff. Sheldon's nonstop whispering almost got them both kicked out of government, which was taught by an old guy who instructed them to read Chapter 5 and take detailed notes.

"He's a math teacher," Sheldon said.

"Why is he teaching government, then?"

"Red Hot Chilly P hasn't found a replacement yet for Mr. Giles, the guy who used to teach this class."

"What happened to him?"

"He was giving everybody As without actually grading any work."

"Huh."

"Also, he turned out to be a convicted felon and the parents went ballistic. Juniper Hill only hires League members, so the pickings are slim sometimes."

★★★★

During lunch, butterflies slammed into Jasper's intestinal wall.

Advanced dueling was next.

"Relax, dude," Sheldon said as they walked across the overgrown soccer field. "Kingsley's a brute, but you definitely want him on your side."

"I'm actually afraid I might—" Jasper made sure Tucker's headphones were on— "shoot myself. I've never held a gun before."

"You won't live-fire for weeks," Lacy said. "You have to learn the Code first—dueling history, etiquette, and strategy. Then Kingsley'll teach you about the weapon, how to take it apart and care for it."

"No matter what he says, just remember he's trying to save your life," Sheldon said.

Jasper heard Nora snort from ten feet in front of them.

In the gym, they climbed a stairwell to a rectangular room that smelled like gunpowder and metal. Kids stuffed coats into lockers, gawking at Jasper's entourage. Through a clear panel on the far wall, Jasper saw a hulking guy in a black tracksuit stalk down the firing lanes to the lobby. He was blockheaded with short dark hair and wore a gaudy gold watch that gave him an out-of-work gangster feel.

"You lot look awful," Kingsley said to the whole room. The accent wasn't as thick as Jasper had expected. "Is that you yawning, Eliza?" A chubby-faced goth girl covered her mouth. "None of you *eejits* are getting on my range until you've woken up. Five laps around the building."

The class filed back outside.

"You, stay," Kingsley barked at Jasper.

He led Jasper into a small classroom and told him to sit. Nora took a desk in the corner and the Donelsons stayed outside.

"This is the history of the Code." Kingsley dropped a binder on the desk with a loud *thunk*. "You learn it backward and forward before you enter my range. If you make it to my range, you do as I say or I'll throw you out. If you think I'm being too harsh, just have a look over at the Wall of Shame." The instructor jerked a thumb toward the opposite wall where hand-sized plaques hung floor to ceiling. "Any questions?"

Jasper shook his head no.

"And you keep your mouth shut," Kingsley said to Nora. "Don't need your peace-lovin' nonsense here."

Nora glared, then tucked her head behind the poetry book.

Jasper started with an article about eighteenth-century "honor culture," which apparently came from a document called the *Code Duello* set up by a bunch of Irish guys in 1777. Basically, it was a blueprint of how rich guys should solve conflicts among themselves. In short, blow one another away with pistols or stab one another with swords. Twenty-five rules covered every possible scenario, from what to do if someone called you a liar to insulted your wife. The worse the offense, the more shots could be fired. An apology could end things peacefully sometimes, but not always. Jasper wondered why nobody in 1777 thought it was weird to spend so much time creating a document that detailed various ways to murder/get murdered.

Next, came a not-so-brief history of the Code. Apparently, Joseph Reed's son, George, got into it with the son of a former Loyalist in 1815 and ended up dueling him. George killed the guy, but also took a bullet in the hip, which crippled him. He was really pissed and got all the Founding Fathers' sons together in some sort of cabal and told them that to really honor their parents' sacrifices, they needed to stick it to the offspring of anybody who stood in the way of Independence. The *Code Duello* wasn't good enough, so George Reed and his buddies decided to write their own version.

Jasper squinted at a cursive document:

The Code
Est. 1820

It being agreed upon that the current remedy to punish certain miscreant, iniquitous peoples has been deemed insufficient to their offenses, we, the remnant of a valorous generation, do hereby enact an immediate solution to secure the satisfaction of our forefathers and the preservation of our posterity. Namely:

1. The vile progeny, regardless of generational distance from his perverse ancestor, shall be held accountable for the actions of that ancestor, as it is universally accepted that vileness, like honor, passes from father to son.

2. Accountability, in these terms, necessitates a single, written challenge to be followed by an exchange of pistol shots predetermined by the act of wrongdoing as follows:
offenses against country, three shots;
offenses against thy fellow man, two shots;
all other offenses unspecified, one shot.

3. The conduct of said exchange, being already well established, shall remain unchanged from that which has been established by accepted convention. Namely:
The challenged shall choose the ground.
The challenger shall choose the distance.
The seconds shall fix the time and terms of firing.

4. Apologies, written or verbal, even when formally accepted as sufficient satisfaction, shall no longer substitute for accountability.

5. *Recreant offspring refusing accountability as enacted herein shall be subject to punishment in the extreme, including punitive measures as befits their misdeed unanswered.*

Jasper rubbed his eyes. These people needed serious instruction on single-clause sentences.

Turning to check the wall clock, he caught a glint off one of the gold-plated plaques on the wall. He got up and crossed the room to get a better look, reading the names and lifespans etched below sets of crossed pistols. They'd all been about eighteen. Burrs, Paines, and a couple Churches. Siblings or cousins of his research team, maybe.

His neck prickled.

"It's a memorial," he said.

"It's bullshit," Nora said.

Jasper spent another half hour reading and rereading as the *pop pop pop* of the range fire echoed through the cinderblock walls. Around two, it went silent and Sheldon gave a thumbs-up through the tiny window of the classroom door. Kingsley shoved him aside and barged in, slamming the door.

"Who chooses the ground, the challenger or the challenged?" he asked, swiping the binder off Jasper's desk.

"Uh—challenged."

"Distance?"

Pause. "Challenger."

"And which is more important: ground or distance?"

"I didn't get that far."

"Ground. Shake up a man by taking him out of his element. That's what helped your little guard dog over there."

Nora kicked a desk over and threw her giant book at Kingsley. It missed, but she was moving before he recovered, closing in fast enough to get off a punch. Kingsley blocked the second, and slammed her face-down on a desk, wrenching her arm behind her back to keep her still.

"*Stay where you are!*" Kingsley yelled when Jasper moved to help her. The pair of Donelsons rushed in, hands moving to their hip holsters. "You can't face yourself in the mirror, that's your problem," he snarled in Nora's ear.

"Go to hell," she spat.

Kingsley twisted her arm tighter. Eyeliner was running down her cheek. "Don't be spewing your shite at me. I got enough of my own."

He let go, and Nora collapsed to the floor.

"If the Counselor wants her around, then she'll behave," Kingsley told the Donelsons. "And if you ever draw those weapons on me, it'll be last thing you do."

Jasper kneeled down and touched Nora's shoulder.

She shrank away, hugging herself.

Chapter Fourteen

The team kept asking what had happened, but Jasper kept his mouth shut. He'd told Nora he wouldn't talk about her anymore. He owed her that.

Still, it made the study room super awkward for a couple days, even if there wasn't really a need to talk anyway. The group read and sorted and logged data, skipped dinner, and went to bed with sandpaper eyes, then repeated the cycle. Nora brooded in the corner, some tape holding together the binding of her poetry book, looking more pissed than normal, which was definitely saying something.

Jasper started getting up early to study the Code over breakfast, which meant Nora did, too. He hated himself for just standing there while Kingsley had manhandled her. She probably thought he was a coward. He kind of was. But he knew that mentioning the incident meant wading into the bad blood between Nora and the instructor.

A week later, Lacy substituted a briefing for the normal research session.

"Okay, here's what we know so far: Jasper's dad went through all the famous biographies on Arnold and took lengthy notes. Ditto for Reed and Washington." She ran a finger down the spreadsheet. "Most of the articles are on Reed: copies of letters, diary entries, and what I think are legal papers. The rest are about this Boswell guy, whose first name was Ira, according to this copy of a muster sheet. He was an officer on Arnold's staff in Philadelphia."

Jasper held the index card mobile, watching it twist and turn. The names came around slowly. *Washington. Reed. Arnold. Boswell.*

Okay, Dad—so they're connected.

But how?

"In other words, we don't really know anything," he said.

"We know your dad was very organized," Sheldon replied. "And he really loved office supply warehouses."

"I was hoping the answer would be obvious. Like, he'd left his thesis statement taped to the inside of the safe: 'Here's what I was looking for.'"

"I think it's going to be like one of those 3-D hidden images," Lacy said. "It's here, but we have to zoom out really wide and get the whole picture."

"I hate those things," Jasper said.

"Yeah, those things suck," Sheldon said.

"We just need to Tucker this thing." Lacy pointed to the kid splayed out on the beanbag chair, face buried in a notebook. "The solution will take shape."

But not yet. This many midnight research sessions in a row was brutal.

Jasper gathered up a stack of notebooks and dropped them back in the safe. He thought maybe he'd heard the bottom plate rattle. He tapped it with his knuckles.

"Tuck, let me see your knife."

Jasper wedged the blade into a hairline crack between the metal plate and the safe wall and pried up a false bottom. Inside was a stack of business cards and an ID badge. The badge showed his dad's face, but the name said *Dan Cooper, Archivist. Historical Society of Pennsylvania.* The business cards showed the same name and title.

"If that said Dan Brown, I was going to freak out," Sheldon said.

Jasper went to a computer and pulled up the website listed on the card. "Guys, this is an actual place in Philly."

He scrolled to STAFF.

No Dan Cooper.

"Your dad made the world's lamest fake ID," Sheldon said. "Why would he do that?"

Jasper took out his phone and dialed the number. It rang three times before somebody picked up. "Yeah, hi. I'm looking for a guy who used to work for you. In the archives." He put the phone on speaker. "His name was Dan Cooper."

"Hold, please."

The group listened to boring transfer music.

"Archives. This is Greg," said an older guy.

"Hey, Greg," said Jasper. "I'm looking for Dan Cooper. Is he available?"

"Ah. Great." They could hear some papers being shuffled around. "Let me guess, he came to your house, said he worked for the Historical Society of Pennsylvania, and looked through your family papers and heirlooms."

Lacy gave Jasper a thumbs up.

"Uh . . . yeah. Yeah, he did."

"Let me get your name and number."

"So, Mr. Cooper doesn't work for you?"

"No." Now Greg sounded pissed. "But you're the third person to call asking for him since I started here last year. Name, please?"

"Right. Um . . . Chester. Ton."

Sheldon was miming the cut-it-out gesture.

Jasper hung up.

"Great work," Lacy said.

"So my dad posed as an archivist to look through people's stuff?" Jasper said. "That's extremely weird."

"Yes it is, Chesterton," Sheldon said. "Yes. It. Is."

★★★★

Lacy sent Cyrus a super-encrypted email over the super-encrypted network connection and then they all shuffled off to bed.

All except Nora.

Jasper wasn't following her, not at first. It was more about wanting to apologize without everybody listening; he still couldn't get that day in the range with Kingsley out of his mind. The coward feeling had never really left.

On the way to the girls' wing, he saw her and some of the Civil War kids heading out the front door.

"Where are they going?" he asked Colton.

"Kinda got a clubhouse in the chapel."

They followed.

Outside, he saw shadows heading into the tiny chapel across from the rundown cottages. Jasper jogged after the group. The frigid air had blasted him awake.

Jasper pulled the door open slowly and stepped inside a greeting area lit by some candles sitting off to one side. A deep bass pumped up from a basement stairwell near the front stage where a wooden lectern stood. Nora sat in a pew, hands clenched, head down, muttering.

"Hey."

"*Shit.*" Nora jumped. "Holy *shit* Jasper! What the *fuck?*"

"Sorry."

"*Fuck.*"

An office door near the altar swung open and a middle-aged guy with brown hair stepped out.

"Sorry, Pastor Bob." Nora's voice had lost its edge.

"Doesn't bother me, but it does . . . scare . . . other *people.*" The guy came over and took Jasper's hand. "Bob. Services Sunday at nine if you're up. The door's always open."

"Thanks."

"You okay?" he asked Nora.

She nodded.

Pastor Bob turned and went back to his office.

73

"What do you want?" she asked.

"Nothing. Sorry . . . about scaring you, but also the other day at the range. That's why I followed you. . . . I feel awful. I mean, you saved my life and then I just acted like a coward, and it's kind of been eating me up ever since."

Nora sank back into the pew. "Whatever."

"I didn't tell the others what happened with Kingsley. A little—okay half—because I was embarrassed, but mainly because of what you did before. The brownie and everything."

He cautiously sat down next to her. They looked at a stained glass image of Jesus on the cross for a while.

"You come here a lot?" he asked.

"When I'm not babysitting you."

The bass turned into some horrible screaming and guitar shredding. "So you think the poetry book would have knocked him out, if you'd hit him? That thing is massive."

"Poets have a lot to say."

"I guess."

Jasper finally got a good look at the tattoo on Nora's arm, and then wished he hadn't. A super creepy girl with deep, black eyes in a dress pointed up at him, mouth wide open.

"Kingsley's a prick, huh?" Nora finally said.

"I'm actually completely afraid of him."

"That's the point. He's trying to mold you into a killer. Don't let him."

"Sheldon says it's self-defense."

"That little prick might as well be a Libertine. Families like his keep this whole dueling BS going."

"I think I saw his brother's plaque on the wall, though."

"Don't rationalize it," Nora said. "That's what the Libertines do—use honor to make murder okay."

"I'm just saying it makes sense that Sheldon feels so passionately about it."

"Then you're an idiot, too."

She shoved past him and headed to the stairwell. "Don't ever follow me again."

★★★★

The Code exam was a beast, mostly because Kingsley leaned on the desk like a gorilla as Jasper took it. He needed a score of at least eighty percent to move on, and he was super ready to get out of these remedial sessions and onto the range with everybody else, mainly because Kingsley had been keeping him almost till dinner lately.

Jasper got a hundred.

Kingsley carried a small, metal case into the classroom and undid the latch. He glared at Nora—daring her to say something. She didn't.

A cold-steel pistol with a form-fitting grip sat resting in foam. "This here's the SIG Sauer 226. Nine-millimeter semiautomatic handgun. In a duel, it'll be your best friend."

"Is it loaded?"

"You treat it like it is *always*."

Kingsley named each piece as he took the gun apart, oiled it, then put it back together. "Now you do it."

With about a million wrong moves, Jasper took the weapon apart, and then reassembled it. Kingsley yelled when he dropped pieces and cursed when he put components in the wrong way—so he pretty much yelled and cursed the whole time. After an hour, Jasper's fingers throbbed, but he could field strip the gun and put it back together in under a minute.

"It appears you can teach a monkey anything," Kingsley said. He left the room and came back pushing a cart full of gun cases. "They won't clean themselves. Get to it."

Halfway through the cart, Jasper's fingers cramped and began slipping on the edges of the pistol he was holding. He thought about asking Nora to help, but then imagined her giant book hitting him in the face. A little while later, Kingsley came back to inspect Jasper's work and found most of it unsatisfactory. Then he made Jasper start all over again.

Around four in the afternoon, Kingsley finally dismissed Jasper. By then, his fingers were swollen and his eyes ached. Nora's left leg was bouncing like a jackhammer—it was her nicotine tell. They trudged outside, through a light rain, to the manor house.

"I was thinking about something," Jasper said.

"Were you?"

"I want to make sure you're not going claw my eyes out if I say it."

"Better not, then."

It was hard to tell if she was kidding.

The rain kept putting her lighter out.

Jasper decided to take a gamble. "I was thinking that this must suck for you. The range—being there with me. All the kids shooting. Piles of guns."

"It's certainly not my favorite place."

Jasper turned and cupped his hands around her lighter. "Right, but you're there because Cyrus put you on guard duty, which means it's my fault."

"The whole world isn't about you, Jasper."

The rain picked up. Nora turned down a path that twisted toward a covered amphitheater behind the east Wing. Weeds shot up in the cracks of the stone benches, but at least the stage was dry.

"Cyrus didn't make me do anything," she said when they were out of the rain. "I volunteered."

"Why?"

"Penance."

"Is that why you go to the chapel so much?"

"It's safer than pills."

"Cheaper, too."

Nora snorted. She offered him her cigarette. He waved it off.

"The cemetery guy told me to pray at my dad's funeral, but instead I just insulted his corpse."

"Did your dad deserve it?"

"Yeah. Actually, I don't know now. You saw that picture Tuck found. Okay, so my dad drank and neglected me and my mom, but Cyrus says he did it to save me. What am I supposed to do with that information?"

"Real people aren't like the ones in movies, you know. They're not either all bad or all good. Most of us are just trying to get by."

"So you think I should forgive him?" Jasper asked.

"I think you should stop trying to figure out if he was the worst dad ever. Just let him be the person he was, even if that guy was a total bastard."

"That's easy for you to say."

Nora took a long drag. "My dad moved us ten times before I came here because he was so paranoid about being found. That's why my parents got divorced. I hate him for it. But I realize now that he was just doing what he thought was best."

The wind changed direction, and rain started blowing onto the stage. Jasper checked his phone and saw twenty texts from Sheldon. Most were cat emojis.

"Let your blisters air out at night," Nora said. "Calluses will build up faster that way. And stop repeating the manual barrel check. If the slide lock slips—which it will—you'll lose a finger."

"Thanks. I've never held a gun before."

"No shit."

Chapter Fifteen

This is it. I can feel it." Sheldon kicked his legs up for the twentieth wall handstand attempt. "I am Atlas. Bow before me *oh balls—*"

His shoulder gave out and he slid down the wall.

The study room smelled like Cheetos and sweat. Jasper was one sentence away from an aneurysm in his eye. Lacy had stopped trying to hide that she was really texting. Nora was still somehow only halfway through that freaking poetry book. But nobody wanted to leave because they hadn't found anything meaningful and Cyrus was coming the next day.

"Maybe he's up here to deer hunt with Chilly P," Sheldon said.

"I just threw up in my mouth," Lacy said.

Jasper rubbed his temples. He probably needed to sleep for a week.

"It smells like boy in here," Lacy complained.

Sheldon flexed his muscles. "You're welcome—"

Colton burst through the door, one of his brothers or cousins on his heels, and hauled Jasper out without a word. Four more Donelsons surrounded them in the library below and formed a shield around Jasper as they charged down the hallway. Colton shouldered his way into a boiler room near the cafeteria, then raced down a flight of steps to a football-field-sized cement basement. The Donelsons flicked on flashlights and ran them over iron beams, before settling the lights on a small room near the back filled with office supplies. Colton shoved Jasper and Nora in and locked the door behind him.

"Secure in the shelter office," Colton said into his walkie.

"Colton, what the hell!" Nora snapped.

"Patrol spotted somebody in the woods outside the south wall. They're chasing him on foot." Colton pulled a handgun from a belt holster and handed it to Nora.

"Get that thing out of my face."

"I'm askin' you to help us if we need it."

"I will cave in your nose with the handle of that murder weapon if you don't get it away from me right this second."

"Won't be on my conscience if Jasper goes down."

Nora sent Colton flying into the door with a two-handed shove.

The room pressed in on Jasper as Nora and Colton ripped into each other. He slid to the floor and counted his breaths.

At two hundred, Colton's walkie crackled. *"All clear."*

Nora dragged Jasper out of the room. She didn't let go of his hand until they reached the main floor.

★★★★

Cyrus was waiting in the study room when they got back from the range the next day. While Jasper unloaded documents from the safe, Larkin and Byron put a new lock on the study room door and handed out keys to the research team.

"Rufus informed me that his men chased the intruder to a campsite before the perpetrator escaped on a four-wheeler," Cyrus said. "Evidence shows he was there for a good while. Perhaps a few weeks."

"Recon."

Everybody turned to look at Nora. She'd been doing that more lately—weighing in without being asked. They were all still getting used to it.

"Perhaps," said Cyrus. "The Donelsons will double perimeter patrols. Now, what have you found out from James's papers?"

Lacy ran down the catalogue of materials and Jasper told Cyrus about the business cards and the fake historical society job. He ended by holding up the mobile, which they'd started hanging from the ceiling fan whenever the safe was open.

"We divided all the readings up, but so far my dad hasn't actually said what he was looking for," Jasper explained.

"By design, I'm sure. He was a careful man." Cyrus went into the hall and came back with a backpack. Unzipping it, he took out two brand-new laptops. "These cannot be connected to the Internet; transfer your data here and keep them in the safe when you are not using them."

"My network is a vault," Sheldon said. "Nobody can get in."

"I'm not doubting your skill, Mr. Burr. I'm exercising caution." He looked at Jasper. "A word, if I may?"

Jasper and Nora followed the Counselor to his car. Cyrus waved Colton and his brother/cousin out of earshot.

"This morning, I told Instructor Kingsley that an assault on you will be regarded as an assault on Jasper," Cyrus said to Nora. "I assure you it will not happen again."

"It was pretty messed up," Jasper said.

"Larkin made sure that Kingsley received the message. But the same is true of the Donelsons. Rufus did not appreciate you laying hands on his son, Ms. Booth."

"I warned him," Nora said.

"I don't care. The Donelsons have chosen to aid us out of good will, but they're still mercenaries. Do *not* jeopardize that partnership again."

"I'm not picking up a weapon," Nora said. "That was our deal."

"And I'll never ask you to do so. But you will defer to the protections I have put in place. Otherwise, I will hold you personally responsible for any harm that comes to Jasper."

The pair watched Cyrus's taillights disappear down the lane. Nora made chimneystacks with her cigarette. Jasper expected her to claw Colton's face when he drifted back toward them, but instead she looked straight through the boy and said, "You think you understand, but you don't. And then, when you do, it's too late. It's just too late. Then it's over, and you want go back to the way things were before, but you can't. There is no going back."

CHAPTER SIXTEEN

Jasper picked at a blister as he waited for Kingsley to roll in the cart. "I'm his gun boy. That's what I am."

"He's punishing you for tattling on him," Nora said. "Shove it in his face by not wincing every five seconds."

Kingsley barged in. This time, there was no cart. Just a single, sleek case. "Suppose you've had enough of cleaning by now."

"Yeah."

Kingsley placed the case on Jasper's desk and opened it. He took out a black bandanna and tied it around Jasper's eyes. "You've got twenty seconds to field-strip and reassemble this weapon. Fail three times and you're back to the carts."

"Twenty seconds," Jasper said.

"Begin," Kingsley barked.

On his first attempt, Jasper's fingers found the familiar levers and edges quickly enough, but he knocked the barrel off the desk during the reassemble.

"Looking for this?" Kingsley asked. "Ah right—you can't see. I forgot."

The second try was a total disaster. Jasper didn't set the takedown lever to the right spot and he almost lost a finger when the rail slammed forward.

"Got a fresh cart of guns waiting if third times not the charm," Kingsley muttered.

Jasper laid his palms flat on the desk and took a deep breath. He saw the gun in his head. He carefully ran through the sequence. It was just mechanics—a metal puzzle.

"Begin!"

Jasper's hands moved on their own. He was on autopilot. There was no thinking. The metal clicked and slid and scraped in perfect rhythm. He reassembled the gun so fast he counted a full five seconds before Kingsley whispered, "Feck me."

Jasper undid the bandanna. "I passed?"

"Barely." Kingsley packed up the gun. "Suppose you're ready for the real thing, then."

Jasper followed his instructor out of the classroom to the empty range. Nora watched through the clear glass. He waited anxiously in the firing lane for Kingsley to come back with a box of ammunition.

"This here's a .357 Sig round, full-metal jacket." He pushed the round into the magazine and slid the whole thing into an opening inside the handle. Flicking the slide catch lever with his thumb, Kingsley armed the gun by sending the slide forward and chambering the round. "Now, your stance: weak-side leg out in front, strong-side back." Kingsley demonstrated, and Jasper tried to mimic the body positioning. "Strong arm fully extending the pistol toward your target, weak arm slightly bent with your hand wrapped around the knuckle of your strong hand. Lean forward a bit, knees bent a touch to absorb the recoil." Kingsley exaggerated the motions, and again Jasper tried to copy his instructor. "Line the front sight post with the rear and aim it at the target. When you're ready to shoot, slide your finger to the bottom of the trigger and breathe in, out, half-in, hold, and then squeeze."

They slid on earphones and protective glasses, which had been hanging from the side of the booth. Kingsley took aim.

BANG.

Jasper jumped. The shot was louder than he'd expected, and it vibrated in his chest. Kingsley went through the steps of safety protocol to ensure that no more rounds were left in the gun before pressing a button on the side of the booth. The target whisked toward them on a metal track, and Jasper saw the neat hole in the bullseye.

"Good shot," he said, turning to Kingsley.

"Now you."

Jasper took a bullet from the box and loaded the weapon, set his feet, and pointed downrange. The target seemed to sway from side to side—or maybe he was shaking? He tried to hold still and slid his finger to the trigger.

Breathe in.

Out.

Half-in.

Hold.

Squeeze.

BANG.

The gun yanked his arm a foot in the air. Jasper fumbled through a safety check and brought the target forward.

It was clean.

"What did you expect on your first try?" Kingsley asked. "Again."

This time, Jasper was ready for the recoil, but he still missed the target.

"Relax your grip."

Jasper kept missing. After each shot, Kingsley would offer some advice. Or curse. Usually both. None of it seemed to help. The ammo box was half-empty and Jasper hadn't so much as grazed the target.

"Maybe you need some motivation." Kingsley ducked into the range office and fiddled with a computer. Downrange, a light flickered on the paper target, and suddenly it had features.

It was Elsbeth Reed.

"Steady, now," Kingsley said. "Nothing to fear from this manky Libertine."

Jasper lifted his weapon. *It's just paper.* The sights swayed back and forth. He swallowed and went through his breathing routine, but the gun still wouldn't steady. Each time the sights lined up, he saw Elsbeth's face and, suddenly, it wasn't just a paper target anymore—it was horrible and paralyzing.

Jasper lowered the weapon. He was sure Kingsley would freak out.

Instead, the instructor gently took the gun and removed the round. "No shame in it."

But Jasper did feel shame—cold and icy, pouring down his back. Elsbeth had murdered his dad and he couldn't even shoot a target with her face on it.

"What does it mean?" he finally asked.

"It means you've got a nervous system."

"But she killed my dad. Shouldn't I want her dead?"

"Wanting someone dead and doing the killing yourself are different things, lad."

"Guess this means I'm not cut out for dueling."

"You can overcome your nerves, if that's what you're worried about. You can teach the mind just about anything. But it's the heart you have to concern yourself with. Not sure what's going on in yours—too early for even you to know, I'd say—but it'll make itself known when it's time." Kingsley jabbed Jasper's chest with a meaty finger. "And when it does, you listen to it."

Jasper picked at his headphones. "Have you ever dueled?"

"Think the headmistress would've given me the job if I hadn't?"

"Right."

"You want to know if I carry any guilt because you think that'll help your decision, when the day comes, is that it?"

"Yeah, I guess."

"It won't. And anybody who says differently is a lying *eejit* who should have their ears boxed."

★★★★

With Thanksgiving break approaching, Lacy pushed them even harder, imposing reading deadlines. It didn't matter much to Jasper and Nora—they'd be staying on campus—but the others would be going home for a week, and they still hadn't found the connection Jasper's dad had been seeking.

Jasper finished his Arnold biographies without finding a single historian who hinted that the general was anything but a gutless traitor. Most blamed Arnold's historically hot and known Loyalist wife, Peggy, for his treachery, plus his giant wounded ego from not getting promoted. Plus the whole court-martial thing. Jasper wondered if maybe this was one of those fake 3-D images, and the artist was playing a trick on them—when you zoomed out and let your eyes settle, there wasn't any hidden object to find. It was all just pixelated, historical chaos.

They'd cleared a wall in the study room and had started taping up a timeline of the Revolutionary War. Their goal was to map Arnold's road to treason and find a seam, anything that could potentially place the blame elsewhere. The Sunday night before break, Lacy called an emergency meeting to try and shake something loose in the hopes that Jasper could dig deeper into it while everybody else binged on turkey.

"Okay, so Arnold captures Fort Ticonderoga, then loses the Battle of Quebec," Lacy said. "In 1777 he wins at Saratoga, where he gets wounded, and also where he gets no credit because of officer politics."

"Dude almost lost his leg for the cause," Sheldon said. "Least they could've done was give him some cred."

"You don't get a prize for starting a race," Tucker said. "You get it for finishing."

"But you get water along the way," Sheldon said. "And people cheering you on."

"Focus, people," Lacy said. "Arnold spends a winter at Valley Forge before Washington appoints him military commander of Philadelphia in 1778."

"Where he basically screwed himself by hanging out with Loyalists," Jasper said. "And marrying one."

"Which brings us to Joseph Reed, my books." Lacy tacked up a sheet that read *Political Enemies*. "As Governor of Pennsylvania, Reed starts a public attack on Arnold for his use of military wagons for a personal business venture, and the Loyalist wife thing. Reed really goes after him with not a ton of evidence. Arnold starts communicating with British spy John André in May of 1779, but then cuts off talks in October. The court-martial clears him of almost all Reed's charges in early 1780, but he still gets a public scolding by Washington for the wagon stuff. In April, he starts talking with André again."

"Washington was the nail in the coffin," Sheldon said. "All traitor after that."

Jasper stared at the timeline. The mobile swayed a little and grazed the top of his head. "Guys, Ira Boswell doesn't fit into any of this."

"Exactly." Lacy said. "And that's your job over the break. Make him fit."

Tucker gave Jasper an accordion folder labeled with a sticky note. *Miscellaneous*. "I didn't read these yet. Start here."

"Has Tuck the Information Annihilator been defeated?" Sheldon asked.

"I've was busy," Tucker said. "Texting your mom."

Nora choked on a strangled laugh.

"Joke's on you because my mom doesn't text," Sheldon said.

"Oh, she texts," Tucker said. "She texts."

"This conversation is making me uncomfortable, and I have to pack," Lacy said. "Jasper, you good?"

"Yup."

Lacy opened the door, and everybody heard Colton say, "Hey, Lace, thought maybe we could get some coffee after my shift ends."

"Sure, Colton. It's almost one in the morning and I'm leaving in five hours and I haven't showered in three days, so yeah I'd like to get some coffee. And maybe we can also go jogging and then look at the stars."

Silence.

"Found a new spot to deer hunt if you'd prefer that."

Lacy sort of laughed. "Sorry. Okay, listen: I'm on the first shuttle out, so I'll be eating a super early breakfast. If you're up and not on Chesterton duty, we can have coffee."

"Where did he find some game?" Sheldon asked.

"Maybe your mom," Tucker said, staring at his phone. "She has game to spare."

CHAPTER SEVENTEEN

Sheldon gave Jasper ten bro hugs when he left at 6:00 AM the next day. Jasper went back to sleep until noon, and probably would have slept the rest of the day if Nora hadn't kicked at the door and said, "It's seriously time to get your ass out of bed."

They made their own breakfast in the cafeteria kitchen—Jasper called it an omelet, but it was basically scrambled eggs with chopped up sausage and a bag of cheese on top. They wandered the empty halls, took smoke breaks in the courtyard, and made coffee jokes loud enough for Colton to hear. At one point, they caught Chillingsworth vacuuming the hallway and then decided they should be nicer to her, but probably wouldn't. Nora showed Jasper the Civil War kids' study room in the library. They'd turned the space into a place to practice graffiti before it was unveiled in more public displays. Nora had carved *Abandon all hope, ye who enter here* on the door. Jasper recognized the knife-work from the Cottonwood Gallows.

NBB.

Nora Something Booth.

Her favorite spot turned out to be the rooftop above the girls' dorms. It had a ratty couch and a terrific view of campus with gables on one side that blocked the wind.

"Sorry you couldn't go home for break," Jasper said.

"We've talked about your obsessive need to make everything about you."

"Right."

"You did me a favor. My dad got remarried and she's almost my age. Calls me 'Nor' like we're sisters. When I go home, there's always a good chance I might assault her."

"You're welcome, then."

Some geese crossed overhead. Colton's boots clacked on the roof as he did the rounds, probably trying not to freeze to death.

"Question," Jasper said. "The awkward tension between you and Lacy. What's that about?"

"She's mad at me," Nora said.

"Because you dueled?"

"Because last year, when I was in a really bad spot, and she was being this super peppy and annoying cheerleader to get me out of my depression, I pretended. I acted like I was coming out of it just so she'd go home for spring break." Nora leaned her head straight back and blew a long trail of smoke into the air. "But really, I just wanted her gone so I could take those pills and not have her be the one who found me."

Jasper wondered how Nora could say that so evenly. "Why don't you just tell her you're sorry?"

"Are you my shrink?"

"I'm just saying, if my friend did that after I tried to help them, I'd be mad."

Nora flicked ash over the side of the couch. "That's because you're self-absorbed."

"She probably feels like you left her."

"That still makes it about her."

"Right, but your deal is kind of all about you, so isn't that the same thing?"

Nora stared at the gray sky. Jasper could see his breath and wondered if it might snow soon. Apparently, winters here were endless. He thought about last Thanksgiving when his mom was on a crazy deadline, and they'd spent a week straight in front of the blazing fire eating takeout. It had been pure bliss.

★★★★

Jasper spent the next day in the study room with a new friend: an accordion folder called *Miscellaneous*. It should have been called *Soul-Crushing Boredom*. There was an email printout confirming his dad's approved access to an archive in the New York Public Library housing some Joseph Reed papers; a list of other archives that held letters and legal papers from Reed's career; and a list of donations collected by something called the "Ladies Association of Philadelphia," which Google said Reed's wife, Esther, started during the war to fund Patriot soldiers' pay. There was also a clipping from a September 5, 1780, *Philadelphia Gazette* article reporting on a particularly deadly outbreak of dengue fever that had killed, among others, Ira Boswell; poor guy had left behind a wife and two kids. Another article from the *Baltimore Sun* in the 1930s went on and on about another Boswell—Charles—who had to liquidate his estate during the Great Depression. Apparently, Charles totally freaked out when they'd put his private library up for auction at a low price—he'd stormed the docket and took the lot off the list.

File all this under "???????"

It was getting late. And it was break, after all, so Jasper figured he didn't have to feel guilty about taking one. In the corner, Nora was doing that jackhammer leg thing she did whenever her nicotine supply got low; pretty soon she'd be pacing back and forth. Jasper started repacking the accordion folder.

And that's when he found it—something so boring and so inconsequential that he'd almost skipped over it.

It was a letter from Joseph Reed to his wife—or a copy of a letter—written in elegant, swirling cursive, the style of the 1700s, and therefore nearly impossible to read. Thank God his dad had transcribed it:

My dearest Hetty,

Knowing well my strong attachment to our family, I am confident of your sympathy regarding the financial troubles of Lt. Boswell and his family. I do not know any thing more disquieting than such a state of Uncertainty, and fear the gloom with which their sickly children suffer will assuredly worsen.

Being that your association has such funds to alleviate their burden, and considering your desire to remunerate the soldiery directly, I request that a sum of forty dollars be dispatched to Lt. Boswell immediately. Yet because the General prefers alternate methods of renumeration, I beg you to keep this act of Charity discreet.

Your most affectionate,

J. Reed

Jasper walked around the room, rereading the letter. He stopped at the mobile, watching it twirl until the names came into view.

Washington.

Reed.

Arnold.

Boswell.

Jasper turned the letter over and saw his dad's big, blocky, hand-writing: WHY WOULD REED WANT TO HELP A MAN WHO SERVED ON THE STAFF OF HIS GREATEST ENEMY??

"Maybe he felt bad," Jasper said.

"Are you talking to me?" Nora asked.

"No. Just thinking out loud."

"It's almost one in the morning."

"Yeah." Jasper piled everything back inside the safe and locked it. The mobile was still spinning as he walked out of the room.

★★★★

Jasper had actually gotten so used to Sheldon's awful snoring that he found it was hard to sleep without it. He stared at the ceiling and thought about Nora lying on the bathroom floor, dying, and then he was putting on Tucker's borrowed jeans and a Whitesnake T-shirt and his coat.

"But seriously," Jasper said to Colton as they walked to the chapel. "How was coffee with Lacy?"

"She said we should do it again."

"That's progress."

They slowed as they approached the chapel door. "Careful with Nora," Colton said.

"Still pissed she almost took you out?"

"She's a black hole is all I'm sayin'. Don't get sucked in."

The deep bass pounded louder than before; Pastor Bob must have gone home for the break. Jasper stood at the basement steps and watched neon lights bounce off the switchback walls. What if he wanted to—*get sucked in.*

Wood creaked underneath his feet. Halfway down the steps, he paused for a whole minute. *Abandon all hope, ye who enter here,* covered the walls in green spray paint. Maybe this was a terrible idea. Maybe Nora would freak out because he'd invaded her space. Maybe she'd finally get around to clawing his eyes out.

But then the music faded for a second, and he thought he heard her sobbing.

Jasper stepped cautiously into the dark room. A giant speaker system armed with lights shot neon streaks in every direction. Nora sat on the couch, wiping her face and nose with the sleeve of her hoodie. She stared up at a massive mural on the celling: a tall, skinny girl with black holes for eyes—the same one as her tattoo. Pink bubble letters read *Hannah Rose Lincoln.*

Nora saw him and screamed, *"IT'S TOO FUCKING LATE!"*

He crossed the room and drew her into a hug even though she fought back, writhing and screaming and cursing. It probably looked criminal to anybody watching.

"I can't fix it." She sagged against him. *"It's too late."*

Chapter Eighteen

After a while, Nora pushed off of him and went outside to smoke. Jasper turned down the music. His ears hurt. He almost tripped over the masses of wires running between computers with towers stacked upon towers. They hummed and beeped, lights flickering and flashing. It looked like a serious gaming setup or something. Nora came back and settled on the couch a foot away.

"So, that's her?" Jasper asked.

"That's her."

"She's really pretty."

"She was." Nora showed him the inside of her left bicep. On it was tattooed the same girl, but older. Little kids were on each side of the figure, holding her hands. "She had a boyfriend. He was her second. Kingsley and I met him at the dueling estate in New York. They probably would've gotten married."

Kingsley.

That took Jasper a couple seconds to untangle.

"He was your second," Jasper said. "That's why you hate him."

"He actually tried to talk me out of it." She kicked her boots up on a splintered coffee table. "I guess I blame him because it's easier."

They stared at Hannah's graffiti ghost on the ceiling for a while.

"So you're a living mural to her," Jasper said. "The life she never had."

"Priests used to flog themselves in the middle ages. This is the modern equivalent." Nora leaned to the side, and lifted her shirt to show her ribs, revealing an old lady in a rocker, surrounded by kids. "This felt like acid going in, but at least for a few weeks I didn't hate myself."

"Right, but eventually you're going to run out of ink space."

Nora pulled her shirt back down. "I plan to have lung cancer by then."

That explained the chain-smoking. "The Libertines would have challenged you anyway. If you'd won that duel, would you feel the same way?"

"It doesn't matter, because that's not what happened. I went after Hannah because I became like them: filled with hate. I blamed them for having to move around all the time. For my mom leaving. So I decided I'd go and get mine. And now I'm paying for it every day."

Jasper saw Elsbeth's face over the target. He tried to imagine how he'd feel if he pulled the trigger for real.

"You know the whole universe isn't about you," he said.

Nora snorted.

"If you'd killed yourself, I'd be dead, too," he said. "That's not BS. It's just plain fact. I get that I can't know how deep this goes, but I don't buy that your life is worthless now because you took somebody else's. I am literally walking proof that that's not true."

★★★★

They fell into a routine. Late breakfasts, hours of silence in the study room, smoke breaks in the courtyard during the day, and rooftop trips at night. They talked about their lives before Juniper Hill and TV shows they hated. Nora came clean about a crush on Alec Baldwin that lasted most of freshman year. Jasper told her about an equally embarrassing Star Wars LEGO collection. They traded Sheldon stories and gave Colton horrible dating advice and stayed out until they couldn't feel their fingers.

Lieutenant Ira Boswell—or actually Boswell's descendants—filled Jasper's afternoons. Jasper's dad had sketched various parts of the Boswell family tree in his notebooks, attaching locations and dates to them. Jasper guessed these were connected to the undercover missions of Dan Cooper, Fake Archivist, to search their stuff. But what his dad was actually looking for, he never said. The chaos continued.

Thanksgiving Day, Nora, Colton, and Jasper made frozen pizza. Nora found outdated packets of cocoa powder that tasted just not-disgusting enough to drink. They mixed a giant vat and carried it up to the roof where they paired the sludge with stale gingersnaps that almost broke their teeth. Colton wore a parka with a furry hood that you could tell he hated.

"This is a stupid question I feel horrible for not asking," Nora said. "Do you miss them? Your parents?"

"He was always missing, so my dad, not really. But my mom, yeah."

"That portrait of her you told me about—the one of above the fireplace? A little Norman Bates. But also kinda adorable."

"It was on the edge for sure."

Nora flung a cookie over the side of the building. The girl had a wicked arm. "When my parents got divorced, I started cutting my dad's hair because my mom used to do it to save money."

"Okay . . ."

"Shaggy is not your look."

"I get it."

Nora sank back into the couch and popped in a piece of nicotine gum.

"Have you decided not to pursue lung cancer?"

"They stop mail during break." She put another piece in her mouth. "The dueling tournament starts next week."

"Sheldon was telling me about it," Jasper said. "Everybody gets paired off. Paintball pistol guns."

Nora nodded. "If you get me as your opponent, try not to shoot me in the neck. The masks don't go down that far and paintballs hurt like hell."

"I'll just miss on purpose. Kingsley won't know the difference. I suck."

"Very true."

Jasper wasn't sure when she'd started sitting this close to him. "Are you gonna sulk until Christmas because I'm doing the tournament instead of joining your pacifist cult?"

"I don't sulk."

"You brood like you're plotting world domination."

Now she was definitely leaning into him. Jasper lifted his arm to move over but she kind of settled into it. He went rigid.

"Relax. I'm just freezing," she said. "We're not going to start making out, or anything."

"Right."

"I don't randomly make out with people."

"That's good."

"Especially not with guys who look like a Chia Pet on steroids," Nora said.

"Your obsession with my hair is making me wonder if you're really the right bodyguard."

Nora nestled her head into the crook of his neck. *Perfect fit*, Jasper thought. He leaned his cheek into her hair and decided it wasn't really that weird to smell it because she'd pretty much orchestrated this whole situation without asking him, so whatever.

"I'm really glad you didn't die," he said.

She didn't say anything for a while. "I wasn't, at first."

"And now?"

"I'm coming around to the idea."

Jasper decided that he was going to kiss her—just on the top of the head. Nothing super aggressive. A sort of in-the-moment thing. That was the play here, right? But then he started thinking about her violent streak and also her comment about how this was really all about body heat and by then, well, he'd completely psyched himself out.

And then she fell asleep.

She turned out to be a mouth-breather. Sheldon would have respected the almost-choking sound she made as she slept.

When the moon was overhead, Jasper went to get up, but Nora grabbed his arm and wrapped it back around her waist.

CHAPTER NINETEEN

B roseph. I missed you."

"Me, too."

"And I got you some sweatpants." Sheldon tossed Jasper a couple pairs of gray cotton pants. "Those should fit your girly legs. Now, be straight with me: did you sleep in my bed?"

"I promise you I did not."

"You can tell Uncle Shelly anything."

"Please never say that again."

Sheldon shoved his clothes back into drawers on his side of the room. "You might be wondering why I'm in such a good mood?"

"Not really."

"I'll tell you why: because over the break, while you were sleeping in my bed and doing weird demonic séances with Nora, I managed to text my way into the phone of Adele Dickinson."

"Who?"

"Dude."

"Oh. World War Two Adele."

"Whose name neither you nor I are even worthy to mention."

"How did you manage that?"

"Great question. My height and lack of game should lock me out of her league, but I am also hilarious and witty. Nobody sends funnier texts than me."

"Or more cat emojis," Jasper said.

"Which turned out to be awesome because she loves cats."

"So, you're going out."

Sheldon thought about it. "We're not *not* going out."

"I don't even know what that means."

"It means we're texting all the time, and there has been some discussion about seeing each other in the caf, and maybe going for a walk later this week."

"Is that like deer hunting?" Jasper asked.

"I really, really hope it is."

Tucker came in reading on his phone and wearing a T-shirt that said GAIUS BALTAR FOR PRESIDENT.

Jasper studied the shirt for a second. "Who's Gaius Baltar?"

"He's the greatest TV character ever made," Tucker said without looking up. *"Battlestar Galactica."*

"This is why most of your friends are online friends," Sheldon said.

Jasper caught them up on his findings at dinner, and then they hit the study room.

Sheldon started building a digital Boswell family tree using Ancestry.com while Tucker plowed through a few of the remaining notebooks. Lacy and Jasper traded theories on why Reed might have paid a big chunk of money to Ira—what Jasper had started calling "The Big Question"—which was basically them repeating the facts over and over with different vocal inflections. Every time Nora left for a smoke break, Jasper thought about the tournament and how he might have to shoot her, preferably not in the face.

The dueling brackets went live at midnight on the Juniper Hill website.

"Balls," Sheldon said, scanning the seeding. "I got Adele's friend."

"Which one?" Lacy asked.

"Brown hair. Skinny."

"They all look like that."

"I know. Isn't it great?"

Jasper scanned the bracket over Sheldon's shoulder. "Who's Eliza Davis?"

"Shit," Nora said.

"At least you'll make it to the second round," Sheldon said, smirking.

"She's a Civil War kid?" Jasper asked.

"With one friend," Nora said. "Me. Which means I'm her second. And she's already pissed because I spend all my time with you anyway."

Tucker came over, headphones on. He handed Jasper a pamphlet and shouted, "THIS WAS STAPLED INSIDE A NOTEBOOK."

The cover read *AA: The Recovery Program.* Jasper opened the flap and saw a summary. *Alcoholics Anonymous is a fellowship of men and women who share their experience, strength, and hope with one another that they may solve their common problem and help others to recover from alcoholism.* The Twelve Steps filled the rest of the booklet with super dramatic drawings of each. Dates were scribbled by each step.

"It's pretty late, Lace," Nora finally said.

Lacy yawned. "Yeah. Let's pack it up."

Jasper slid the pamphlet into his coat pocket.

At the dorm steps, Nora pulled him toward the front hall. They walked over to the chapel, she lit a candle, and they sat and stared at stained-glass depiction of Jesus.

Nora prayed while Jasper read the Twelve Steps. The bass pumped below their feet.

"What do you think the pamphlet means?" he asked her when she was through.

"I think you know what it means."

"He was trying to get better."

"Looks like it."

Jasper felt that shift again—the cracking up of things once settled. "I'm pretty sure if I stop hating him, I'm going to fall apart. I think it's the only thing keeping me together."

"You can hate and love somebody at the same time."

"I don't want to love a dead person who sucked. I want him to come back and redo everything and not suck." Jasper rubbed his temples. He really needed to look into reading glasses. "I just want him to be a total bastard or not a bastard at all."

"But that's not real life, Jasper. Everybody is a bastard on some level."

"I'm not going to forgive him if that's where all this is leading. You don't understand how he treated my mom and me. He doesn't deserve to be forgiven."

"Probably not." Nora went quiet for a while. "Neither do I. What do you think I'm doing here? I'm begging for forgiveness. 'Cause maybe there's a chance I can get just a little."

Jasper shoved the pamphlet back into his coat pocket. "I always thought praying was kind of stupid, to be honest."

"A lot of things seem stupid before your life goes to shit."

"So, what do I do?"

"Pastor Bob says you just spill your guts. Ask for things you want. But not things like a new car."

"God doesn't care about my ride?"

"Probably lower on His priority list."

Jasper put his hands together like he'd seen Nora do. He thought about bowing his head, but that didn't feel right. Too scripted. "God, this is Jasper."

"He knows your name."

"Just making sure." Jasper closed his eyes. "So, things are kind of messed up right now. My dad was a bastard, but it turns out he was trying to save my life, so if you could help me sort this out, I'd really appreciate it because right now I'm on the razor edge of a breakdown. Also, I kind of really miss my mom, and yeah—" The words were flowing now, hard and fast and his eyes burned. "Life without her kind of sucks because I'm pretty much alone, and I've got new friends but I still feel like I'm on a planet by myself . . . and I just wish she were here. Also, I'd really like to not die or kill anyone, so if you could help our mission, that would be great." He choked on the last words, more sobbing than speaking. "I think that's all."

"You can say 'Amen,' but it's not mandatory."

"Amen." He wiped his face. "And God, help Nora stop smoking so I don't get secondhand lung cancer."

"He filters out sarcasm."

When Nora got up to go to the basement, Jasper stayed and prayed some more.

And then he prayed some more.

Chapter Twenty

"Point and shoot," Sheldon said. He loaded Jasper's paintball pistol and handed it to him. "Point and shoot."

Jasper looked across the small clearing at Eliza. She was a shorter, chubbier, and angrier version of Nora. "This is pretty cruel."

"Her fault, dude. She could shoot back if she wanted to."

Kingsley waved them to the center. Trees formed a wall on every side. The sun was barely up, and Jasper couldn't feel his toes. "Eliza here has refused to choose a firing distance. Leaves it to you, Jasper."

"Fifteen paces," he said. That put the distance to target at thirty paces, which he could miss without trying.

"And since you're the only one with a weapon, I assume you'll be firing first. Back to back, then."

Jasper slid on the mask. He still hadn't managed to look Nora in the eye this morning.

"Fifteen paces," Kingsley said. "March!"

Snow crunched under Jasper's feet. Crazy how snowfalls quieted everything.

"Halt and face!"

Eliza looked farther away than he'd imagined. He wondered if he even had to try to miss.

"Fire at will!"

Eliza ripped off her mask and dropped to her knees. "Please . . . don't kill me."

Jasper froze.

"You *get up right now, Eliza!*" Kingsley roared.

"Eat me," Eliza shouted.

Then she started screaming for mercy.

Literally.

"*Mercy!*" she yelled. "I'm so young, Jasper! I have so many years to live."

"This is *jacked* up, Nora, even for you," Sheldon yelled. "Tell her to stop!"

"You think I told her to do that?" Nora shouted back.

"Think about my parents," Eliza moaned. "They'll be heartbroken."

"*Jasper, you pull that bloody trigger,*" Kingsley screamed.

Jasper took aim. His arm shook. He tried to block out her face, but the screaming was too much.

Mercy.

Have mercy.

"Jasper, just freaking *shut her up!*" Sheldon yelled.

He closed his eyes and pulled the trigger.

Shunk.

The screaming stopped.

Jasper opened his eyes and saw a lump of black on the ground. He ripped his mask off and bolted across the clearing.

Eliza squirmed on the ground. Red paint covered her . . . neck.

"Shot me in windpipe, you tool," Eliza gurgled.

"Ah, crap—I'm sorry," Jasper said.

Kingsley knelt on the ground and took off his gloves. Jasper was sure he was going to choke Eliza at first, but Kingsley gently tilted her head back and wiped away the paint. Almost like a parent.

"No damage," he muttered. They did some intense glaring at each other, but Kingsley finally cleared his throat and said, "I'd put some snow on it on the walk back." He stood and marked his clipboard. "Jasper advances to the next round."

Eliza kept clawing at her throat like she was bleeding to death.

"You're fine," Nora said, helping her up. "Didn't even break the skin."

"Your boyfriend shot me in the throat. Pretty sure I'm not fine."

"Sorry," Jasper said. "I wasn't even—"

"Yeah, yeah we're all sorry." Sheldon pulled Jasper toward the path that led back to the manor house. "Kingsley will wreck you if you admit to throwing a shot. Just let it go."

"I closed my eyes."

"Yeah, I saw." He glared at Nora and Eliza limping behind them. "Bro, are you gonna start wearing eyeliner soon?"

"What?"

"Nora's cult. Tell me she's not recruiting you."

"She's not."

"Because it's your freaking decision," Sheldon said. "Not hers."

"I got it."

"Do you?"

They put some distance between Nora and Eliza. Colton walked the path ahead, shotgun scanning the woods.

"I freaked out, okay," Jasper said. "In the range. Kingsley put Elsbeth's face on the target, but I couldn't shoot it. I got scared. And then, when Eliza pulled that crap, I froze again."

"Hmmm."

"And, yeah Nora gives a new angle to all this dueling stuff, but I'm not saying I agree with her. I'm just trying to figure out what I'll do while not pissing myself from terror. I mean, I never even saw a gun up close until I got here. Now, I'm training to point one at actual people. Cut me some freaking slack."

Sheldon made a snowball and nailed a tree. "Nora beat me in the spring tournament her sophomore year, you know. Just a few weeks before she challenged that Lincoln girl."

"Really?"

"She'd been training one-on-one with Kingsley for like a year, and was way out of my league. She shot me in the chest—twice. There was this rage in her eyes that I'll never forget—like a dog bred for fighting about to be released from its cage. And even though I lost, it was probably my most important match because it showed me how hard I had to train if I wanted to survive."

"You could survive by hiding," Jasper said. "That's Nora's whole thing."

"Yeah, but what Nora forgets is that the Libertines will just go after someone else. They want blood—whose blood it is isn't really the point. That's what my family understands . . . what my brother understood. We're soldiers, and there's a war on. Every kid here is trained to fight, but we don't all do the fighting. And that's okay. Still, a select few *have* to fight so that everyone else can live in peace."

"You're not out for revenge, then?"

"I'm out for honor," Sheldon said. "Not the jacked up Libertine kind, but the real thing. Honoring my brother's memory by following his example—by volunteering to go to the front, like he did, so that others don't have to."

"I never thought of it that way." Jasper threw a snowball, but missed his tree. "You're not afraid of what happens if you win? The regret?"

"Dude, I'm not looking for a fight. I'm just sticking around for one that I know is coming."

They stomped in silence until they hit the soccer fields.

"So, you're her boyfriend, huh?" Sheldon asked.

"That's not what it is."

"If you start wearing eyeliner, I am taking back all of my sweatpants."

"I was actually thinking of going the tattoo route," Jasper said. "Get a giant spider on my face."

"Like the body in the middle and the legs spreading out across your cheeks?"

"Exactly."

"She'll probably want to make out with you all day if you do that."

"That's the point."

"I just tasted my own bile."

★★★★

Snow fell for a week. Drifts on the soccer field came up to their knees. Jasper swore to never complain about Pennsylvania winters again.

"It looks like a breakout of leprosy on her neck," Nora said as they trudged to the range. "Eliza keeps telling people it's a hickey. No one believes her."

"I still can't believe I hit her," Jasper said.

"We're all surprised."

Ahead, some kids huddled outside the gym door. Colton pulled on the handle but it didn't budge.

"What's going on?" Sheldon asked.

"Gym's locked." Colton radioed the same into his walkie. A minute later, it crackled back, "Headmistress called an assembly. Y'all have to head back."

Students plodded down the path to the auditorium in the west wing. The stage was full of old TVs on carts and extra chairs. Jasper and crew stood in the back as kids hunted for fold-down seats that weren't broken. Kingsley stalked into the room and stood against the stage, arms folded, staring murder. Jasper had never seen him this angry. Chillingsworth joined him a minute later and everybody quieted down.

"You have been called here because of an outrageous occurrence," she said. Shrill. On edge. "A handgun has gone missing from the range armory."

"Not missing," Kingsley said. "Stolen."

Jasper's neck prickled.

"Never in my twenty-two years at this school has a weapon gone missing—"

"Stolen."

"Yes, stolen." Students squirmed in their seats as Chillingsworth performed a wall-to-wall scan of the room. "As we speak, campus security is searching your rooms and you will stay here until they are finished." She waved off the protests. "You do not have a right to privacy in this school—consult the Supreme Court if you disagree. Until the weapon is found, the range will be closed. And the dueling tournament is canceled."

Students booed. Somebody threw an empty water bottle at the stage. Kingsley marched up the aisle, dragged out the offending student, and barked in his face.

"This is a problem," Nora said.

"Maybe Kingsley miscounted," Jasper offered.

"He doesn't make mistakes when it comes to his guns."

"Then, what do we do?"

"Hope they find it."

An hour later, Rufus came in and talked with Chillingsworth in hushed tones. There was a lot of head-shaking and scowling on her part. Twice, she jabbed a finger at him.

He shrugged and walked up the aisle toward Jasper. "Gonna have to ask for your keys to the study room. Headmistress wants it searched. I'll need the combination to the safe, too."

"Not a chance," Nora said coldly.

"Are you gonna make us?" Jasper asked. There wasn't much they could do to stop Rufus or the Donelsons.

"I take my orders from the Counselor," Rufus said. "He don't tell me much, but he did tell me that what happens in that room ain't my business. But the headmistress, she's threatenin' to close the library unless she gets in there."

"Can you do the search for her?" Jasper asked.

Rufus shook his head. "Afraid not. She don't exactly trust my judgment these days."

"She's pissed that Cyrus keeps going over her head," Lacy said, yanking one of her curls.

"We can*not* let her in," Nora hissed.

"We have to," Jasper said evenly.

"What?"

"What if Cyrus is right, and that cook was like an agent of the Libertines or something? Maybe they could get to a student, too."

"He's just paranoid," Sheldon said. "That's his thing."

"Maybe it should be our thing." Jasper watched the assembled students, wondering who among them might have the weapon. Wondering if he was their target. "Either way, we can't wait out this power grab. I'll open the safe, let Chillingsworth see there's no gun, then she'll leave us alone."

"And what if she sees something?" Sheldon asked.

"What's there for her to see? We're reading about Benedict Arnold? We've been staring at my dad's research for months, and still don't even really know what we're looking for."

"This is a bad idea," Tucker said.

"Agreed," Sheldon and Nora chimed in at the same time.

"Right, but it's my stuff, so it's my call. I'll deal with the fallout."

★★★★

In the library, Chillingsworth stood on the catwalk, arms folded. "This is not your private locker room," she said as they climbed the steps. "You are guests in *my* school. Now open this door."

Jasper unlocked it.

"Stay where you are." She pushed her way in and turned on the light. Starting in the near corner, she worked her way around, sifting and poking things that apparently might be hiding guns. She looked under couch cushions, in the fridge, and behind every book on the shelves.

111

Then she turned to the safe.

"Open it."

Jasper blocked the combination with his body so she couldn't see as he twisted the dial.

Chillingsworth made neat stacks as the folders and books came out. Jasper flinched when a bunch of documents came loose, but she didn't seem to care. When it was empty, she stuck her head in and looked around, knocking on the sides. Then she knocked on the bottom. She turned to face Jasper, and held the gaze for a few seconds, then grabbed a pair of scissors and pried up the false bottom.

The mobile. The letter from Reed with "The Big Question" written across the back. He'd been putting them there for a while now.

Chillingsworth looked the documents over, then left them on the nearest pile.

"Like I said, Headmistress"—Jasper cleared his throat—"none of us took the gun."

She straightened the bottom of her suit jacket, and walked out of the room.

CHAPTER TWENTY-ONE

B ut what," Sheldon said, "was he looking for?"

"Sheldon, if you ask that one more time, I'm going to murder you," Lacy snapped.

Jasper had spread out all the pieces of the Boswell family tree in a grid on the floor. Sheldon was pacing up and down the row of papers to reach one, and cross-referencing it with the Ancestry.com version. Without the shooting range to fill their afternoons, the team had been pretty much living in the study room. Jasper actually missed it—not the guns or their cursing Irish instructor, but the mechanical repetitiveness. Every choreographed move and step and breath and the single purpose of getting a piece of lead in the center of a target thirty feet away. He'd recently started to "not totally suck," as Nora put it.

"All of these people are direct descendants of Ira?" Jasper asked.

"Affirmative," Sheldon said.

"And we know my dad visited the ones who are still living and looked through their family heirlooms—papers and documents. Looking for something inherited."

Sheldon nodded. "That is correct, Detective Chesterton."

"And he checked into a hotel near this family in Virginia," said Jasper, tapping the names Milford and Anna Boswell. "So that's probably who he was planning to meet with next."

"Yes. We've said that forty times," Lacy groaned.

"He was on a trail," Jasper continued, "but to what?"

He dragged a chair over and stood on it. He blurred his eyes and let the papers fade to a white blob and then slowly focused. He was right on top of it—he could actually feel it bubbling under the surface.

And then the solution broke through.

"Something to answer the Big Question," he said.

He jumped off the chair and grabbed the *Miscellaneous* folder. He found the *Baltimore Sun* article from 1932 and started scanning it, reading fast enough so he could filter out the irrelevant details. He jabbed at the page and started shout-reading:

"'Councilman Charles Boswell's personal library is rumored to contain a number of first editions and a host of unpublished family papers dating back to the American Revolution. A bidding war drove the price to nearly one hundred dollars before the councilman, seeing the crowd descend upon his family history like scavengers on a carcass, ran to the podium and declared the auction over, claiming that he would rather starve than sell his century-old lineage to a seething mob.'"

Sheldon was already scanning the Ancestry.com tree. "Holy. Balls."

"Tell me Charles is a direct descendant of Ira," Jasper said.

Sheldon nodded.

"And all the people my dad visited . . . They're direct descendants of Charles."

"Yup."

Jasper's fingers tingled. He bounced on his heels. "We need to get inside that house my dad never made it to. Look for the thing that might have been passed down by Boswell."

He was met with dead silence.

"Tuck, headphones." Sheldon waited until Tucker pulled them on. "Bro, that's deep Libertine territory. We're talking the Jefferson clan's backyard. We get caught there, and we won't be taken prisoner."

"We could ask the Directors to submit a travel request to the Libertines like normal," Lacy suggested.

"Which the Libertines would reject. . . . Or accept so they can ambush us," Sheldon said.

"Okay, then we can't get caught," Jasper said. "It'll be just us and a few Donelsons. We get in and out."

"It's not that simple, dude."

"Right, but since my other option is to wait around here and maybe get shot, I'm up for it. I mean what are we even doing here if we're not going to act on what we find out?"

"He's right."

Everyone looked at Nora, who had stopped bringing her poetry book altogether. She said about as much as Tucker during their sessions, but was now definitely more than just a bodyguard.

"Oh, because you're going to carry a gun and have our backs," Sheldon said.

Nora raised an eyebrow at him. "I thought you wanted to die with honor. Change your mind?"

"This isn't a duel. They have machine guns."

"You're scared. The mighty Sheldon Burr is afraid."

He took a step toward her, fists clenched. Tucker saw something was going down and pulled his headphones off.

"Some of us still have things to live for," Sheldon said, close to a growl.

"Like a duel? You're pathetic."

"That's enough," Lacy said. "Nora, shut up. Sheldon, get some air."

He was already out the door.

Tucker got up and hovered awkwardly close to Nora. Jasper didn't even see him reach for the knife—he must have had it in his hand before Sheldon stormed out.

"Tuck," Jasper said. "Tuck—*whoa.*"

Tucker held the knife a couple inches from Nora's face. She froze.

"Aaron Clark," he said. His robotic voice sounded colder than normal. Subzero. "Do you remember him?"

115

Nora stared the blade down. "What about him?"

"Do. You. Remember. Him?"

Jasper looked to Lacy for help, but she was as wide-eyed as him—terror all around.

"That psycho who got expelled for fighting," Nora said through gritted teeth. "With Sheldon."

"Sheldon caught him messing with me. Told him to stop." Tucker rotated the blade. An inch closer and it would've grazed her cheek. "Aaron pulled this on him, but Sheldon didn't back down. I wasn't even his friend, but he stood up to that animal. For me."

Nora's scowl was disappearing. She leaned away from the blade. Jasper could tell she was getting it—they were all getting it now.

"Sheldon is not pathetic," Tucker said. It was almost a whisper. "He's brave."

"Okay."

"Say it."

Nora looked at her hands, then cleared her throat. "He's brave."

Tucker nodded. With a flick, he folded the knife back in its sheath and walked out.

The three of them just sat there for a couple minutes before packing everything back into the safe. Nora helped, which was a giant tell: she felt awful.

"Would the Directors even let us make the trip?" Jasper asked.

"Cyrus has pulled a lot of strings already, so who knows," Lacy replied. "We'd have to make a solid case. And get the Donelsons on board."

"Think you could talk to Colton? Feel him out?"

"Sure."

There was a joke there, but Jasper let it go.

CHAPTER TWENTY-TWO

That night, Jasper dreamed that somebody was yelling in his face. It was weird because the shouting was pretty loud for a dream.

"Get up! Get up! Get up!"

Somebody lifted him from the mattress, and dragged him out of his room and down the hall.

It was freezing cold—and he only had sweatpants on. Definitely not a dream, then.

"On our way," another guard yelled into a walkie.

Jasper found his legs on the stairs. "What's wrong?"

"Wall sensor went off."

"Where's Nora?"

"Colton's going to the girl's dorm now."

More Donelsons met them in the hallway. They raced to the boiler room and down the steps, sprinting across the bomb shelter, before shoving Jasper into the small room. He locked the door from the inside and stood against the wall, panting in the dark. Shivering, he decided to start sleeping in sweatshirts.

The room was so quiet that Jasper was sure he could hear something. At first, he thought it was the blood pounding in his ears. But the sound was lighter. Softer.

Another person.

Breathing.

"Hello?"

"I'm sorry." It was half whisper, half cry.

Then a flashlight beam blinded him.

He shielded his eyes, and saw the gun first.

Then the face.

"If you open the door, I'll have to shoot them, too," Adele whispered. "I can't look at you when I do it. Turn around. Kneel down."

"Please."

She stepped forward, and put the gun to his temple. Her hands shook. She was crying. Jasper got why Sheldon liked her. She was unbelievably gorgeous. Even now.

"I'm so sorry," she said. "It's the only way. They know where my family lives."

Was it possible this was one of those layered dreams? Maybe he'd wake up *for real* when she pulled the trigger and be in his bed and tell Sheldon about it and they'd laugh about how messed up it was. About how he'd dreamed that his roommate's crush had murdered him.

He turned around and knelt on the cold floor. The weird part was, he wasn't scared at all. He couldn't really understand that it was the end. That a bullet was about to enter his brain and he would stop existing. That he would be no more and life would go on after him and without him and that it had all been meaningless until now.

"I'm sorry." She sniffled, then put the muzzle on the nape of his neck and turned off the flashlight. "It won't hurt."

He recognized her breathing routine.

In.

Out.

He heard bare feet on the cement floor—tiny strides heading his way, hard and fast.

Nora.

But she wouldn't make it in time. She'd see him dead, and it would ruin her.

Half-in.

Hold.

Jasper went prone as Adele fired. He thought maybe he was dead and this was hell because it felt like grenades were going off in his ear canals. He dove for the door and screamed for help, but couldn't hear himself. Only the gun vibrating as Adele shot wildly in the dark.

Bangbangbangbang.

He felt for the lock and turned it. *Click.*

The door swung open and Adele fired at the light. A body fell. Jasper saw a shadow dive through and tackle Adele, then wrestle the gun away and start punching. Methodic and vicious. *Thud thud thud thud.* The sound was far away like he had headphones on. Adele went limp but Nora kept hitting her.

"She's gonna kill her," Colton yelled. "Get her off." He shook Jasper's shoulder. "You hit?"

"No, I don't think so." He looked for the body. "But that guy—"

"Don't know if she meant to help me, or just get in first. Saved me from a bullet, either way."

Nora threw herself at Jasper, running her hands over his chest, checking for wounds. When she was satisfied he was okay, she turned to Colton. "We're leaving."

"You crazy? It ain't safe."

"*Safe?*" she yelled. "She was waiting in this room, Colton. *This. Fucking. Room.* Somebody told her where to go."

Colton's walkie crackled. "I'm coming with you, then."

Nora led them to the Civil War study room. They barricaded the door with a bookshelf and a busted recliner. Jasper found a sweatshirt that smelled like mildew, but at least he'd be warmer.

As Nora paced, she picked blood off her knuckles. She looked out of place in shorts and a T-shirt that hung off one shoulder.

"She kept saying she was sorry," Jasper said. "That they—*they,* Nora—knew where her parents lived." Jasper grabbed Colton's arm. "Cyrus wasn't paranoid at all. He was dead right."

"Obviously." Nora tested the barricade with a shove. "But the Libertines didn't tell her where to go. We did that."

"What?" Jasper asked.

"The guy, before Thanksgiving—he was recon," Nora said. "The Libertines were trying to see what we'd do with you, and we showed them."

Colton shook his head. "That don't explain how she knew about the safe room."

"Because you have a leak, Colton. One of your people talked."

Rufus was freaking out on the walkie channel, barking for somebody to report in with Jasper's location.

"You're not bringing anybody back here until you've figured out how she knew," Nora said.

When Colton left, they reinforced the barricade with a desk. Nora unscrewed the legs of a coffee table and tossed Jasper one to use as a club. She made them sit in the dark in case anybody was prowling around outside and hissed every time he made a noise.

An hour later, boots clanged on the metal stairs.

"Open up, Nora," Rufus demanded. "It's all right."

"There's a leak."

"Yup. I believe we found it."

They took down the barricade and let the Donelsons in.

And someone else.

"What's he doing here?" Nora asked.

Sheldon's face was as white as a sheet. He looked like he'd recently thrown up.

"We'll get there," Rufus said. "Cameras showed a man climbing over the east wall. That's what tripped the sensors. My boys gave chase, but the target got away again."

"He wasn't trying to get in," Nora said. "He was trying to get Jasper to the shelter."

"Looks that way." Rufus glanced at Sheldon. "Adele woke up. Girl can barely talk on account of her jaw being broken, but she said enough. Said a burner phone was mailed to her over the break. Man called and said he'd send some Libertines to visit her family if she didn't kill Jasper. Had her steal a gun from the armory. Told her to find out where we keep him during a breach, and report back when she found out. Sent her a text yesterday to go there and wait."

"But *how* did she find out?" Nora asked.

Sheldon pulled out his phone and gave it to Rufus.

"No—nononono," Jasper said.

"Jasper sent Sheldon a text over the break," Rufus said. "Something about the chapel basement being like the bomb shelter we put him in. Adele said she looked through his phone one night when they was hanging out."

"I didn't even think about it—"

"Shut up—just *shut. Up.*" Nora grabbed the phone and read the text. "That little—and *you*—" She threw the phone at Sheldon. "She's a *ten*—what the hell would she want with you?"

"Easy," Jasper said. "It was my fault."

"'Cause you're always a victim. The poor orphan boy who can't get his shit together."

He bit back a nasty reply. She wasn't exactly wrong. "I messed up. I'm sorry."

"You're *sorry*." Nora put her fist up to his eye. "That's more blood. On my hands, Jasper. *Mine.*" She pressed her knuckles into his cheek, and smeared bits of dried blood on it. Water pooled under her eyes. "I volunteered for this job, but it costs me a lot. Don't waste it on your own fucking stupidity."

CHAPTER TWENTY-THREE

B yron watched Jasper and Sheldon change. He'd been attached to Jasper since he'd arrived the night before.

"At least you don't have to help me go the bathroom anymore," Jasper said.

"The Counselor is waiting."

Apparently, the bodyguard still hadn't discovered a sense of humor.

"Right at the end last night, before he kicked us out," Sheldon said, "I thought Cyrus was going to have Larkin murder us."

Jasper reached for his phone and then remembered Byron had taken everybody's cells last night right after the epic scolding session. He'd probably crushed them with his giant fists. "I think I said I was sorry three hundred times."

"Yeah, you had major *I'm sorry* diarrhea."

They joined the small army outside their dorm room. Nora and Byron, plus about ten Donelsons, acted as a human shield as they walked to the library.

The halls were less crowded—some kids had taken off early for winter break—but anybody still at Juniper Hill had to back against the wall as the entourage passed by. The procession bordered on the absurd, but reminded Jasper of the terrifying. He kept reliving the seconds in the bomb shelter, the feeling of cold metal on his skin. That it was his own fault didn't make the memory any less paralyzing. In the safe room, he'd crept even closer to the edge than when he'd nearly drowned in the Delaware River. Almost dying was becoming habit.

Lacy and Tucker were waiting outside the library.

"Did you pitch Cyrus the Virginia trip when we left?" Jasper asked.

Lacy nodded.

"And?"

She shrugged. "A granite wall of silence."

"But he enjoyed reminding us that he'd been right about the Libertines having people on the inside," Tucker said. "Guess we deserved that."

Cyrus was reading something on a laptop when they came into the study room. He let them settle down. "I spent the night reviewing your research," he said. "I'm convinced of your primary theory: that Jasper's father was seeking out the descendants of Lieutenant Ira Boswell and the records they may have inherited."

Jasper let out a breath.

"But the Directors will not approve the mission without a more thorough argument—specifically, how the supposed items connect Boswell to Arnold. Or Reed and Washington, for that matter. Do you have a theory?"

"More of a gut feeling," Jasper said. "Nothing I can prove."

"Explain, please."

Jasper watched the mobile twist on its string. "All these historians make one thing pretty clear: Reed hated Arnold. My dad visited a bunch of Joseph Reed archives, found this letter about him giving Boswell money, then started tracking down Boswell's descendants and was killed."

"I have yet to hear a theory."

Jasper took a second to arrange the details. "The answer to our Big Question—why did Reed donate off-the-books cash to Boswell?—is the same as why the Libertines killed my dad: Boswell. I think he knew something, and I think he wrote it down, and the Libertines don't want us to find it. Something about Reed or Washington. Something damaging."

Cyrus pressed his fingertips together. "That would explain their decision to break the Code. And to infiltrate our organization."

"Right," Jasper said. "And Elsbeth is in the driver's seat of this, obviously—so maybe Reed was too, back then."

"Perhaps, but we are widening the extent of our speculation. Restrict your argument to Lieutenant Boswell, focusing on his close relationship with Arnold, and connecting that to Reed's public campaign against him. You have one week."

Jasper blinked. "Until what?"

"At my request, Lacy's father has called an emergency meeting of the Board of Directors. They arrive Friday. You must convince a majority of them that the trip is worth potentially angering the Jeffersons, as well as any transportation and protection expenses."

"We're doing this, then?"

"We are." Cyrus looked among them. "Be certain you understand the implications of your request. If your mission is compromised, you'll have to fight your way out."

"We're in," Sheldon said. Adele's attempt on Jasper must have swayed him.

"I will remain on campus to plan the expedition should the Directors grant their approval." Cyrus stood and buttoned his jacket. "And now, if you'll excuse me, I must have a discussion with the headmistress."

"I would kill to have Chilligraphy duty today," Sheldon said. "He's gonna light her up like a bonfire."

★★★★

They decided to go the old-school research-paper route to build their case. Lacy divvied up sections, and Tucker became everybody's walking citation. It took three days to get together a first draft, which

Sheldon said sucked worse than the dystopian novella he wrote in seventh grade. They ate and slept and drank Lieutenant Boswell until he started appearing in their dreams. If anybody thought about going home for Christmas, they didn't say it.

At Cyrus's instruction, Kingsley reopened the range for the group. It was more real this time, the pointing and shooting; Jasper missed the target less and less frequently. He wondered if it was the practice, or maybe he'd finally gotten to the heart of the thing—this was war and if he wasn't willing to pull a trigger, he'd die. Nobody cared that he was scared or that none of this was his fault. They were after him, so he had to do something about it. He maybe had to kill.

"Reading in church is a sin," Nora said one night.

Jasper crossed out a line in their latest draft. Sheldon really needed to cool it with the word *thus*. "Pretty sure God wants me to succeed, so He'll forgive me."

"Because you have a direct line to Him."

Byron roamed up and down the aisle like he was searching for a bomb.

"You don't have to come if our mission gets approved, you know," Jasper said. "Byron's pretty good at his job."

"I can keep you from dying without a gun. We've established that. Multiple times."

"I mean, if you don't want to be around all the possible shooting— if it's too hard—it's not a problem."

"Penance is supposed to hurt."

"Is the plan to die protecting me?" he asked. "Is that why you just charged in and went after Adele? And why you're coming with us now?"

"The plan is to do things that make me feel less shitty about my past," Nora said.

"Right, but I'm asking about the logical conclusion of that process. If you're aiming for martyrdom here. Because I would have a serious problem with that."

"I keep forgetting that my life is really about your self-obsession."

He put the paper down. "I was sort of okay with our consumer relationship because it's kept me alive and made you feel less awful," he said close to her ear. She smelled like lilac and smoke. Spring on fire. "But I'm over it now. I'm not really sure when that happened, and I don't know if it even matters because of all your emotional baggage, but consider me no longer okay with being your guilt outlet if you're just using me to get to some ultimate solution."

"So you don't mind if I die protecting you," Nora said. "You just don't want it to be my main goal."

"Maybe you forgot that I've buried both of my parents in the last six months. Forgot how burying one more person—specifically, you, who despite trying to make chain-smoking cool again, has definitely become my closest friend—might be more than I can take. How it might break me."

She put her palms on the pew and pressed down. "It's my life, Jasper. I can do whatever I want with it."

"But you don't live in vacuum."

"Still my life."

The pounding bass quieted as the song changed. Jasper heard dogs barking in the distance. The pair went to the door and watched a steady stream of cars and pickup trucks park at the cottages.

The Directors had arrived.

Chapter Twenty-Four

The guy in the back who looks like an out-of-shape linebacker is Lacy's dad," Sheldon said.

"No wonder Colton's terrified of him," Jasper said.

Lacy leaned on their shoulders and peeked over. "He's a total pushover."

Jasper went to the next window to get a better look at the Directors parading toward the manor. The group was watching from the closed, north-wing dorms that overlooked the front entrance. Jasper could see his breath. "And the old lady he's helping?"

"Mary Greenhow," Lacy said. "Related to Rose Greenhow, the Confederate spy. The grandmother you always wanted."

"So that's two votes for us." Jasper squinted at a couple around his parents' age arguing pretty loudly. "Which one is Oswald?"

"Lady in the red coat," Sheldon said. "And the guy who looks like he walked out of a copy of *GQ* is her ex-husband, Director Forrest."

"A guy whose ancestor was a Confederate general turned KKK leader married the daughter of a Russian spy?" Jasper asked. "That has to be awkward."

"Not a lot of gift exchanges happening at the holidays, I'm sure," Sheldon said. "They divorced after their son died in a duel."

Jasper spotted Cyrus in the rear chatting with a shorter, thin man in his fifties. He leaned on a cane. "And that's Chairman Hickey."

"He's kind of a legend," Lacy said. "Survived a three-shot duel against a Washington in the seventies. Took a bullet in the femur and ribs."

"He might be the only League member hated more than you, bro," Sheldon said. "His ancestor plotted to kidnap and assassinate Washington during the war."

"People say the range targets at the Libertine schools have his face on them," Lacy said.

Nora opened the door and Tucker came into the room carrying the final draft. They paged through it one last time, even though everybody knew it was too late to make changes. Lacy put the printouts in five folders and had a Donelson deliver them to the auditorium.

"Should've left in some of my *thus*es," Sheldon said. "The power of a good *thus* cannot be overstated."

The group skipped lunch and instead paced outside the auditorium door. Jasper reviewed Cyrus's outline for the Virginia trip in case the Directors asked for a summary. Sheldon kept trying to fix his tie, but just kept making the mess worse. Tucker had gone with jeans and a blazer over a T-shirt that read DIE above a gigantic, twenty-sided die.

"It's been three hours," Jasper muttered.

"They are taking forever to read it; thus, they hate it," Sheldon said.

Lacy smoothed a wrinkle from her black dress, and went back to pulling her curls out.

The door opened.

"They are ready for you," Cyrus said.

The four tromped up the steps to stage left and sat on stools by the podium. Nora camped out by the door. The Directors sat at two tables below, hands folded on top of the report.

"Good morning, I am Director Greenhow." The old lady examined them over her reading glasses. "Which of you is responsible for the annotated bibliography?"

Tucker raised his hand.

"Outstanding, young man," she said. "Simply sublime."

"If only the same were true for the rest of the paper," said Director Forrest. His blue suit was basically painted on. "To start, how do you know that James Mansfield didn't already visit the home of"—he checked his notes—"Milford and Anna Boswell before his death? If he did, this entire trip is a waste of resources, and that doesn't even touch on the inevitable political fallout with the Jeffersons."

Jasper walked to the podium. "When he visited a descendant, my dad made notes on that part of the family tree. There were no notes recorded on this section."

"Maybe he forgot. Or he just didn't get around to it," Director Forrest argued.

"Which is exactly why they're requesting to go—to find out," said Director Oswald.

"Are you going to argue for him?" Director Forrest asked.

There was a moment of tense silence.

"He checked into a hotel in Charlottesville in the afternoon, and died a couple hours later," Jasper said. "That also supports our theory that he never made it to see Milford and Anna Boswell."

"Maybe he was on his way back," said Director Forrest. "Your supposition is thin, if you ask me."

"This money Joseph Reed gave to Lieutenant Boswell is what I find troubling," said Director Greenhow. "It could simply have been a gesture of good will. After all, we know historically that his wife wanted the money she raised to be paid directly to the soldiers. Why do you find the payment so nefarious?"

"Reed hated Arnold," Jasper said. "So it's really odd that he would pay that much money to somebody who worked so closely with him. But it's even more shady because of what has happened in the present—in light of my dad's murder."

"*Alleged* murder," Director Forrest corrected.

The other Directors watched Jasper.

"*Alleged* murder," he repeated, "followed by my very real kidnapping and torture, which I'd be happy to review in graphic detail, since I was there—"

"Easy," Sheldon whispered from behind him. Cyrus was giving him a death glare.

Jasper cleared his throat. "My dad's alleged murder by Elsbeth, my kidnapping, and the two attempts to kill me here are more evidence that the True Sons of Liberty don't want us looking into Boswell. So while we argue that giving money to the guy whose boss would eventually betray America is odd, the attempted cover-up has made it very . . . nefarious."

"I'm inclined to agree," said Director Oswald. "But you don't say what this evidence contains."

"We don't want to speculate," Jasper said.

"In other words, you don't know," said Director Forrest dryly.

"No."

The Directors traded pointed looks.

"But whatever is in that document, it's big enough to blackmail two people at Juniper Hill into attempting murder," Jasper said. "That seems like something we should check out."

Lacy's dad stirred in his seat at the end. "On behalf of the board, I would like to apologize for not doing more to protect you. We're investigating both incidents thoroughly."

"Have you considered dropping the matter entirely?" Director Forrest asked Jasper. "It could be the safest option for you. For all of us."

Jasper thought the man must be kidding. "So my dad died for nothing?"

"We've all lost someone; it's part of League membership."

Chairman Hickey put a hand on Forrest's shoulder, and patted it twice. "Jasper, Counselor Barnes tells me there is a plan in place." His voice was a little raspy. Slow and steady. "Please, share it with us."

Jasper scanned the outline. "We stay at a motel ten miles from the Boswell home near Charlottesville. Sheldon will set up a secure Wi-Fi network and digital scanner so the item can be transmitted immediately in case we run into problems."

"Counselor Barnes's paralegal, Sybil, will pose as an archivist from the University of Virginia. I'll be her assistant. The cover story is that Lieutenant Boswell was recently discovered to be a close friend of Thomas Jefferson, and the university is looking for any correspondence between them. And is willing to pay."

"How very generous of the university," said Director Forrest.

"The Counselor offered to use his own money."

That shut him up.

"Once we have the item, we'll head back to the motel, scan, and upload it. Pack up and head out. If all goes well, we're back on campus by noon the second day."

"And if all does not go well?" asked Chairman Hickey.

"We've mapped several routes to the Donelson property in Tennessee," Jasper said. "If things go wrong, we'll head there to wait it out." Jasper looked at his friends. At Nora. "We know what we're asking. We're still on board."

"Very brave of you."

"I wouldn't call it bravery. I'm terrified. But sitting around here waiting to die scares me way more."

Chairman Hickey looked down the table. "Are there further questions?" The other Directors shook their heads. "Let's proceed to a vote."

Jasper gripped the podium. He didn't expect an answer so soon.

"Those against?"

Director Forrest shot his hand up right away. No shock there.

But then Director Church raised his, too.

"Dad," Lacy said.

He wouldn't look at her.

"Dad."

"Those in favor?" Chairman Hickey asked.

Director Oswald and Greenhow lifted their hands. Chairman Hickey inspected them, then his notes. Spent some time deep in thought, tapping the top of his cane with a pointer finger.

Then he said, "I am also in favor."

Jasper almost pushed the podium off the stage. This was really happening—they were really going on this trip.

"On behalf of the board, and the entire League, I wish you luck," Chairman Hickey said. "If the past is any guide, you're going to need quite a bit of it."

Chapter Twenty-Five

I actually never thought they'd say no," Jasper said. "I'm not sure why."

"You're an optimist." Sheldon sat on his suitcase, which was outrageously overpacked. "It's your second best quality after your hockey hair."

"That was pretty awkward with Lacy's dad."

"That, I get," Sheldon said after a while. "Parental instincts."

"Not sure if I made this clear but—"

"Yeah, about a thousand times. *You're welcome.*"

Jasper zipped his own bag shut. "Before this—in my old and boring and not dangerous life—my friends barely wanted to drive the forty minutes to hang out at my house. Now, I've got people pledging themselves to protect me."

"Forty minutes is a long way to drive to just hang out," Sheldon said. "An hour-twenty round trip."

"You know what I mean."

Sheldon gave him a bro hug. "If Iron Man wasn't watching, I'd make up a special handshake that only we knew about so we could do it front of everybody else and make them jealous."

"We're going to the armory," Byron said flatly.

The guy was so quiet, Jasper kept forgetting he was there.

In the range, Kingsley waved them into the classroom. On each desk sat a series of gun cases—the ones that were always locked up in a separate cage in the armory. Jasper opened the one in front of him, and saw it wasn't the black, worn practice pistol he was used to, but silver and brand new. These were the real deal—dueling pistols. The ones saved for killing.

"Oiled them myself," Kingsley said.

He brought out some ammo boxes, and they filled two clips each—hollow point rounds, the big league stuff that expanded on impact. Lacy jammed bullets into her clip like a possessed person; she was all in, no matter what her dad said. Nora and Tucker watched everybody like they were juggling dynamite. Kingsley passed out black, leather holsters that fit snuggly on their belts. Jasper's was different—it was made for the small of his back so he could carry it secretly into the Boswell house. Last were Kevlar vests. Jasper would have to take his off during the actual mission.

Kingsley stopped him on the way out. "You asked me a question before. About me killing anyone."

"Yeah."

"I told you it was none of your damn business."

"I remember," Jasper said.

The instructor rubbed his chin with a meaty hand. "I've got plenty of regrets. Every man does. But winning my duel, that's not one of them. You understand me."

"I think so."

"You and I, we were drafted into this fight the day we were born. I sleep easy knowing I did my duty." Kingsley grabbed Jasper by the shoulder and kind of just shook him a little—probably the closest thing the guy knew to a hug. "You bring that gun back to me or I'll kill you myself."

★★★★

The caravan left at dawn, Rufus's truck leading, followed by the van driven by Byron. The white landscape raced by as the group passed through small towns and rural byways. It felt good to be outside the walls—Jasper had actually started to forget that there was a world still carrying on. People were going about their non-Revolutionary off-spring lives, not worrying about dueling or hiding or maybe becoming murderers or getting murdered. It seemed hilarious and stupid and completely ridiculous—them, not him. He'd been in the incubator too long, obviously. He couldn't imagine what it was like for the other League kids. This was the only world they knew.

Normally, the trip would take about ten hours, but Rufus was sticking to back roads, stretching the journey to fifteen. Eventually, the terrain flattened out and Jasper saw the ground—patches of brown that told him it was getting warmer. He dozed off after a late fast-food lunch and woke at five in the afternoon. Larkin had switched places with Byron behind the wheel. Tucker and Sheldon were snoring on the benches. Lacy and Cyrus stared out their windows.

"You should sleep," Nora said. "Still another three hours."

"I think my neck is permanently crooked."

"Lie down."

He stretched out and put his head on her lap. She put her hand on his chest and he laced their fingers.

"Relax," he said. "We're not going to start making out or anything. I don't do that with random girls. Especially ones running for the President of the United States of Emo."

Her lips were doing weird stuff to his face; she must have missed his mouth. It took him a couple of seconds to figure it out, and then the whole thing got better. But it still hurt. She kissed like she did everything else: a little angry.

"Don't take this the wrong way," he said. "But your mouth kind of tastes like an ashtray."

She played with his hair. "Don't make everything a joke. If this isn't what you wanted to happen, then just say it."

"I didn't not want this to happen."

"Good, 'cause I'll be pretty pissed if you start kissing other people," she said.

He traced some tattoo lines on her arm with his thumb. It was weird how things changed—how for a while you were one thing with somebody, and then the line blurred and then you were another.

"I'm staying back at the motel tomorrow with Tucker and Cyrus," she said. "I'll just get in the way, otherwise."

"I get it."

"I'm not abandoning you or anything."

"I said I get it."

They made out some more—less teeth-colliding this time. Big improvement. Not that he had much experience.

"You're still gripping the gun too hard," she said. "That's why you're pulling right."

"I never thought you'd give me shooting advice."

"What I did . . . before . . . is different from this. I still hate this, but it's different."

"Necessary, you mean."

"Maybe. I don't know. Just relax your grip, okay."

Tucker sat up, looked at them, and then lay back down. "This is not your personal deer-hunting vehicle, Chesterton."

★★★★

Two hours later, they met Sybil at a motel outside Charlottesville. An overweight, skeptical lady showed them to rooms that stank of sweat and bleach. Sheldon set up the network and scanner while everybody else tried to sleep. That turned out to be impossible, so they sat around and watched horrible TV because it distracted them from the reality: they were completely freaking out. Jasper changed into dress pants and a sweater that fit his fake job better. He and Sybil went over their routine until she seemed satisfied he wouldn't screw up their cover. He went to Nora and Lacy's room afterward, but they were asleep. On the way back to his own room, he ran into Cyrus at the vending machine. The lawyer was staring at a dangling Twix bar.

"Sybil likes them," he said brusquely.

"You think he'd be proud?" Jasper had been wondering about how his dad would feel about this mission for a while. "It sounds silly, but I'd really like to know. Do you think our efforts would make him happy? Is this what he wanted for me?"

"It's hard to say."

"Yeah."

Cyrus gave the machine a right hook and the Twix fell into the collection tray. "He wanted you to escape, and we're on that path—wherever it leads. I think that would've pleased him."

"It's funny, caring what he thinks when he's dead," Jasper said. "After hating him for forever."

"If anything else," Cyrus said, "he would be proud that you're attempting to remake the past instead of allowing yourself to become a prisoner to it. That is something none of us has had the chance to do."

None of us. Jasper never thought to ask Cyrus about his lineage. It seemed way too personal. Like walking in on him going to the bathroom. Maybe he'd ask Sheldon about it later.

Jasper broke the silence. "I meant what I said to Chairman Hickey. I'm terrified. I've never been this scared in my life."

"Hold out your hand."

Jasper did as he was told.

"Do you see what I see?" Cyrus asked.

"You mean my hand shaking like I have pneumonia?"

"Exactly."

"That has to be a terrible sign."

"Nerves only reflect anxiety—the mind anticipating the event. All that matters is what you do in the moment. That is all there is. And when it comes, you will move or you will not. There will be no nerves. Only action or paralysis."

Jasper put his hand in his pocket. It was still shaking. "I better try and get some sleep."

CHAPTER TWENTY-SIX

S till going with the long hair, I see," Sybil said.

"I've been a little busy. You know, not dying."

She checked her lipstick in a compact mirror. "I suppose it fits your cover as a lazy college student."

Jasper steered her car around a long, slow bend in the country road. His palms sweated against the wheel. He kept pushing back against the seat to feel the gun holster beneath his suit jacket, and looking in the rearview mirror to make sure Rufus's truck was still behind them. Lacy, Sheldon, and Colton were in there, guns ready, and another pickup rode behind them in case things got really crazy.

"This is it," Byron said from the back seat. He hunched below the windows, almost prone. "Take it slow."

Jasper turned up a long, gravel driveway that snaked toward a brick house in the middle of a clearing. The trucks stayed down by the road. Split rail fences broke up the plot, carving out fields where a couple horses grazed. Jasper pulled up to the house and he and Sybil got out, then walked up to the front door and knocked.

And then they knocked again.

"I called yesterday to let her know we'd be stopping by," Sybil said. "She said she'd be home."

Jasper raised his fist to knock again when the door opened the length of a daisy-chain lock. A short old lady, more wrinkles than actual face, poked her head through the opening.

"What do y'all want?"

"Ms. Boswell, good afternoon," Sybil said. "My name is—"

"What are y'all, papists?"

"I'm sorry?"

"No, not papists, no—today's Sunday. Jehovah's Witnesses?"

"No, Ms. Boswell. We're with the University of Virginia's library. We spoke yesterday."

"What about?"

"Thomas Jefferson and his friendship with your husband's ancestor, Ira Boswell, a soldier in the Revolutionary War," Sybil said. "We discussed the possibility that your husband, Milford, inherited some letters?"

"I remember. Y'all got a card?"

"Of course." Sybil handed her a crisp cream rectangle.

"Can't be too careful these days. All kinds of evil out there." She closed the door and undid the daisy-chain lock. "Well, come on in, then."

The house smelled of mothballs and ashtrays, which probably explained Anna's haggard face. Jasper made a mental note to push Nora harder on the Nicorette. The old lady showed them to a sitting room where they settled down on a musty couch. Vintage frames with pictures of a man—Jasper guessed Milford—covered every tabletop, and available square inch of wall space.

Anna poured three cups of brown liquid. Jasper sipped it and wished he hadn't.

"What's his story?" Anna asked, nodding at Jasper.

"A graduate student," Sybil said. "My assistant."

"He a hippie?"

"No. Just lazy," Sybil said.

"My Milford hated hippies. Wouldn't stand for one being in his house."

"I'm not a hippie," Jasper said.

"Oh, so he *can* talk. How 'bout that." Anna bunched her face up and made a noise Jasper guessed was a laugh. "All right, all right, don't get all worked up, now."

"As I mentioned over the phone," Sybil said, "we appreciate your seeing us on such short notice."

"Bit strange, coming on a Sunday."

"With primary documents, every second counts. Entire collections have been destroyed because of a slight change in temperature. Considering the season, we didn't want to take any chances."

Anna rocked slowly in her recliner. "How much you gonna pay me?"

"That depends on the condition of the items, but the university authorized me to purchase any verified period artifacts at market value."

"I like the sound of that."

"Have you had a chance to look through your late husband's things?"

"Honey, that would take years. But I know where you and the hippie can start."

She hobbled ahead of them down the hall to a tiny office. An inch of dust covered the desk and bookshelves. Two filing cabinets stood in a corner with an old-school antenna TV perched on top.

"The man loved his space," Anna said. "Hid in here so I wouldn't bother him. Said he was payin' bills, but I mostly heard the football game." She banged the filing cabinet with an elbow. "Well, have at it, honey."

Sybil put on a pair of latex gloves and opened the first drawer. Like a good graduate assistant, Jasper catalogued items on a clipboard as she drew them out. Most of the papers were normal household crap—bills and receipts and paperwork from daily life—and lots of it. Milford kept detailed records. Things got more pack-ratty in the second filing cabinet; the bottom drawer was just a bunch of bowling-league trophies.

"Now, that's a real sport," Anna told Jasper. "Not like the soccer you long-haired kids play."

Sybil started on the desk. Jasper scribbled like mad to keep up. He glanced at the wall clock and saw they'd been there for almost forty minutes.

"Is there a key for this?" Sybil tugged on the center desk drawer.

Anna came over and gave it a jiggle, then a bang, then a hard tug. It popped open.

"Thought I didn't know about his little gambling habit," she said. "Always made me sad he thought he had to keep it from me. Wasn't an addiction or nothing. Guess he just liked his privacy."

Sybil took out a stack of envelopes that turned out to be nothing more than get-well cards. Jasper counted almost fifty. She held up some childish drawings of a family. "You have grandchildren?"

"In Richmond. They came out more when he first got the cancer. Not so much, now."

Jasper was actually starting to feel sorry for the old lady.

Sybil moved to the bookshelves and started on the top row. Jasper saw the prize before she did, but when she saw him get all fidgety, she flared her eyes like she'd murder him if he didn't play it cool. It was the frayed edges that gave it away—brittle and worn like dry leaves in November. He could see them wedged between a King James Bible and a large-print edition of *Moby Dick.*

"Now, what's this?" Sybil said. "I believe we have something interesting here." She removed the other books on the shelf first, exposing the documents, which weren't really documents at all, but the outward facing pages of a book—no, three books.

"Thought you was looking for letters," Anna said.

"Such is the way with archival work. We take what we can find." Sybil gently lifted the books off the shelf and laid each one on the desk. Jasper actually bumped into her trying to get a better look at them. They had light-brown covers and were in the same state of rapid decay. The first cover almost tore off as Sybil carefully opened it.

"What are they?" Anna asked.

"I believe—"

142

"Diaries," Jasper said. He couldn't read the tiny cursive writing, except for the date scrawled at the start of the entry. "This one begins in January, 1775."

Sybil carefully turned to the back. "Looks like it covers almost two years." She made the same inspection of the other two. "Oh, my. Almost six years of entries. This is something special indeed, Ms. Boswell."

"Probably worth quite a bit."

"If Ira was the author, then I'd say so." Sybil was working hard to keep her voice even. "But you see, here—on the inside of this cover?"

Jasper squinted alongside the old lady.

"Looks like it reads Alice to me."

Jasper felt his heart do a double beat.

He knew that name. He'd seen it once—the article on Ira's death from dengue fever.

"His wife's diaries," Jasper said.

"Still valuable," Sybil interjected. "Historians researching women during the Revolution would naturally love this in their collections. Unfortunately, I am not authorized to pay a premium for anything but Ira Boswell's own documents."

"How much?" Anna asked.

Sybil put a latex finger to her lips. "Based upon condition—very poor—and content—interesting, but not exactly what the university is seeking—"

"Oh just say the number, sister."

"I could go as high as . . . three hundred a piece?"

Anna smiled wide enough for Jasper to count her missing teeth. "Sold."

Jasper took out some legal documents Cyrus had drawn up that would fool even an actual lawyer.

"I'll need your signature here," Sybil said. "And here and here." Anna scribbled like a demon. "Would cash be acceptable?"

"Darlin', cash is king."

143

Sybil removed nine crisp hundred-dollar bills from a bank envelope and handed them to Anna. Jasper took out a special plastic bag and Sybil placed the diaries inside, and then back in his bag. He wanted to take off sprinting to the car.

"On behalf of the university and archivists and historians of the Revolutionary era, I thank you, Ms. Boswell," Sybil said. "Please, do reach out to us if you locate anything else you think might be of interest to our collection."

"Sure you don't wanna look in my cellar?"

"Unfortunately, we have to be on our way. But you have my card."

"Yes, I do." Anna walked them to the front door. "Bother me on a Sunday any time you want."

"Take care, Ms. Bowell."

Gravel crunched under Jasper's feet as he struggled to walk slowly back to the car. The short walk was an eternity. His heart beat hard and fast as if he'd just run a marathon, and all he could think of was his dad—how this is where he would have come. How now, he was finishing his dad's work.

Sybil got in the front passenger seat. "Go," she ordered when Jasper fired up the ignition. He put her car in gear and eased back down the driveway as Byron got on the walkie to Rufus. The trucks fell in line behind them as they pulled out onto the road.

"Oh my God," Jasper said, gripping the wheel. "Oh my God. We did. *You* did it! That was amazing."

"We probably could have started at fifty a piece," Sybil said. "But the Counselor can afford it."

"We did it. We actually—"

The seatbelt choked the rest out of him as he slammed on the brakes, skidding the car sideways. Two black SUVs blocked the road ahead. The Donelsons' trucks rolled up on either side of Jasper. Sybil pulled a coal-black pistol from her purse and chambered a round.

"Jasper," she said evenly. "This is where you get your gun out."

CHAPTER TWENTY-SEVEN

Jasper slid the pistol from the holster and pulled the hammer back with his thumb.

"Reverse if they start shooting," Rufus said over Byron's walkie. The bodyguard stowed Jasper's bag with the diaries under his seat and chambered a round.

For about ten seconds, the two sides just stared each other down. Jasper couldn't see into the black SUVs—the windows were tinted. He remembered what Sheldon had said about the Jeffersons and machine guns, and wondered if Rufus had brought enough firepower.

A short, muscly guy in his thirties stepped out of one of the SUVs and walked toward Sybil's car. He wore a dark blue suit, pistols hanging beneath his armpits in shoulder holsters.

"Exit your vehicle," he ordered. His blond hair ruffled in the wind.

Nobody moved.

The man signaled back to one of the SUVs. A window lowered and Jasper spotted a muzzle. He didn't even have time to duck before a string of bullets ripped across the windshield, spidering it badly. Sybil let out a sharp scream.

"You are trespassing," the man yelled. "Now, step out of your vehicle and explain yourselves."

Rufus slowly climbed from his truck and walked a few steps toward the guy. "William, good to see you again."

"I can't say the same, Rufus. Neither would my brother if he knew you were here."

"Last-minute kinda thing, you understand. These folks are guests of mine and are making their way to Tennessee."

"I wasn't notified of this journey through the proper channels," William said.

"Well, I'm sorry 'bout that, but just the same."

"Would you stop me from interrogating trespassers on my land?"

Rufus scratched his cheek. "The way I see it, I'm helping you avoid what could otherwise be a messy situation—what with the buckshot my boys got loaded in them widow-makers. So why don't you head on your way, and we'll do the same."

The two men were close now, maybe a couple feet apart. William looked off to his right, like he was thinking about something.

Then he went for his gun.

It was a blur—Jasper couldn't believe Rufus could move that fast—but the older guy tapped into some hidden energy reserve and hit William with a sharp jab on the chin. It stunned the man just long enough for Rufus to step behind him, and throw the guy to the ground. By the time his back slammed into the road, Rufus had his gigantic revolver pointed at William's chest.

"Now, be a good boy and tell your people to back on outta here," Rufus said. "Like I said, we'll be on our way."

The passenger door of one of the SUVs opened, and a woman stepped out.

The woman.

The Iron Woman.

Jasper saw the gun in her right hand, the black duster jacket sweeping around as her arm rose up to aim. It was like watching a movie, except it wasn't in slow motion. Elsbeth, the death-dealer.

But then Jasper wasn't watching anymore, because the camera moved. *He* was moving. He didn't even realize until Byron yelled something and tried to grab him, but it was already too late. Jasper opened his door and raised his gun.

In.

Out.

Half-in.

Hold.

This must be what Cyrus had meant—the automatic reaction. You didn't tell your body what to do. It just did it and you were along for the ride.

Jasper settled the sights on her dark torso and steadied his arm. Her gun was almost in position—she'd be firing soon.

This was it. The moment. If he missed, Rufus would be dead. Maybe they'd all die. But he wasn't afraid anymore. He felt no emotion.

Squeeze.

BANG.

Elsbeth spun around like she'd been hit in the shoulder by a truck. A bullet cracked in the car windshield; she'd still gotten a shot off.

Then there was yelling: Donelsons screaming at the dark-suited guys with machine guns who had poured from their SUVs. Rufus started backing up slowly, screaming orders, gun never leaving William. Rufus made it to the truck before the first Jefferson machine gun went off.

Rattattattatat.

The Donelsons returned fire, their shotguns creating deep bass *KABOOMs*. Byron finally got ahold of Jasper and shoved him in the back seat. Sybil was looking at something on her chest, studying it like an experiment. Jasper saw a dark circle getting bigger and bigger until it covered her entire right side. She touched it with a finger and then slumped toward the console. The back of her shirt was soaked through.

Byron grabbed a first aid kit from the glove compartment and started stuffing gauze onto the wound. "Jasper, put pressure on this while I drive. *Jasper! Pressure!*"

Jasper ducked as a machine gun round shattered the windshield completely. He felt blindly for Sybil and pressed against the wound as

Byron threw the car into reverse. The transmission whined as he red-lined it and cut hard to right the wheel.

"Sybil's hit," Byron yelled into the walkie. "Bullet went through. She's bleeding out."

Jasper put his other hand on Sybil's chest and pressed as hard as he could, trying to keep the life inside her.

CHAPTER TWENTY-EIGHT

Wind tore at Jasper's face as they flew along the roads. Every time he opened his eyes to check on Sybil, a piece of windshield glass or road debris got in his eye.

There was so much blood.

It covered her entire torso, the seats, and Jasper's arms. It really did have a smell—dull, metallic. He felt like he'd showered in it.

"Is she going to die?" Jasper shouted.

"Pressure!" Byron yelled back.

Eventually, the car rocketed over a set of railroad tracks into a small town with a single traffic light. Byron screeched to a halt in front of an old square building with a medical cross insignia and carried Sybil's unconscious body from the car. Rufus leapt out of his truck and banged on the aid station's door, bellowing for help. A guy in a white doctor's coat came to the door and unlocked it.

"Gunshot wound," Rufus shouted as they carried Sybil inside. "Bullet went clear through."

"My Lord," the doctor said. "Bring her back here." He glanced at Rufus's gun. "I guess y'all haven't called the police?"

"No police," Byron said.

Jasper followed them down the narrow hallway, hands still pressing as they lay her on a gurney.

"Let go, son," the doctor said as he pried Jasper's hands off. "I'll take it from here."

Jasper stumbled into the lobby. He would've collapsed if Sheldon hadn't caught him. His body shuddered. The blood on his arms was sticky, pulling at the hairs. His breathing got shallow and quick until it was almost impossible to breathe at all, and he started to cry. He grabbed his knees and rocked back and forth, trying to ignore the sounds coming from the OR down the hall.

★★★★

Jasper didn't remember moving. But somebody—Byron, probably—must've carried him because he woke up under a heavy blanket in the back of one of the pickups. A billion stars shone overhead as a cold wind rushed around him. Six or seven Donelsons sat nearby, shotguns ready. Byron practically sat on top of Jasper.

Sheldon was snoring near the gate.

A shadow stirred on his other side and handed him a water bottle.

"She made it through surgery," Colton said. "Bullet just missed her lungs. Sybil's tough, that's true enough."

Jasper downed half the bottle in one gulp. "Where is she?"

Colton nodded to the cab. "Others are in the truck behind us."

"Nobody else got hit?"

"They was spraying wild to cover Willy."

Jasper yawned. The air felt good, like cool water over a fresh wound. "Who was he?"

"You know Asher Jefferson?"

The name registered from chatter at school. "The head of the Jefferson clan?"

Colton nodded. "That was his little brother, William."

"We just shot up a big-time Libertine's little brother."

"Seems that way."

Jasper could feel the hyperventilation creeping in again. He gulped some more water to keep it at bay. The whole point of this had been to keep a low profile.

Not start a war.

"Nice shot," Colton said.

Jasper replayed the scene—saw Elsbeth Reed in his sights. It felt like a week ago. "Did you see her, Elsbeth, get up?"

"Saw somebody haul her through a door."

"So I didn't kill her."

"Bullet looked high right. Shoulder, I'd think, by the way she went down."

That actually made Jasper a little less tense. He tried to concentrate on how he'd feel if Colton said she'd stayed down, but it was all too blurry. Maybe it was better this way.

"Means you gotta name her now," Colton said. "Your gun."

Jasper shifted around, felt the butt of the weapon in the small of his back. "What are the rules again?"

"Girl that broke your heart, or mom. Moms and sisters are risky, though."

"Right." Jasper thought about his limited romantic past. "I went out with this girl named Jackie once in tenth grade for like a week."

"Jackie."

"Yeah."

"Sorry-ass name for a gun. Maybe it'll do just till you and Nora split."

Sheldon snorted so loudly, he woke himself up for a second, then settled back to sleep.

"Shame about that old lady you visited," Colton said.

"What?"

"That the house was empty," Byron cut in. "That you found nothing."

Headlights from the next truck lit his face enough to make it crystal clear.

Keep your mouth shut.

"Yeah," Jasper said to Colton. "It sucks."

"'Least nobody died," Colton said. "And y'all get to see Tennessee while Sybil heals. Real mountains. Won't be a total waste, is what I mean."

Jasper tried to catch Byron's eye. The bodyguard gave him absolutely nothing.

★★★★

The ride got bumpy as the trucks crossed a skinny ridgeline around dawn. Descending the winding slopes, the caravan crawled along a dirt road for another hour before stopping at a monstrous log cabin. Sheldon didn't actually wake up until the truck gate opened and he rolled out into the dirt.

"Frickin' freezing," he said. "I thought it was supposed to be hot in the South."

The cabin's front door opened and a dark blur bolted straight for Jasper. Nora rammed into him in a sort of hug/body check that took the wind out of him.

"You need to stop scaring the shit out of me," she hissed in his ear.

Cyrus and Larkin helped Rufus carry Sybil inside while Tucker tried to high-five Sheldon, but ended up just slapping his forearm instead.

"I shot Elsbeth," Jasper told Nora.

"I know."

"She was gonna kill Rufus."

"You did what you had to."

"I didn't kill her."

Nora touched his bloody hands and forearms. "Did you want to?"

"I don't know."

She rubbed the sticky residue between her fingers, lost in some thought. Then she snapped straight. "Doesn't matter. You're not dead. Mission accomplished, even without the documents. We'll keep looking."

So she was in the dark, too. Jasper looked around, eyeing the Donelsons unloading. Did anybody know what really happened?

"What?" she asked.

"Nothing. Crazy day."

Nora watched him for a beat—really bore into him—then she dragged him toward the cabin. "You need a shower."

★★★★

Under the steaming water, Jasper watched tiny streaks of Sybil's blood run out from beneath his fingernails. He wondered if he'd ever be able to forget that horrible drive, pressing her wet skin with his bare hands. Bile surged into his mouth, and he put a hand against the tile to steady himself. Maybe stop reliving that moment until he had some food in his stomach.

Or forever.

Somebody banged on the bathroom door and then barged in.

Byron.

"*Jeez*," Jasper said, grabbing for a towel. "Naked here."

Byron held out a flannel shirt and jeans from the Colton Donelson collection. Jasper could hear Nora's combat boots treading the planks outside.

"What's going on?" Jasper asked in a low voice. "Why are we lying about the diaries?"

"Because that's what the Counselor wants."

"But you have them, right? They're safe?"

Byron nodded. "You should have stayed in the car."

"A little late for that."

"The Counselor was very upset you took such an unnecessary risk."

"I got you in trouble. I get it. Sorry." Jasper cinched his towel tighter. "Maybe you could lecture me later?"

Byron left and Jasper got dressed.

"You two having a moment in there?" Nora asked when he came out. Some suspicion in her voice.

Jasper deflected by shrugging. "Byron needs a lesson on boundaries."

"You're not kidding."

Downstairs, the pair joined the others around a giant oak table. Jasper shoveled in ham, eggs, biscuits, and grits while Nora filled in the group on how they'd bolted from the motel after the shootout. Jasper was on his third cup of muddy coffee when Cyrus appeared in the kitchen doorway and signaled for him and Byron. Nora got up, too.

"Stay," Byron told her.

"The hell I will."

The room went silent.

"It's fine," Jasper said. "I'll be right back."

Nora looked back-and-forth between Byron and him. Her eyes narrowed; she could sniff BS from fifty feet away.

Cyrus silently led Jasper and Byron down a hallway to the other side of the house. "Have you told anyone?" he finally asked.

"No."

"It must stay that way."

"Why?"

Cyrus stopped before a mirror and adjusted his tie. "Because we have been betrayed."

A set of double pine doors opened up ahead. Rufus appeared in the doorway and waved them inside.

"Can't be him," Jasper said. "He almost died with us."

"Perhaps, but we're done trusting our closest allies. I'll share with Rufus only what is necessary to secure his continued service. But the diaries remain a secret."

The den was big and warm and ringed with trophy bucks. Byron and Larkin roamed among windows, hands hovering close to their guns. Rufus stoked some logs in the large fireplace and motioned to a pair of leather couches separated by a coffee table.

"How is she, Counselor?" Rufus asked.

"Resting. Thank you for your quick thinking."

"That river splits two ways." Rufus walked over and held out his hand to Jasper. "Glad you learned how to aim that thing."

"Me, too." Jasper shook his hand. No way this guy would betray them.

Right?

Cyrus brushed a piece of lint from his pant leg. "Have Asher Jefferson or any of the other Oligarchs reached out to you?"

"Nope," Rufus said. "Which don't sit right, considering we probably wounded a couple of them back there, maybe even killed one or two."

"It sits perfectly," Cyrus said. "Elsbeth has been leading this operation with their support since the beginning."

"Whole thing has felt too organized; she'd need help from somebody at the top." Rufus rubbed his chin, thoughtfully. "So y'all didn't find what you were looking for in that lady's house."

"Unfortunately, no," Cyrus said.

Jasper put on his best downcast face paired with a headshake—not too much, just enough to sell it. He wished he could lie professionally like Cyrus, without skipping a beat.

"Cryin' shame to come all this way for nothing." Rufus drifted back to the fire and poked at it. "But you got bigger problems: someone told them Jeffersons about the whole trip. Wasn't no accident they knew where to find us."

There it was, out in the open.

"It is equally clear that we have a leak, yes," Cyrus said.

"I can write up a list a people who knew we was coming, but I'd be on it. My kin, too."

"Your loyalty is not in question, Rufus."

"It would be, if I was you."

Cyrus nodded.

"Here on out, you oughta be more careful about who you tell your business to."

Cyrus cleared his throat. "We are obviously beyond the bounds of our current contract, and yet your services are needed more than ever. Perhaps we can come to a new arrangement?"

Rufus watched the fire for a while. "I been both sides of this thing. Can't say I like either one. But I'll tell you what: I never slept better in my life than after them Oligarchs gave us the boot."

"Considering the circumstances, I'm sure the Directors would allocate more funds—"

"You Yanks never could let a man get to the end of a sentence," Rufus said. "Contract's fine the way it is. Keep your money."

They shook hands, then chatted about security before Rufus left to see how repairs on the trucks were going.

Cyrus waited a moment, then motioned for Jasper to join him by a window. "You will return to campus and begin transcribing the diaries alone and in secret," he said, barely above a whisper.

"How am I supposed to do that?"

"Consider the facts: the entire mission was a failure. There are no documents from Lieutenant Bowell. Sybil nearly died in your arms."

"You want me to act depressed?"

"Withdrawn, yes. I'll help the ruse along by informing Ms. Booth that Byron will be taking over for her."

"So, lie to everybody?"

"Is that a problem?"

"Yeah, it's kind of a freaking problem," Jasper replied. "Those people are my friends. They helped me figure all of this out. Oh, and they also almost got ripped apart by machine-gun fire."

"The perfect cover for a mole."

Jasper blinked. "You can't seriously think it's one of them."

"General Washington never imagined that your ancestor would betray him," Cyrus said. "And now Arnold's name is a synonym for traitor. Consider that the next time you put your full trust in anyone."

Jasper racked his brain for an argument, but came up short. Cyrus had logic on his side. Somebody had talked, nearly ruining everything they'd been working for. "It feels wrong," he finally said.

"Unless you'd like to inform Sybil that the entire mission was blown because you feel bad, we will honor her sacrifice by protecting what she almost died to obtain." Cyrus set his jaw. "Deception is our only ally now."

Chapter Twenty-Nine

Jasper walked into the woods until he couldn't see the cabin anymore. For once, Byron was giving him some space.

The worst part, though—and Jasper hated himself for it—was that he couldn't wait to get started.

Every time he thought about the diaries, his heart beat faster. This was what they'd risked it all for. Those awful nights in the study room clawing at clues, digging and outlining and scraping until they'd finally cornered the thing and unearthed it big time.

And now he had to lie about it. It was like finding a cure for cancer and then hiding it under your mattress, awkwardly peeking at it every night to make sure it was still there.

He felt like a traitor.

The irony.

Eventually, he ran into a Donelson patrol. Colton peeled off from the group to show him the way back.

"Maybe we can take the scenic route," Jasper said. "I'm not really in a rush."

They found a stream and followed it for a while until it hit a waterfall that dropped twenty feet below.

"Great spot to jump in the summers," Colton said. He pointed to the far side where a giant boulder stuck up out of the water. "Just gotta make sure you don't go in at a bad angle or the pressure will push you under that rock and you'll drown."

"How do you make sure that doesn't happen?" Jasper asked.

"Just gotta be real careful."

Along the way, Colton named every tree, plant, animal, and most of the birds. Jasper could tell he knew these woods, and loved them. It was weird to think about Colton having this whole other life down here, away from Juniper Hill and the guns and security details. Jasper felt kind of selfish for never even considering that Colton's life was about more than just protecting him.

They'd stopped by the side of the creek and were skipping stones across the surface. Jasper was barely keeping up.

"How come you guys help the League?" Jasper asked. "I get that the Libertines kicked you out because of the not-dueling and everything, but you don't have to help us. You could just live your lives."

Colton winged a rock across in one skip. "Jackson wasn't a big fan of the Indians. Said they was in the way of progress and signed a law that made sure they left. You heard of the Trail of Tears, right?"

"Yeah. Bunch of Cherokee got pushed off their lands by the US government."

"A lot a other tribes, too, but people only talk about the Cherokee." Colton turned a stone over in his hand, ran a thumb along the edge. "Thousands in total died from starvation and disease during them marches. Women. Kids."

Jasper nodded, really letting it sink in. It was looking like he didn't have a monopoly on the whole inherited villainy front.

"Now, my daddy says that ain't on us," Colton said. "We wasn't there, we didn't do it ourselves—but as Jackson's kin, it's our job to help fix the harm his actions caused."

"So, you try to do good to make up for what he did. Like helping us."

"Something like that," Colton said.

"The world needs more people like you and your dad."

Colton shrugged, then threw another rock. "Ain't none of us oughta be controlled by our past. But you can't run from it, neither. Guess that's what it comes down to for us."

When the sun started to dip below the horizon, they started back. Jasper's stomach knotted tighter with every step. He knew Nora was waiting, probably stewing in a cloud of smoke on the porch right now. And he had to face her—look her straight in the mouth and lie. The others would maybe buy the "poor, traumatized Jasper" routine, but not her. Her fantastic BS radar would out him in five seconds.

There was one way—a grenade he could use. It would pack enough boom to give him the space he needed. But pulling the pin, that would take guts.

If he went there—if stooped *that* low—there'd be no going back. He'd blow Nora apart and find himself covered in debris.

It would be the end of whatever they were.

★★★★

Jasper and Colton got back to the cabin after dusk. Nora sat on the porch swing wrapped in a blanket, watching Jasper approach like a cat. An ashtray with about twenty butts in it sat beside her.

"Hey," he said.

She took a pull and stared straight ahead. It was like that day in the courtyard after he'd come out of his coma. They were strangers again.

"Cyrus fired me," Nora said.

"I know."

She pointed her cigarette at Byron who was pacing by the door. "You think this is a good idea?"

"Wasn't really my decision."

"Bullshit actually does have a smell, Jasper."

"What do you want from me?"

"How about the truth." That was the old Nora. She was giving him a chance to come back from the edge. "What's going on?"

Jasper gripped the grenade, fingers on the pin. He braced himself. This was going to be ugly. "It's not my fault that you need this bodyguard duty to not feel awful about yourself. You're just gonna have to find some other pet project to make up for what you did."

She took it like a Marine: no flinching. Or maybe the insult had been so bad, it had obliterated her ability to speak.

He turned his head away. He couldn't even stand to have her in his peripheral vision.

And then his neck was burning—a hot, searing knifepoint on the left side. He screamed and pulled away but it followed him.

Nora followed him, jamming the cigarette tip harder into his skin.

Byron grabbed her by the wrist and threw her against the porch railing. Jasper kept screaming. The pain actually got worse by the second. Nora stood there and watched, her face scary calm. He'd expected yelling and swearing and maybe even crying, but not this.

This was way worse.

The door burst open and people streamed out, but Byron held a hand up to keep them back. It was like a wild animal was on the loose and nobody wanted to spook it.

Jasper pressed his palm harder into his neck, not really sure if the pressure was even making a difference. It hurt so much. Obviously, that was the point.

"I'm sorry," he said to her. And he really was. He'd been inside the blast radius, too, and the shrapnel had gone in deep.

Nora stared for another second, then pushed past the crowd to get inside.

Cyrus watched her go, his face empty. No sympathy for Nora's suffering, no guilt for making Jasper do it.

Pure granite, to the bone.

CHAPTER THIRTY

The alarm went off at 5:30 AM. Jasper slammed the button to silence it after two beeps, not that it mattered. Sheldon could sleep through the apocalypse.

He sat up and rubbed his eyes, which had started throbbing a week after they'd gotten back to campus and the pain was only getting worse. Maybe he needed glasses. He couldn't remember the last time he'd been to the eye doctor. Juniper Hill didn't have a nurse that pulled you out of class to do vision tests.

He dressed in the dark. Layers were a must after the New Year's Day blizzard that had turned the campus into a tundra three weeks before. He'd heard two kids had gotten frostbite walking from the gun range to the manor. He put on another sweatshirt, pulling the collar wide as he stuck his head through. The burn mark had scarred over, but it stung every time Jasper caught something on it.

Byron waited outside the door, looking like he'd slept like a baby, even though he'd probably only gotten four hours at most. The shift-change with the Donelsons happened somewhere around midnight—Jasper hadn't nailed it down precisely—but it couldn't leave much room for REM sleep. The guy was a robot.

"Hat," Byron said.

"Right." Jasper ducked back inside and got the thick wool cap Lacy had given him for Christmas.

They stopped in the cafeteria for some fruit, then started for the gun range. An arctic blast ripped through Jasper's layers. The Donelsons had shoveled a path across the field and marked it with reflectors so if the snow drifted, you wouldn't stumble around getting hypothermia. Bits of ice blew into Jasper's eyes and he squinted through his hands most of the way. Byron unlocked the gym door and then relocked it behind them.

"Let's shoot first," Jasper said. "My eyes are killing me."

Byron went to the armory and got Jasper's gun, the one Kingsley had assigned him before the trip. Jasper thought it was stupid that he couldn't carry it around—it would be easier to be protected if he could protect himself—but Kingsley would never allow it. They were lucky he even let them up here without personally supervising their practice. Cyrus had definitely gone over his head and Chillingworth's to the Directors to get that kind of access.

Jasper put on his eye protection and headphones. He filled the clip, shoved it into the gun, chambered a round, and took his time. Shooting had become a reprieve from staring at the diaries, so he made sure to extend practice as long as possible.

Bang . . . Bang . . . Bang . . . Bang.

He barely noticed the recoil anymore. It was kind of scary how repetition got you so used to something.

"Pulling right," Byron said.

"Yeah."

Jasper finished the clip, then loaded another and emptied it even slower. He pushed a button on the booth that retracted the target.

"Still pulling right," Byron said with a tiny shake of his head.

"Yes, I can see that."

"Can you?"

So Byron had found some sarcasm. Good for him.

Byron returned the gun to the armory and they went to the classroom. From the special lining inside his jacket, Byron drew out a plastic sleeve containing the notebook, which Jasper had been using for transcription, and a diary covering the years 1779–1780. Jasper had started with this one because it spanned the years of three key events: Arnold's first contact with André, Reed's request to send Boswell money, and Arnold's act of treason. The other two diaries were buried under the planks in Byron's cottage. The bodyguard pulled out latex gloves from another pocket and Jasper put them on.

His cover was simple: Jasper, being super late to the League game, needed tons more weapons training. Winging Elsbeth had been a fluke. So, every morning and every night, Jasper and Byron had the range all to themselves. Jasper shot enough so that the ammo logs corroborated his story, and then spent the rest of the time transcribing the diaries of Boswell's wife, whose life turned out to be incredibly boring.

"I bet she's gonna tell me about the weather," Jasper said. He squinted at the entry, *March 1st, 1779.* "Yup. 'Cold.' There it is. Always starting with the important information." He jotted down the next sentence, but got stuck on a word. Alice's cursive was tiny, faded, and slanted so far, it was basically falling over.

Was that an *H*? A *B*? Jasper reread the sentence, scanning for context. He'd ferreted out the most confusing words by now and had made a list, but this was a new one.

"It's an *L*," he announced to Byron, because one, this work was incredibly boring and he needed to share it with somebody else, and two, he knew it annoyed the crap out of Byron. "'Lucy stopped by with a letter from . . . Paul.'" He added both names to an index in the back of the transcription journal. It was over twenty names long at this point, and Jasper still didn't have the faintest clue who these people were. "I wish Alice was more like you: no friends and less chatty," he said to Byron. "I'd be done with this in a month."

"If you talked less, you'd be done sooner."

"Careful, Byron. You're becoming hilarious."

Jasper cruised through two days worth of the diary, but got held up by the writing on the backside of the page bleeding through. Paper quality back in the 1700s really sucked, not to mention the two hundred years of decay. A random capitalization—"Providence"—screwed him up on March 7th, and he added that to the list of words Alice randomly capitalized for who-knows-what reason. By the end of two hours, he'd managed to get through half the month. It was a big improvement. He'd started at an entry a day.

"You know what's weird?" he said, breaking the silence. "She doesn't talk about the war at all. I mean, she mentions stuff in passing—rumors, mostly—but life goes on like, 'Lucy paid a visit. Somebody sent a letter. Ira dined with the officers. It snowed.' *Blah blah blah*."

Byron checked his watch. "Time to go."

"Right." Jasper packed everything back inside the plastic bag.

"How many days today?"

"Fourteen. No, fifteen. This would go faster if you helped."

"I have a job."

"If you can't read, you can just tell me. I won't judge you." Jasper was getting less and less careful about poking the beast. He liked seeing the tiny cracks in Byron's facade.

"Anything to report?" Byron asked.

"It's all just names right now. Neighbors. Friends. Her two kids are always sick. Nothing ground breaking about Ira."

"The Counselor says—"

"Yeah, I know. It's all useful. I got it."

Byron put the diaries back in the lining of his jacket.

Kingsley was pacing at the door when they left the building. He muttered something as Byron handed him the key, but the wind carried his words away. Jasper wondered who would win if the two men fought. Byron was made of steel, but Kingsley would fight dirty. It would be an interesting match-up.

"You think he knows?" Jasper asked.

Byron pretended not to hear and tucked his chin into the collar of his black overcoat for the trek back to the manor house.

Halfway across the field, Jasper looked up and saw the dark silhouette on the rooftop. Nora had started the routine a week after they'd gotten back, watching him from their old spot like a gargoyle. Neither snow nor sleet nor thirty-below temperatures stopped her. Jasper liked it better this time of day, when he could see her in the morning light.

He waved.

She crunched a cigarette under her boot and then climbed back through the window.

CHAPTER THIRTY-ONE

Bro." Sheldon patted Jasper on the back, then rubbed his shoulders. "Brohemoth."

"What."

"I hate seeing you like this. Sulking is not your thing. You need to get back in the game."

"The game?" Jasper asked.

"You should take a crack at the World War Two girls."

"I think we established that's not a good idea."

Sheldon stopped the rubbing.

"Sorry," Jasper said.

"Low blow, but true." Sheldon went back to his seat and his bag of Cheetos. "They can't all be murderous spies. It's just a matter of numbers."

"You should ask out Sarah Franklin," Tucker said. He was halfway through a volume of an old-school encyclopedia—the letter *E*—as part of a New Year's resolution to become a human Wikipedia. Humanpedia. "She's nice."

"How would you know?" Sheldon asked.

"Because she started making out with me last week when we were redoing that chemistry lab."

Jasper and Sheldon looked at each other.

"You made out with Sarah Franklin," Sheldon said.

"She really sucks at chemistry." Tucker turned the page, finger tracing the lines as he speed-read. "Which is a deal breaker for me. You can ask her out, though."

"Pretty sure nobody wants to get near me, Sarah Franklin included," Jasper said. "I'm kind of a liability. And I have Byron."

"He does cramp your style," Sheldon said.

Byron prowled the shelves, eyes scanning up to the catwalk. Jasper didn't like hanging out in the study room anymore. It felt like a graveyard. Lacy went up there sometimes to cram for a test, but mostly they hung out in the main reading room.

"Still can't believe Cyrus took the safe back," Sheldon said.

"Yeah. It sucks." Jasper's mopey face was pretty good by now. "The Directors pretty much ordered him to."

"Dude, I'm on board if you wanna dig around with what we already know. Say the word. Tuck's in, too."

"I am in," Tucker said, eyes never leaving the encyclopedia.

Jasper stared at his chemistry notes. Lying was harder when you had to look people in the eye. "I've gotta move on, start to figure out what's next. . . ."

The library door banged open. Nora glared at them, then walked by and clanked up the steps. They heard her rummage around in her study room and come back with a bunch of cables and power cords. She walked out without saying a word. Or looking at Jasper.

"The tension is real, yo," Sheldon said.

"You have no idea."

"At least you'll save money on tattoos."

Jasper didn't have to fake feeling like crap this time.

"Too soon?" Sheldon asked.

"It's fine. Whatever."

Sheldon crumpled up his Cheetos bag. He tapped Tucker on the shoulder and motioned for him to put on his headphones.

"You still pulling right?" Sheldon asked.

"Yeah," Jasper said.

"You've gotta relax your grip."

"You know, people keep saying that like the words will actually make it happen."

"Take it down a notch, diva," Sheldon said. "Why don't you let me come to your super-awesome range workouts? I've got two dueling tournament titles."

Jasper felt around for an excuse. Why hadn't he already come up with a response for this scenario?

"He has plenty instruction," Byron said from across the room. Bodyguard to the rescue.

Sheldon leaned toward Jasper. "Brody, if you're trying to make me jealous, mission accomplished."

"I'm trying to stop pulling right," Jasper said.

"You're really thinking about dueling, then?"

"I don't know." And he didn't. If the diary research didn't pan out, he'd be forced to make a decision. "Trying not to think about it."

"This is the part where Uncle Shelly dispenses wisdom." Sheldon picked something out of his teeth. "Don't."

"I did not expect *you* to say that."

"Bro, you didn't touch a gun until you got here. You really think your nerve is going to hold in a three-shot duel?"

"I did okay in Charlottesville."

"You did amazing!" Sheldon said. "But that was a firefight. You were operating on instinct. The duel is a ritual. I was my brother's second, so I know what it's like. You go up to the grounds Friday night, have a five-course dinner with your opponent and their guys. You eat this huge meal and chat with them like you're at a dinner party, staring them in the face. And the whole time, while you're making small talk, you know only one of you is going to be standing the next day."

"Why are you trying so hard to talk me out of it?"

"Because you—you'll die for sure."

"Thanks for the confidence vote," Jasper said.

"Chairman Hickey was an epic shot, and it was a miracle he made it out of his duel alive."

"You could die, too, ya know."

"True."

Jasper stared at Sheldon. "What's wrong with you?"

"We've been over this."

"Right. You're some soldier for the cause. But you don't want anyone else to be. . . ."

"Not everybody has to be on the frontlines," Sheldon said. "Guys have to be in the back of the platoon, too. And they're more likely to survive. Like you."

Anger and guilt collided in Jasper's gut. If, by some miracle, the diary contained something—if he actually got out of this whole mess—they'd all still be here.

"This is so messed up," Jasper said.

"It's the life we got, dude. None of us chose this."

"The life we got sucks."

They watched Tucker turn the page and start tracing the next line. Jasper tried to not picture him standing beside the coffin at Sheldon's funeral.

But he saw it anyway.

And it was awful.

Chapter Thirty-Two

Jasper murdered his eyes the next week. Byron got some Tylenol from Nancy, the chubby, middle-aged nurse, but they barely put a dent in the ice pick that was poking the back of his left retina. But he kept up the pace. It was like running from Godzilla with a busted ankle—you could cry about it, but that wasn't going to stop you from getting stepped on. You just had to suck it up and power through, even if you shredded your tendons along the way. Godzilla was coming whether you moved or not.

Jasper had started getting up earlier, sometimes even before his alarm went off. Alice's boring life had become his. He thought about her all day and dreamed about her at night. When Alice's friend died of smallpox, Jasper spent two days sulking—he actually felt like he'd lost someone, too. He found her two kids increasingly annoying, always sick and whining. Or maybe Alice just complained a lot about them. And what kind of mom was she, journaling instead of parenting? And why did he even care?

Jasper really needed to get his life back.

One morning, he started feeling dizzy and had to lie down before he puked. Byron took him to Nancy who diagnosed him with "eye strain." Apparently, the dry winter air and the weird fact that his eyes didn't shut completely at night was making his condition even worse. She gave him this ointment to smear on his eyes at night to seal them shut, and a drop to use hourly during the day. There was also an eye test that showed he was far-sighted or maybe had an astigmatism.

"What does that mean?" Jasper asked.

"Something is wrong with your eyes," Nancy said.

"Right—but what?"

"I'm not an eye doctor."

This was all very helpful.

"Does he need glasses?" Byron asked.

"He needs a full eye exam."

"Do you have any reading glasses he could try?"

Nancy brought out a shoebox and Jasper put a few pairs on. Most gave him vertigo, but there was one pair with hot pink frames that actually made the words a little clearer.

"Can I have these?" he asked.

"Your eyes must really hurt."

At least the case was black.

Let the slaughter continue.

Some nights he needed more time to work, so they started sneaking into the abandoned north-wing dorms. It was cold and bleak and Jasper had to wear a headlamp to see, but at least he could keep moving. Keep running from Godzilla. Plow forward until he couldn't keep his eyes open or his hands went numb, and then he'd start the process all over again.

During Nurse Nancy's mandatory "eye breaks," he'd watch the chapel and, every now and then, see a Civil War kid trickle in or out. It became a kind of a game—could he spot Nora before he had to get back to work? Most nights, the answer was no, but occasionally he'd see her scurrying along in the dark, her boots clacking on the pavement. Did she miss him? Was she still pissed? He wondered if when this was all over—whenever he got to the end of whatever this torturous quest was—she'd understand what he'd had to do. If she'd ever hear him out.

A dime-size scar on his neck said things weren't looking good.

He kept watching for her anyway.

And that's when he started noticing.

It didn't seem like a big deal at first—a couple of boxes in the mail room. Maybe somebody's parents were shipping late Christmas gifts. But at night, from a window in the north wing, Jasper swore that he saw the Civil War kids hauling those boxes to the chapel. It was probably more gaming equipment. Why did he want to know? He had enough to do. Break over. Back to work.

But he couldn't let it go.

Jasper started dropping by the mail room and looking at shipping labels—all addressed to Eliza. The packages were mostly from tech companies, and not very descriptive. But a couple had their contents printed on the side: Gridiron Server, BMD—Beast Mode Driver. The words didn't mean a thing to him, but it seemed like some serious gear.

It wasn't like he could tell Byron. The guy would probably raid the place and smash everything with his giant fists. And it wasn't like Jasper had any reason to tell him, anyway. He had no idea what the Civil War kids were doing. But he wanted to find out.

So he waited until the midnight shift change on a Wednesday. Colton's night.

Jasper got out of bed as quietly as he could. He hadn't even taken off his shoes. Zipping his hoodie, he cracked open the door and stepped into the hall.

"You all right?" Colton asked.

Jasper started toward the bathroom. Colton followed him.

"I want to go to the chapel," Jasper said. "I want to see her."

"That ain't a good idea."

"It's definitely not. But I want to go anyway."

"I oughta check with Byron."

"He'll say no."

Colton shifted Lacy to the other shoulder. Jasper found it weird that it was no longer weird to be around a sawed-off shotgun all the time.

"Give me ten minutes with her," Jasper said. "Please."

"Really shouldn't."

Jasper stared at the tile floor. Bleach stung his nostrils. "I helped you out with Lacy. Come on."

"That ain't the same thing and you know it."

"Colton," Jasper said. "I need to see her. Tell me you don't understand."

Colton tucked a strand of hair behind his ear. He studied Jasper and the wall behind him for a solid minute before finally saying, "I ain't leaving you two alone."

"Deal."

The winter was just being nasty now—wind that carved at you like knives. Jasper thought it had to be near zero. He pulled down his wool hat and burrowed his face in the coat. Patches of snow the Donelsons couldn't plow had turned into ice sheets and he almost bit it near the chapel.

"You really thought this one through?" Colton asked. "As I recall, the last time you spoke, she put a cigarette out on your neck."

"What is she gonna do, kill me?"

"A couple more witnesses wouldn't hurt, is all I'm sayin'."

"You're scared of her."

"I am."

Jasper shuddered as they approached the chapel. "Me, too, actually."

He pried open the door with frozen fingers, and the boys stepped into the entryway. Jasper was careful to ease the door shut so the lock wouldn't clang. He listened for the bass—he was actually counting on it to cover the creaking of the wooden planks as they crossed the floor—but tonight he could have heard a pin drop.

The pair eased along the wall, stopping suddenly when a board underfoot groaned.

At the top of the stairwell, Jasper heard buzzing. Or was it humming? It was kind of like the noise he'd heard when he'd stood too close to a power line on a school trip. And it only got louder the lower they went. Now, it almost sounded like wind.

Crunch.

Jasper froze.

He carefully lifted his right foot and saw shiny pieces glittering in the green light bouncing off the walls. A black wire stretched across the step, an inch from Colton's boot.

Jasper could feel a prickling along his neck. "Don't move," he whispered.

"What's wrong?"

"Don't—"

Colton's boot caught the wire as he tried to reverse up the steps. Jasper heard a *ding,* like a bell being set off. It wasn't loud, but he still screamed. He fell to the landing, tripping another wire—*dingding-ding*—and kept rolling down the stairs until he landed at the bottom with a thud.

A flashlight beam blinded him.

He felt something hard and cold jammed against his neck.

"*Drop it!*" Colton shouted from the steps. "*Put it down!*"

"I almost killed you," Nora hissed in Jasper's face.

"*Put. The knife. Down!*"

Jasper blinked away the spots floating in front of his eyes and saw Eliza wielding a giant Maglite. Nora was pointing a six-inch blade at Colton. "Easy," she said. "I thought he was someone else."

Colton lowered his gun and helped Jasper up. "Don't think Chilly would like you riggin' up tripwires on her campus."

"And I don't think Byron would like Jasper wandering the grounds this late," Nora said. "Why don't we go wake him up and ask?"

The humming was intense now. And the rushing sound really was wind—three window fans were pointed at two racks of computers. Eight monitors blinked hundreds of lines of tiny numbers and letters. This wasn't gaming.

It was something more.

Jasper looked Nora right in the eye. "I came to say I'm sorry."

"You said it. Now get the hell out." She pushed him back up the steps, blade still out.

What was she hiding? What was happening down here?

"I mean it," he said. "I'm sorry."

"I'm not."

She marched them to the top of the steps, then disappeared back down.

"Byron doesn't need to know about that," Jasper said as he and Colton headed back to the dorms.

"Fine by me," Colton replied. "Could have my daddy poke around their little hideout during the day. See why they're so private all a sudden."

"Let's just pretend it didn't happen."

But Nora had given away more than she'd meant to.

I thought you were someone else.

Someone she'd been ready to kill.

CHAPTER THIRTY-THREE

Jasper fogged up the hot pink reading glasses and then cleaned them with his shirt. They were working pretty well—the ice pick was almost gone from his head—but they also had left a permanent dent on the bridge of his nose. Thankfully, the safety glasses from the shooting range supplied a perfect cover.

"We need new latex gloves," Jasper said to Byron. "There's a hole in this pair."

"You need to be more careful." Byron checked his watch. "Eight minutes."

Jasper put the reading glasses back on and dragged his eyes to *June 13th, 1779*. He tried to focus, but his thoughts kept drifting to breakfast (he was starving) and the calculus quiz he was nowhere near ready for (which he'd be taking in about an hour), and Nora and this person she was ready to kill and what all those computers were doing in the chapel.

And that's how he almost missed it.

> *I woke last night to the sound of heavy boots. I went to the steps and saw Ira salute a man dress'd in a heavy coat and plain clothes. They sat by the fire and spoke in low voices. He left and Ira smok'd for some time. When he return'd to bed I asked who the man was, and he said it was Mr. Reed of the Pennsylvania Council, but would not say what they spoke of. very warm to day.*

177

He scanned to the next few entries for similar cursive patterns but came up empty. More weather and whiny children.

Until a week later.

I wish there was something I could do to aid my husband. He is much troubl'd by the visit from Mr. Reed. I ask'd him but he refus'd to tell me—very mild weather.

"Time to go," Byron said.

Come on, Ira, Jasper thought. *Talk to your wife.*

little Sarah very poorly with a fever and violent cough— sent for Dr. Teller—Ira confid'd about his visitor last week said Mr. Reed ask'd him to persuade Gen. Arnold to aban- don our Cause. G. Washington had lost faith in him as we all know from the court martial. Mr. Reed promis'd a high commission and money if Ira did so. I am much troubl'd as many gossip that we are Tories. fine weather today.

"Byron."

Maybe it was the edge in Jasper's voice, but the bodyguard's hand flew to his gun.

"Byron. Listen to this."

He read the passage out loud.

Byron took out his phone and sent a text.

"Did you hear what I said?" Jasper shouted. His ears were pound- ing and his eyes had stopped burning and, just for a second, he wasn't having horrible flashes of Sybil's blood all over him.

This was it.

The answer to the Big Question.

"Joseph Reed bribed Boswell to turn Arnold into a traitor!" Jasper said, jabbing at the page. "*This* is what they didn't want us to find!"

Byron's phone buzzed. He glanced at it and started carefully packing up the journal. "The Counselor is on his way to inspect the diary himself."

Jasper clapped and let out a whoop, then went to hug Byron, but realized that was a bad idea when the bodyguard shoved him away.

It had all been worth it. The kidnapping. The torture. Sybil.

All of it.

Nora.

Maybe not all of it.

Jasper bombed his calculus quiz and smiled doing it. Who cared? What did it matter? He'd finally found it. This wasn't fool's gold; it was the motherlode. It was like finding out that magic was real and that he was actually a wizard-king. Every time he thought about the journal, his fingers tingled and the world faded away.

Joseph Reed—war hero, one-time bff of Washington, abolisher of slavery in Pennsylvania—had been *deep* into something very shady. Something the Libertines would kill to keep from going public.

By the time Cyrus knocked on the door of the frigid north wing, Jasper thought his heart was going to beat out of his ribcage. Larkin locked the door and Byron gently took out the diary. Using Jasper's headlamp, Cyrus read the transcription first, then the diary, then reread both. The whole act took less than five minutes.

"Isn't this crazy?" Jasper asked. "Can you freaking believe it?"

Cyrus stood and paced the room. Maybe it was the shadows, but his granite face looked harder than usual.

"It is extraordinary," he finally said.

"I know, right?"

"More than the League could have ever imagined."

"That line about George Washington losing faith in Arnold is crazy," Jasper said. "Like maybe Washington was involved in the whole plot?"

"Perhaps," Cyrus said. "Or Reed made that up to urge Ira on."

Jasper's stomach rumbled. He'd been too excited to eat. "Cyrus, tell me this is my way out."

"It is." The Counselor lowered his voice to a whisper. "For us all."

CHAPTER THIRTY-FOUR

Whatt?"

"The True Sons value honor above all else," Cyrus said. "Imagine how this information would challenge the historical narrative. This, Jasper"—Cyrus held the diary in front of his face"—this is why they murdered your father. Why they have done all of this."

"Right . . . because it makes Reed look like the bad guy—maybe even Washington. So we make a trade with the Libertines: no one challenges me, and I keep it quiet."

"No, Jasper," Cyrus said. "This is far bigger than you now."

"I don't . . . exactly know what that means."

Cyrus grabbed Jasper by the shoulder. "We will make a trade, yes—but it will not just be for your duel. It will be for every duel." He was so close, Jasper thought they might hug. "We will use this information to leverage a permanent peace for *every member* of the League."

The tingling in Jasper's fingers had spread to his face and down his spine. He was on fire. He could see his breath—giant clouds—as he heaved in and out. "We threaten to tell everybody—the world. Historians and professors and colleges. The Libertines would do anything to keep that from happening."

"Precisely."

Jasper felt lightheaded. This was a total rush. "So we set up a meeting," he said, then realized how stupid that sounded. "Nope. They'll definitely murder us."

Cyrus nodded. "We're going to have to seek an audience before the Arbiter and convince him to broker this deal."

Jasper waited for an explanation.

None came.

"Who's the Arbiter?" Jasper asked.

"In times of conflict, the Arbiter is an impartial judge who acts as an intermediary between our organizations. The True Sons respect his office and would never attempt violence if he is involved."

"Please don't say it's the President," Jasper said. "Or anything to do with the Illuminati."

"Don't be ridiculous."

A sliding scale for sure, Jasper thought. "So, who is it?"

"The Chief Justice of the Supreme Court."

Jasper wondered why he was even surprised.

Nicolas Cage, eat your heart out.

"Are you sure the Libertines won't agree and then just massacre us?" Jasper asked. "That's definitely something Elsbeth and her people would do."

Cyrus was silent for a moment. "We have no other choice."

"Freeze."

Larkin's voice on the other side of the door was like a diesel tractor engine.

"Hands up," he said. "Walk forward. Slowly."

Feet scuffed down the hallway. Jasper would know the sound of those combat boots anywhere.

Byron packed up the diary quickly and unlocked the door just in time for Larkin to march Nora inside at gunpoint.

"You should find a better hiding spot," she said. "Eliza spotted your headlamp up here weeks ago."

"Why are you here?" Cyrus asked.

"I go to school here, remember?"

"Explain yourself, Ms. Booth."

"I saw your car pull up tonight," Nora said. "It saved me from having to talk with Jasper's babysitter."

"What," Cyrus said, "do you want?"

"I need to show you something."

Cyrus stared at her. "We'll be with you shortly."

"Not him," Nora said, nodding at Jasper. "He's seen enough."

Larkin marched her back out into the hall.

"What does she mean? What have you seen enough of?" Cyrus asked.

"Yeah . . . I . . . uh." Jasper cleared his throat and tried to avoid Byron's stare. "She caught me spying on her."

"Keep him here," Cyrus said to Byron. "Can you at least manage that?"

Jasper watched from the window as Cyrus and Nora marched out the front of the manor and to the chapel. Byron put a hand around the back of Jasper's neck. He kept it there for a full thirty minutes until Cyrus and Larkin came back.

"You will not step foot in that basement again," Cyrus said. "Is that understood?"

Jasper nodded.

"The diary is all that matters now. I will take all three back to Philadelphia and store them in your father's safe." Cyrus began pacing the room again, but it was different this time. His steps were faster, his swivels more jagged. "I will request a meeting with the Arbiter and summon you if he agrees to hear us out."

"What if he doesn't?"

But Cyrus was lost in something else, staring at the floor as he paced.

"Whatever it is that you're not telling me," Jasper said, "should I be worried?"

Actual worry lines creased Cyrus's face. Cracks in the granite. "The safest place in a tornado is the eye. That is where we are right now."

"So I should be pretty worried."

"Byron is here with you," Cyrus said. Then he added, almost under his breath, "And it seems others have been here with us all along."

CHAPTER THIRTY-FIVE

Jasper slept the entire next day and most of the following night. He woke up at 4:20 on Sunday morning and started getting dressed before he realized there was no more work to do. He lay in bed and reviewed the entries in his head. The thrill even blocked out Sheldon's epic snoring. At 5:00, Jasper got up to take a shower, ate a breakfast that was actually hot, and finally got around to watching the vampire ninja movie Tucker had been raving about on the TV in the study room.

"It was actually as bad as I thought it was going to be," he said to Byron.

"Worse."

Winter hadn't left, but he could tell spring was calling ahead to book reservations. The giant piles of snow had melted to gravelly peaks streaked with black, and most of the paths around campus were clear. Jasper had to squint as he walked off the eight eggs he'd inhaled for breakfast. He felt like he'd come out of a yearlong coma.

"What's the date?"

"March 3rd," Byron replied.

"Wow."

When they reached the amphitheater, Jasper saw Colton and Lacy sitting exactly zero inches apart on the stage, sipping giant mugs of something hot. They waved him over.

"You're alive," Lacy said.

"Barely."

"White as a sheet," Colton said. "Like them vampires in that movie."

"I want that hour and twenty-six minutes of my life back," Lacy said. She patted the stage. "Talk to me about things. You doing okay?"

Jasper sat. "Actually, yeah. Everything is better."

"I was getting worried about you. Not as worried as Sheldon, but almost."

"She asked about you every day," Colton said.

"It was all kind of a lot," Jasper said. "I needed some time to figure things out."

Lacy nodded slowly. "And you thought the best way to do that was to completely ignore everybody who cared about you—people that also might be a little shaken by everything."

Jasper guessed he deserved that—knew he deserved it.

He took in a deep breath, then let it out slowly. "I'm really sorry, Lace. I guess I'm so used to being on my own I just went back to old habits."

She looked at him, her face harder than he'd ever seen it. The reaction really surprised him—that his absence had made her that upset. That he'd been equal parts oblivious and selfish to everyone around him.

"You can only play the orphan card so many times, you know," Lacy said.

"That's true."

She finally smirked. "That was your last time. I hope you enjoyed it."

"You know, I really did," Jasper said.

Colton gave him a tiny nod, and he felt the tension seep out of the moment.

"So," Jasper said. "Did I miss anything good?"

"Let's see," Lacy said. "Chillingsworth finally caught the kid who was shoving paper towels into the toilets in the boys' bathroom by the library—nobody knows how. Then there was that tenth grader who slipped on the ice out front and broke her arm. Am I missing something?" she asked Colton.

"That other thing."

"Oh, yeah. I got into college."

"College?" It sounded like a different language to Jasper. "Right. College. That's great. So, you're not going to duel, then?"

"I will be majoring in business administration at a small school in St. Paul, Minnesota," Lacy said. "It's not exactly Harvard, but they gave me a partial scholarship. Student loans will cover the rest."

"That's amazing." Jasper saw Colton try really hard to smile. "Congratulations."

A door banged open and Jasper saw Kingsley stalking along the path through the soccer fields. Behind him, just above the snowdrifts, bounced Nora, hood up over her head. They disappeared into the gym.

"That's . . . weird," Lacy said.

"Kingsley don't open the range on Sundays," Colton said.

"Pretty strange." Jasper snuck a look at Byron, who stared bullet holes into him. *None of your business. Don't even think about it.*

"Could be she left something in there," Colton said.

"Like what?" Lacy asked.

"Don't know. Bookbag, maybe."

Lacy put a hand up. It was dead quiet, not even a breeze. "Wait."

They listened for at least two minutes. Jasper strained his ears until his brain just started making up noises.

And then he heard it.

A light *pop* followed by another set of three.

Pop pop pop.

Lacy was up before Byron could stop her, charging through the snow and slush to the gym. Jasper and Colton could barely keep up. She threw open the door and ran up the steps.

They found Lacy staring at a girl in the firing line who looked exactly like Nora.

But Jasper knew that wasn't possible because Nora would never be in the firing range, eye protection on, headphones slung around her neck, glaring at Kingsley who stood, arms folded, doling out advice she clearly didn't want. Nora would never be breaking down a handgun and rebuilding it with robotic precision or slamming the clip home and racking the slide.

But then the girl took off her hoodie and Jasper saw her tank top. And the tattoos. He watched her raise her weapon and fire off volleys of three, one right after another.

Pop pop pop.

Pop pop pop.

Pop pop pop.

Nora cleared the pistol and pressed the zipline button to bring the target forward. Ripping it off the wire, she examined the holes and put it aside. Kingsley said something, she yelled something back, and he roared louder. She just kept pointing to a part of the gun. Her eye caught Jasper's, and she paused, staring at him for a few seconds, before slamming a fresh clip home and chambering a round.

Pop pop pop.

Pop pop pop.

Pop pop pop.

CHAPTER THIRTY-SIX

Sheldon wouldn't believe Jasper until Nora showed up on the range for class the next afternoon. He spent most of the hour gawking at her.

"Maybe she's having a psychotic breakdown," he said as the group walked back to the manor later.

"She is not having a psychotic breakdown," Lacy said. "You saw her. She's perfectly calm."

"Then maybe she's defaulting to her natural state like the head vampire ninja guy in the movie," Sheldon said. "For a while, he stopped slaughtering innocent villagers, but eventually he just had to give in to his monster instincts and get down with his bad self."

"That's not it," Jasper said, sidestepping an icy patch. He'd tossed and turned most of the night wondering how her sudden willingness to pick up a gun fit into what he had discovered, if at all. Byron either didn't know or wouldn't tell him. Jasper figured it was the second one.

"Something's not right," Lacy said. She was yanking a curl that stuck out under her winter hat. "Why is Chillingsworth letting her handle a gun? She knows about Nora's past."

It was actually a great question—one Jasper had asked himself.

Maybe that's why he answered it out loud, totally oblivious that he was wading into some of his own secrets, too.

"Maybe she was ordered to by somebody higher up," he said.

Jasper felt Byron pull the back of his coat, then release it as Jasper wiped out completely on the walkway.

Lacy and Sheldon turned around.

"Nice, dude," Sheldon said.

"It's icy," Byron said. He didn't offer to help Jasper up. "You should be more careful."

Jasper got up and wiped bits of snow off his butt. Lacy held his stare for a second too long—three seconds too long, actually—then turned around and they kept walking.

Byron looked straight ahead like nothing had happened.

"You should just ask Nora," Sheldon said.

"Maybe," Jasper replied, distracted. *Somebody higher up.*

Somebody like Cyrus.

"Bro, that was a joke."

"Right."

But the weird thing was, Nora seemed to become less pissed at him as the week went on. When they'd come back from Charlottesville, she'd outright ignored him, except for those daily staring contests on his way back from the range. Now, she'd catch his eye as they passed in the hallway. So there wasn't any high-fiving or fist-bumping, but the loathing was gone, that much was obvious. Jasper just couldn't figure out why. What had changed?

★★★★

A week later, Jasper woke up in the middle of the night. Byron was looming over him, a finger pressed to his lips. The bodyguard let Jasper put on his coat before he pushed him out into the hall. There was no Donelson guard. Just a small travel bag, which Byron made Jasper carry to a bathroom on the first floor.

"Change," Byron ordered. "You have one minute."

"What? Why?"

"Fifty-eight seconds."

After Jasper changed, they ducked out a side door. Snow crunched as they walked to the tree line, single file. Byron stopped twice, turning around and scanning the woods. When they got to the outer wall, they followed it south, eventually coming to a small hollow. Byron made a sort of whistle noise and a shadow slid from the trees.

"You're late," Nora said. Her gun glinted in the moonlight as she lowered it.

Byron reached into his coat and handed Jasper his holster and weapon. "He's a heavy sleeper."

"What's going on?" Jasper asked.

"Lower your voice," Nora said.

Jasper shivered, then clipped the holster onto his belt. "Where are we going?"

"Over the wall."

She climbed the tree, a great big cottonwood with branches that reached over the brick. Twenty feet up, she shimmied out onto a branch until she could step easily onto the top of the wall. Byron dug out a thick rope from the underbrush, tied one end around the trunk and tossed her the other. She hauled it up and threw the rest over the other side.

"Move," Byron said.

On the way up, Jasper lost his footing on a busted branch and nearly broke his neck. Nora had made the shimmying part look easy— he got pretty close to crushing some vital equipment down there before making it to the wall. She rappelled down first and switched on a headlamp so he could see where he was going. Jasper grabbed the rope and slowly eased himself down to the slope below.

"Cyrus told you what we found," he said when he had his feet back on solid ground.

"Good work, detective."

Jasper pulled his coat tighter. "That stuff I said, I didn't mean any of it—I had to say it. It was horrible. Cyrus told me to—"

He flinched as her hand moved toward his face—he'd been expecting that. But instead of slapping him, she stuck her hand into his coat collar until she found the scar. She gently ran her thumb over it, back and forth.

"Does it hurt?" she asked.

"Not anymore."

"I wanted it to hurt."

"I mean, it really hurt for a while."

"Good."

Jasper heard Byron's feet scraping the brick above.

"Why are you doing this?" he asked. "You said you'd never pick up a gun again."

"The universe does not revolve around my self-pity. Some things are bigger than me."

Byron landed nearby.

"What took you so long?" Nora asked.

"Heard something."

Nora led the way down the slope, faster this time. She'd occasionally stop and switch on her headlamp to examine a notch in a tree, then change direction slightly. Jasper wondered what else she knew that he didn't—what she and Cyrus were keeping from him.

They hit a logging trail and followed it to a clearing carved into the forest. A white van sat there, engine running. Nora used her headlamp to flash a signal, and Larkin emerged from the driver's seat. He shook hands with Byron and they all piled inside. Headlights off, Larkin eased down the logging road at a crawl. Jasper spotted a long case on the back seat that definitely looked like it had a big gun in it. More than a few duffle bags of ammo were lying on the floor.

"I thought this was a neutral meeting."

"The plan is to keep it that way," Nora said.

A dark blur ran across the road, then another. Larkin jammed on the breaks and everyone drew their guns, scanning the woods.

"Byron, on me," Larkin said. "Three, two, one. Move."

Larkin lit up the woods with his high beams right before he and Byron exited the van. Jasper tracked a figure running off the road into the underbrush.

"Step out of the woods," Byron said. "Hands up."

Five seconds passed before Tucker shuffled onto the road, followed by Lacy and Sheldon. Colton came from the other side, bringing up the rear.

"*Shit*," Nora whispered.

"Walk to me," Byron said. "Hands on your heads."

"It's us, Byron," Lacy called.

"Hands on your heads."

They obeyed the command. Jasper saw the fear and surprise and confusion lining their faces. They were in the dark with him.

"Clear," Byron said after patting each of them down. He took Colton's walkie and made sure it was off.

Larkin finally lowered his gun. "Why did you follow us?"

"The better question is, why did you disable the wall sensors and sneak Jasper over in the middle of the night?" Lacy asked. She sounded pissed.

"That's not your concern."

"Cyrus made Jasper our concern when he got here, and we already screwed up that responsibility once. Wherever he's going, we are, too."

Larkin pointed back up the hill. "Return to campus."

"Where I will call my dad immediately," Lacy said. "I'm sure the Directors would love to hear all about this."

Nora climbed over Jasper to the front seat and slid out the driver's side door. She muttered something in Larkin's ear. He growled and shook his head. But after a glare from Nora, he relented.

"Get in," Larkin said.

"Where are we going?" Lacy asked.

"You don't get to know that."

193

CHAPTER THIRTY-SEVEN

Nora pushed at Jasper's shoulder until he shifted to the back row, gun still drawn.

She rode like that the whole way.

Nobody talked. Jasper stared at the back of Tucker's head thinking how weird he looked without the giant headphones slung around his pale neck. Sheldon snuck glances over his shoulder every now and then, but when Nora scowled at him he turned back to the front. They paused once for Lacy to take a pit stop—the sun was rising and Colton held up a jacket to give her some privacy.

At nine, Jasper spotted the Philadelphia skyline. Larkin got off I-95 at the Center City exit and cut through heavy traffic to Independence Mall. Lines of yellow school buses waited to drop kids off at the Constitution Center. Larkin pulled into a parking garage one street back, winding up the tight lanes to the third level, where he parked near the beat up Crown Vic. Cyrus exited the car and climbed into the van holding a briefcase.

He examined the four who hadn't originally been invited to the party. "You should not have interfered."

"You blasted us for not noticing the brownie guy," Tucker said. Jasper actually heard some emotion behind it. "We took notice."

"Like martyr Nora taking over the gun range," Lacy snapped. "I asked Sheldon to keep a closer eye on Jasper, and last night we thought he'd been kidnapped."

"Your concern is admirable, but misplaced," Cyrus said. "Stay in the vehicle with Larkin until we return."

Lacy stopped the door from closing. "Either we come, or I call my dad."

Jasper felt the tension in the air, like they were tiptoeing through a minefield.

"I could have Larkin physically restrain you," Cyrus said.

"Try it," Lacy shot back. Jasper caught a little trace of Nora in that response. Maybe they weren't so different after all.

Cyrus took a slow, deep breath. "I *need* you here, in the event that things go . . . poorly. You will be shadowing us and provide cover fire for a quick escape. Does that satisfy you?"

Lacy looked to Nora, who nodded. "Fine," she said. "Now get me a weapon."

Larkin handed pistols to her and Sheldon. Tucker grabbed a box of ammo and mumbled something about being on reloading duty.

Jasper got out of the van with Nora and followed Byron and Cyrus to a stairwell, up one floor, then across the parking garage to another stairwell, and all the way down to the street. They walked past busy professionals and aggressive joggers and a homeless guy who was adjusting his sign—people running through the motions, oblivious to Jasper's world of ancestral ties and diaries and minors packing serious heat.

This was his life, the only one he got.

A block behind Independence Hall, they crossed into a small park and followed the brick path toward a big statue in the center. On the other side of the park, three men in dark suits and red ties were walking toward them. Out in front was a guy who stood over six feet and was built like a Mack truck. He had brown hair and a big hawk nose that matched everything else giant about him.

"Black sedan, south side of the park," Byron said.

"I see it," Cyrus replied. "They'll wait until we leave to make a move."

Jasper scanned the streets for the car but couldn't find it. Nora let out three deep breaths.

On a park bench near the statue sat a barrel-chested man in his six-ties sipping coffee and reading a paper. Twice he adjusted a gray fedora that he didn't look comfortable wearing.

"Your Honor," Cyrus said as he sat down on the man's right. "I'm Cyrus Barnes."

The linebacker Libertine settled on the man's other side. "Silas Washington, Your Honor." Washington's voice was a triple bass. Jasper worried the two security guards back near Independence Hall might hear everything he said.

"Murder." Chief Justice Addison Fletcher snapped his paper to straighten out the page. "Reshuffling my day—my week—for this was absolutely *murder*. Do either of you have any idea what my schedule is like?"

"I apologize, Your Honor," Cyrus said. "It was our only option."

"Why?" Silas asked, looking past the Chief Justice at Cyrus. "I have met with your Directors several times in the past without the Arbiter present."

Cyrus glared at the Libertine. "I am less trusting, and with good reason."

Silas stared back, brows knitted. "Are you accusing me of some-thing, Counselor?"

"Okay, let's keep it civil," Fletcher grumbled. "Not sure you people existed, to tell you the truth. My predecessor left very vague notes about my responsibilities on the off chance I was contacted. Apparently, you didn't need his services. Lucky him." The Chief Justice glanced at Cyrus. "Which, eh . . . *organization* . . . do you hail from?"

"The League of American Traitors, Your Honor."

"Out with it then, Mr. Barnes. The longer we sit here, the more likely some spoiled law student will recognize me and ask to clerk this summer."

"The matter is simple, Your Honor: we would like you to broker a per-manent ceasefire between the True Sons of Liberty and our organization."

"And how," Fletcher asked, "do you expect *me*—who until five minutes ago had you in the same category as Bigfoot—to do that."

"By hearing our evidence," Cyrus said.

"Evidence of *what?*" Silas asked.

"That Joseph Reed bribed a Continental officer to provoke Benedict Arnold into committing treason."

It was quiet for a few seconds. Jasper could hear a group of students on a field trip, giving their parent chaperone absolute hell.

Cyrus cleared his throat, then continued on. "Joseph Reed served as George Washington's personal secretary and, later, as governor of—"

"I know who he *is*, Mr. Barnes," the Chief Justice snapped. "Did you bring this evidence?"

"Your Honor," Silas Washington interjected. "Even if this assertion were remotely true—which it is most certainly not—Counselor Barnes is suggesting blackmail. As an officer of the court, surely you cannot entertain this 'evidence.'"

"But this is not a court of law, Mr. Washington," Fletcher said. "This is an off-the-books, did-not-happen meeting. And I can entertain blackmail as much as I can overlook the number of concealed weapons your friends there are carrying."

Cyrus slid over and motioned for Jasper to join them. "Your Honor, this is Jasper Mansfield, the sole surviving heir of Benedict Arnold. He made the discovery."

Fletcher gave Jasper a once-over and then snapped his paper back in place. "Do I have to drag it out of you?"

"We found a diary." Jasper fumbled with the briefcase and finally got it open. Keeping his winter gloves on, he took the diary out of its plastic sleeve and saw someone had marked the entries with little neon strips. Sybil, probably. "Actually, we found three but this is the one that matters. It belonged to a woman named Alice Boswell, who lived in Philadelphia. Her husband, Ira, was on Arnold's staff."

Fletcher shielded the diary with his newspaper. It only took him a minute to read each entry. Jasper figured old people could read cursive because it was still being used when they were in school.

"Interesting." Fletcher handed the diary back to Jasper, and he locked it back up. "You are implying that this nation's most hated traitor was, in fact, inspired to commit treason by this state's greatest founder—and perhaps Washington himself."

"We are, Your Honor."

"I have a right to see this evidence," Silas said. "And to validate its authenticity before an agreement is even discussed."

"That you do, Mr. Washington. But not here. We've been loitering about long enough."

"The matter must be resolved here and now," Cyrus said. "It is imperative."

"In a park at nine thirty in the morning? No, Mr. Barnes. This matter requires time. Consideration. A hearing and sifting of evidence."

"In the past, the Arbiter has—"

"We are not in the past. This is the present—something both of your organizations seem to have trouble grasping. And in *this* present you have come to *me*—and *I'm* in charge. And I have decided to hear your case—properly." Fletcher folded his paper. "If you defend your evidence and convince me that it means what you hope it does—what Mr. Washington clearly hopes it does *not*—then I will gladly order a ceasefire. God knows we don't need any more gun deaths in this country. What do you say to that, Mr. Washington?"

Silas leaned his head forward. "The True Sons of Liberty will, of course, abide by the ruling, Your Honor."

"And you, young man?"

Jasper thought that was weird—the Chief Justice calling Cyrus young.

"Young man."

Cyrus elbowed Jasper.

"Yes, Your Honor," Jasper said. "Wait—what?"

"You found this evidence? You transcribed it?"

"Yeah . . . I mean—yes, sir."

"Your ancestor is the individual in question?"

"Uh huh."

"Did you think someone else would argue the case?"

Jasper felt that tilting sensation again—the same one he'd had in Cyrus's office when the lawyer had dumped all this into his lap back in October. Only this time, the park took a little longer to level out. "Right."

"Perhaps read a thesaurus in the meantime." Fletcher sighed. "I have your contact information, Mr. Barnes, and will reach out with the date. You will reply with copies of this diary and any other evidence required for review by Mr. Washington. I expect briefs from each side no fewer than three days before the arranged hearing, at which time you will each have thirty minutes to present your arguments and answer any questions I may pose."

"And the matter of authenticating the diary, Your Honor?" Silas asked.

Fletcher turned to Cyrus. "I suppose you aren't willing to part with this evidence, Mr. Barnes?"

"We are not, Your Honor."

"Hmm. What about the other diaries—the two without the sensitive information. Would you part with one of them? I have a friend at the Smithsonian who could take care of the matter discreetly."

Cyrus thought about it, then nodded to Byron. He removed one from inside his coat and handed it to Fletcher.

"Does that satisfy you, Mr. Washington?" Fletcher asked.

"It does, Your Honor."

"Well, isn't that grand." Fletcher cleared his throat and squashed the fedora farther down his head. "I really do hate this thing. Terrible idea for a disguise."

And then he walked off.

Chapter Thirty-Eight

Jasper sat perfectly still. The briefcase felt like a ton of bricks on his legs. He wondered if he could get to his gun fast enough if he had to.

"I am still confused, Counselor," Silas said. "Why did the Directors not communicate this to me personally?"

"There is no need to pretend anymore," Cyrus said icily. "His Honor is gone."

Silas looked at his guards. At Jasper and Nora. "Pretend?"

This guy was an even better liar than Cyrus, Jasper thought. He was really selling this performance.

"Are you seriously going to deny that you know *nothing* of Elsbeth Reed and her attempts to bury this diary?" Cyrus asked.

"Elsbeth Reed?" Silas boomed. "Attempts to bury—*what* are you referring to?"

"Leave the briefcase," said one of Silas's bodyguards.

He stepped into view, gun drawn low at his hip. Nora's coat made a swishing sound behind Jasper.

"Wesley," Silas said. "What—Put that down!"

"Reach for it," the guard said to Nora, "and the boy dies."

"*Wesley*," Silas growled through his teeth. "I have just given my word to the Arbiter. Do you know what that means?"

"Leave the briefcase on the bench," Wesley said. "Walk away."

The Libertine bodyguard would pull the trigger. Jasper could see it in his eyes. They showed the same strain of metal as the EMT's, the same as Elsbeth—big league assassins who actually meant what they said. This guy wouldn't lose a minute of sleep.

So the question was, *Is this worth it?* Cyrus had asked Jasper this on the rooftop, but he'd never gotten around to answering. He could go on—live his one life in hiding. *Forget that awful year when I learned to kill and saw people get shot.* His quest could be over right now. It would be a huge relief, wouldn't it?

Jasper sat up straighter, giving Wesley a better target.

"Even at this range," Jasper said, "I'll live long enough to watch you bleed out next to me."

The Libertine's eyes twitched.

Didn't expect that, did you, Wesley?

Silas lunged at his bodyguard and drove him to the pavement. The gun went off. It was muffled, silenced by the mass of Silas's body. Wesley wriggled beneath him for a couple seconds, and Jasper still wasn't sure who'd shot whom. The other bodyguard had his gun out, swinging it between Byron and Wesley, uncertain who was the real threat. He made his choice, but it was the wrong one.

Another shot ripped across the park, this one louder. Wesley had taken out Washington's other bodyguard and was now aiming at Jasper . . .

But he didn't have a chance. Byron and Nora unloaded their rounds into his torso. His head smacked against the pavement. Silas fell face-down next to him.

Cyrus crawled to Silas's side and heaved his body over. Confused eyes stared straight up to the sky.

A kid from that field trip group screamed nearby. Security guards were herding fleeing tourists into Independence Hall. Tires screeched somewhere behind the park.

"We need to *leave*," Byron said. *"Now."*

Jasper's feet slammed into the sidewalk. Nora was screaming at him to go faster. He clutched the briefcase to his chest, scared he might rip the handle off. Horns blared as they cut across traffic; some idiot on a Vespa almost turned Jasper into roadkill. Byron led them down an access road and then up an alley to a tiny lot where the white van was waiting, engine running.

A gun cracked and Jasper heard something whistle by his ear. He turned and saw Elsbeth Reed fifty yards behind them, gun aimed in his direction. Ahead, Colton leaned out of the driver's side window and loosed two shots from something long and sleek—*crackcrack*. The van doors flew open and Jasper launched himself inside, bowling over Sheldon and Tucker.

Larkin peeled out of the lot. Colton fired off another round from the machine gun. Windows shattered and glass flew everywhere as Elsbeth returned fire, taking out the van's back windows. Jasper saw her jump into a black sedan, which was now tailing them. Larkin picked up speed, brushing a few cars along the narrow alley before cutting back toward the congested Philadelphia streets.

Sirens wailed in the distance—how would that play out when they were caught? Three dead bodies in the park? They'd only killed one of them, but good luck explaining that to the police.

Larkin blew through a red light, but the black sedan stayed with them. Nora was trying to get a shot off, but couldn't steady her sights long enough. Elsbeth fired and the van lurched right: a tire blown out, maybe. Larkin wrestled the wheel and nearly hit a SEPTA bus as he careered into the other lane and down a side street. The van sagged on the blown tire and almost flipped as he jerked the wheel right, sending them underground to the parking garage Cyrus had first brought Jasper to. They flew down two levels, tires squealing on the tight turns. Headlight beams bounced off of the walls behind them. Just a couple more turns and they'd be at the elevator. Help had to be waiting, right?

We're going too fast, Jasper thought, right as the van lifted sideways. Larkin had gunned it around the final bend and the back tires hadn't had time to settle. It was physics—momentum and speed and distance. Jasper tried to grab onto something but all he could find was the case, and so he hugged it closer and closed his eyes as the world tipped and he slammed into the window, which had suddenly become the floor. The van skidded a few feet before coming to a rest.

Jasper smelled oil and burnt rubber. He tried to move. Bad idea. Pain shot through his ribs. The briefcase must have broken something. Somewhere behind him, Lacy was mumbling, "Tucker . . . Tucker, wake up." People shifted on broken glass and on one another. Jasper saw Nora, unconscious with a gash on the left side of her face. Byron and Cyrus were splayed near the front of the vehicle. Larkin stirred by the driver seat. Colton was just gone—probably thrown right out the window on impact.

"Are we dead?" Sheldon asked from near Jasper's feet.

"*Shhh*," Jasper said. A car door slammed. Footsteps. He reached for his gun and swallowed a scream. It felt like somebody was prying his ribs apart with a fork from the inside.

"Throw the briefcase out."

Jasper knew the voice. It was like a memory he'd tried to bury, but his mind had insisted on keeping a small scrap on file.

Elsbeth.

"That's all we want," she said. "Toss it out, and everybody walks away. Or don't, and we kill you all."

Jasper closed his fingers around the handle of his gun and tried to orient himself. Was her voice coming from behind or in front? Which way was even up?

"Sheldon," Elsbeth said, "if you can hear me, I think you know our original deal is off."

Jasper thought maybe he had a concussion. Or maybe it was all the close-quarters gunfire. He turned his head and looked at his friend, crouched on the ground—actually crouched upright now, since the van had tilted.

Sheldon was staring at the seat.

"You were hiding things from us," Elsbeth called out. "That can be forgiven. All we want is the diary, and we'll honor the arrangement."

Cyrus or Byron—somebody near the front—groaned. Jasper saw feet dart across the back of the van. Sheldon's breathing was getting louder like he was hyperventilating. He was reaching for something next to him, closer to Nora. Something in her hand that he had to pry out of her grip—her gun. He weighed it for a second. His eyes met Jasper's, and then Sheldon pointed the weapon at him.

"I want a new deal," Sheldon said, voice shaking. "No duels for any of us."

"Fine," Elsbeth said. "Toss the diary out."

"Sheldon . . ." Jasper said.

"Shut up, Jasper." His eyes were wide, flicking all around the wreckage. "We're all going to walk away from this. None of us will have to duel. Just give me the diary."

Jasper hugged the case closer with his left arm. His mouth was a desert. "She'll kill us," he croaked. "You know she will."

"No." Sheldon shook his head—quick, tiny jerks. "We'll be okay. Just give me the case."

Jasper shifted, trying to get some space so he could bring his right arm out.

"Don't." Sheldon was crying now, big rivers of tears racing down his cheeks. He reached over slowly and grabbed the briefcase's handle.

Nora's gun remained inches from Jasper's face.

"What did you do?" Jasper demanded hoarsely.

"This wasn't supposed to happen."

"You're *letting* it happen."

"It was never supposed to be like this. It's not what you think, I swear."

And that's when Jasper understood—when he really got what it meant to see this quest through. How had he not known this before? Somewhere in the split second between a shout outside of the van and Sheldon looking for the source of it did the truth sink in: dying wasn't the worst thing. Anybody could die for a cause. Yeah, it was tragic and heroic, but it was also easy. You didn't have to stick around to find out what happened—learn if your death meant anything.

Killing for a cause—that was worse. Dealing out death and then living with the consequence.

Jasper wrenched his right arm free and fired.

For a split second, he thought he'd missed.

Then Sheldon collapsed onto him. Jasper heard the crack of a machine gun. He let go of the briefcase, hugged his friend, and moaned. Sheldon's weight pushed on his broken rib, but there was worse pain to deal with. Warm liquid spread over his chest, and he squeezed Sheldon tighter, sobbing as his friend panted into his ear, mumbling something Jasper couldn't make out.

Larkin staggered back and tried to shift Sheldon's weight, but Jasper fought him off until his rib felt ready to snap. Voices and footsteps surrounded the van and then things blurred into a waking nightmare and there was only the sharp smell of blood and then nothing at all.

CHAPTER THIRTY-NINE

Jasper stared at himself in the giant bathroom mirror. He'd showered twice, but still felt the blood tacky on his skin. A sourness pulled at his gut and he dry-heaved into the sink, then almost fell over as pain ripped up the side of his stomach; apparently every muscle in the human body was connected to his cracked rib. When the nausea passed, he washed his face and put on the shirt Sybil had left, fumbling with the buttons. His hands were shaking. How long would that last? Or would it come and go?

Maybe that was part of the deal.

Nora was waiting in the hall when he came out. A line of tiny bandages ran from the middle of her forehead to her temple like little railroad ties. Her flat, guarded stare was gone. They were in the same club now. No need for the badass routine. He'd been to hell and back, too.

"How's Byron?" he asked.

"No change."

Jasper felt like he might throw up again.

"You need to eat something," Nora said.

She took his hand and led him to a break room down the hall. In between playing nurse, Sybil had ordered in a ton of food. Nora sliced chunks off an apple and forced Jasper to eat some.

"This is the part where you start filling in the gaps," Jasper said. "Bring me back in the loop."

"I was pissed as hell after Charlottesville," she said. "But I got it—Cyrus didn't trust anyone. So I went digging on my own. That's what you saw in the chapel."

"Digging for what?"

Nora pulled her legs up, knees tucked to her chest. "We were trying to see if the school network could be hacked. Eliza did most of the work. I didn't understand how the Libertines got to that cook and then to Adele. How would they have known where they worked and lived? The League buries those records under layers and layers of encryption."

"Did you crack it?"

"Just a little, nothing deep. But we found Sheldon's network—the one he made to protect your research."

Jasper shuddered. He wondered if that would happen every time someone said his friend's name out loud. "So Sheldon was passing intel to the Libertines the whole time?"

Nora shook her head. "That was the strange part: Eliza said his network was the real deal. A top-level firewall. Steel vault. He really was trying to keep anybody from finding our stuff."

Jasper rubbed his eyes. It felt like he'd been awake for a week. He thought of what Elsbeth had said to Sheldon. *We know you've been hiding things from us.*

"I'm lost," he said.

"I thought we'd hit a dead end, and was getting antsy to move onto something else. But Eliza had coded all the programs and her dad had bankrolled all those towers so she kept at it. A week later, she found the back door."

Jasper picked at a bad spot on the apple slice. "Is that a technical term?"

"Eliza said it was like somebody on the inside of a house had changed the locks on an entry point. We still couldn't get in, but if you had the new key . . ." Nora picked at her bandage and examined her fingers, then flecked off some dried blood. "It was one of the computers in your study room. That was the door."

"You're saying Sheldon 'changed the locks' to let someone in."

"I didn't know who did it," Nora said. "That's why Cyrus didn't want any of them coming with us to see the Arbiter. After I showed him what I'd found, he didn't trust them."

Jasper shook his head, which somehow made his busted rib hurt. "This doesn't make any sense. Why would Sheldon make some deal to screw the League and then bother to protect all of our work?"

"Maybe he felt guilty. I don't know."

They were quiet for a while.

Finally, Nora nodded her head. "Larkin will find out."

There was that sourness again. Jasper figured he should be happy that somewhere below them, Elsbeth was getting exactly what she deserved.

Still, he just wanted it all to be over. FADE TO BLACK. ROLL CREDITS.

They shuffled to the conference room, which Sybil had turned into a triage center. Cyrus stood over Byron, who was laid out on the table. Jasper pulled up a chair and held onto one of the bodyguard's giant hands. They were cold and clammy. A bandage was wrapped around most of his head.

"We need to take him to a hospital," Jasper said.

"You know that's not possible."

"He's gonna die."

Cyrus lowered his chin. "And he would do so gladly."

In the corner, Lacy was sitting beside Tucker as he stared deadpan at nothing. No headphones to keep this nightmare out.

Colton limped into the room, left arm in a sling, clothes torn like he'd been dragged across a field of rocks. He whispered something in Cyrus's ear.

"I will not force you to attend," Cyrus said, turning to Jasper, "but I would prefer if you joined us. I was . . . not exactly right concerning the Oligarchs' role in all of this. I would like you there when we learn the truth."

Jasper watched Byron's chest rise and fall. Were his breaths getting shallower? Was he in pain?

"She talked?" he asked.

"She has expressed a willingness to speak, yes."

So Larkin had tortured the crap out of her.

Nora laced her fingers in Jasper's as they rode the elevator to a lower level. It had all been a blur once he'd shot Sheldon, but there were still flickers: Larkin pulling him out of the van; the others groaning awake; Colton, half dead, machine gun trained on Elsbeth. He'd been the real hero, crawling to his weapon and taking out the other Libertine just as the League cavalry arrived. He'd saved them all.

And that's what made it all so horrible. It was what Jasper played over and over in his head: If he'd waited just a few more seconds, what would've happened? What would Sheldon have done? He'd be alive now, that's for sure.

The lower level was dark and industrial. Cyrus led them past machines that hissed and belched steam. Larkin was standing outside a supply closet along with some other League guards dressed in dark suits. His shirtsleeves were rolled to the elbows and two of his knuckles were split.

He opened the door.

Elsbeth Reed sat on a chair against the back shelf, arms tied behind her back. Her face was so swollen that Jasper barely recognized her.

"You murdered James Mansfield in his motel room last September. Is that correct?" Cyrus asked evenly.

Elsbeth spit at him—blood, mostly.

Cyrus coolly wiped specks off his face. "I could give you more time with my associate."

"He got too close." Her voice was ragged and scratchy. She panted and stared at the floor.

"To the truth about Reed's provocation of Benedict Arnold? You knew about it."

A few moments of silence passed. "We knew Reed would do anything to hurt Arnold," she said. "We watch the archives in case anybody digs too deep, finds something they shouldn't."

"The New York Public Library . . ." Jasper said, scrolling through a mental list of the safe documents.

"That's when we first noticed him." Elsbeth rolled her left shoulder and winced. It must have still been healing from where Jasper had shot her. "We followed Mansfield to other archives. When he started paying visits to Boswells, he had to be dealt with."

"Just to protect some stupid legacy?" Jasper snapped. "Nobody would even care! It all happened almost three hundred years ago!" He was yelling now, borderline screaming: "WHAT IS *WRONG* WITH YOU?"

She didn't flinch.

"On whose authority did you act?" Cyrus asked. "We know it wasn't Oligarch Washington's."

She remained silent.

Cyrus motioned to Larkin. The bodyguard put a hand on her shoulder and pressed his thumb over the gunshot wound. Elsbeth writhed and screamed and bared her teeth. Jasper looked away and fought off another dry heave.

"On whose authority did you murder James Mansfield?" Cyrus demanded again.

"Tallmadge."

Cyrus and Larkin exchanged a quick glance. "Tallmadge?"

She nodded.

"Who's that?" Jasper asked.

"He runs the True Sons' security division," Cyrus said, eyes drifting as he tried to fit this new piece of information into the puzzle.

But Jasper, who had spent months buried in Revolutionary history, beat him to it.

"The Culper Ring," he said quietly. *You have to be kidding.* "Washington's spy network during the war. It was run by Benjamin Tallmadge."

Cyrus's gaze snapped back to Elsbeth. "Is this true? Has Benjamin's descendant resurrected that network without the Oligarchs' knowledge?"

Elsbeth was slower to nod this time, but it came.

"Their own little CIA," Nora murmered.

"And the boy—Sheldon Burr—how did you get to him?" Cyrus asked.

"We approached him at his brother's duel," Elsbeth said.

"How were you able to do that?"

She coughed. Winced. "We have people at the dueling estate."

"Other . . . Culper agents," Cyrus said. "Like you."

Jasper thought she might refuse to answer again, but she nodded.

"And you told him he could avoid his duel in exchange for what?" Cyrus pressed.

"We gave him a flash drive to plug into a computer at Juniper Hill. He got us in the network."

There it was. Nora had been right.

But that didn't explain everything.

"Sheldon was hiding things from you," Jasper said. "How did you know we'd be in Virginia?"

Drool seeped out the corner of her mouth. "No shortage of traitors who don't want their daughters to duel."

Jasper blinked, then reeled. Only a handful of people knew about that trip—and only one had a daughter.

Nora beat him to it. "Director Church."

"It wasn't hard to convince him," Elsbeth said. "You people rarely are."

"Send a car to his home immediately," Cyrus ordered Larkin.

When the door shut again, Cyrus took a step toward Elsbeth and backhanded her across the face. She slumped against the wall, eyes wide.

"That was for Silas Washington," he said. "A decent man, slain because of your interference. You've taken a shaky truce and ignited it into outright war." Cyrus took out a handkerchief and wiped blood from his hand, his stony face returning. "Are you familiar with the security protocols in the capital?"

Elsbeth moved her jaw around. Jasper heard a *pop*. She nodded.

"Familiar enough to get us to the Supreme Court building, undetected?" Cyrus asked.

"I tell you, and then you kill me."

"Unlike you, Ms. Reed, the League does not deal in that sort of deception," he said. "Help us, and we will spare your life; refuse, and we will leave this room and lock the door behind us. You will die in that chair, in the dark, thirsty and hungry and soaked in your own urine. I leave the choice to you."

★★★★

Jasper stood on the rooftop. Sirens wailed in the distance. Cops were still crawling the streets for them, clearing bodies. The city really pulled out all the stops for domestic terrorism. Jasper thought about Silas's kids—did he have any? Did they know yet that their dad was dead? He hoped they had somebody with them when they found out. Getting that news alone was awful. He wouldn't wish it on anyone.

A door opened, and Cyrus came up beside him.

Time is funny, Jasper thought. *How you can be standing in the exact same spot, but things can be so different. Infinitely worse.*

"The Arbiter has been in touch," Cyrus said. "He is livid, to say the least, but he will still hear our case."

Jasper heard Cyrus's inflection go up a little at the end. "If . . ."

"The True Sons have requested they be granted custody of you should the Arbiter rule against us."

"So it's really me on trial."

"It is."

Jasper had expected that. Events had always been leading to this conclusion from the second Cyrus had knocked on the car window all those months ago.

A showdown with no way out.

"Your position isn't different from the Founders whose offspring target us," Cyrus said. "You can go into hiding, keep your head down and suffer tyranny, questioning every parked car, every shadow, every footstep." He faced Jasper. "Or you can take a stand and fight for a future that you create. Prove that this diary implicates Reed and leverage that information for a peace that has eluded our side since the nation's birth."

Jasper had looked over the edge of this particular cliff more than once. He'd even pushed his friend over it. But this felt different. They were so close to escaping the cycle. Collapsing of heatstroke a yard from the finish line was way more soul-crushing after the first twenty-six miles of the marathon.

"This is where you say it's up to me, even though that's basically just a huge guilt trip," Jasper said.

"I will support whatever you decide. Chairman Hickey and the remaining Directors have been apprised of the situation, and they echo my support."

"That's actually way worse."

A wind kicked up. "But Jasper, our window is rapidly closing."

"You trust her?"

"I trust that she believes I will keep my word if we walk into an ambush," Cyrus said.

"She could just not care about dying. We don't seem to." Jasper closed his eyes and pictured his dad, standing here, on this roof, diary in hand. Would he have had the guts to go through with this? "Sheldon acted so tough. You should've heard him talk about dueling. He was gonna be some great warrior for the cause. Burrs don't hide. That's what he used to say."

"I'm sure that he acted that way because he wanted it to be true."

The scene from the van replayed in Jasper's head. He tried to shove it aside, but it was in IMAX 3D, surround sound. The corners of his eyes burned. The tremor was back in his hands.

This is what Nora had talked about. The cost.

And that's why he would do it.

Not because he was brave, but because you don't run this far and climb over this many bodies to stop at the last mile marker. You risk heatstroke and heart attack because on the other side of the tape is water and rest. Making it there wasn't a sure thing. You hoped.

You never despaired.

CHAPTER FORTY

Jasper watched the lights of the Chesapeake Bay shoreline whizz by. The windbreaker cut out none of the cold, but that was okay because Sybil insisted he stay wide-awake. In T-minus ten minutes, she'd call him back into the main cabin and continue force-feeding him chunks of the brief they were crafting. This was nothing at all like TV, where you got up and gave some big emotional speech that convinced a jury to side with you or you flipped the bad guy on the stand and proved your whole case. This was boring, tedious work. All those hours of *Law and Order* had seriously let him down.

They'd waited until the third night after the shooting to drive to a charter yacht service in Delaware. When the place opened, Larkin booked it and cruised farther down the Chesapeake to a cove and picked up the others—Sybil, Cyrus, Jasper, and Nora. Returning the boat was something they could deal with later.

The cabin door opened and Nora came out on deck with a cup of something hot.

"You know what goes great with coffee?" she asked. "A cigarette."

"Good luck lighting it."

The yacht rose and fell on a small wave and Jasper winced as he grabbed the railing to keep steady. A cracked rib wasn't helping him find those sea legs.

"Byron died," Nora said.

Jasper had been waiting for this moment. "When?"

"Yesterday morning. I'm so sorry."

Another one down. And this one hurt the worst. "I was such a prick to him."

"I'm sure you weren't."

"He never complained once about having to babysit me." When would they even find time for the funeral? Maybe Jasper wouldn't be alive to see it. "Byron was so tough. I didn't actually think it was possible for him to die."

"He was a true badass."

They watched the shoreline until the horizon turned gray. Then Nora tugged Jasper's arm and led him into the cabin.

No rest for the weary.

Sybil and Cyrus were sitting on benches along one side, hunched over laptops. Larkin manned the wheel up front, overseeing all of the dials and buttons and switches. A nautical map lay open next to him, and he checked it every couple of minutes. Jasper wasn't sure when, exactly, but they'd be reaching the mouth of the Potomac River and follow it north to the capital. Cyrus had kept the rest of the plan to himself.

"There are only two *ts* in the word entrapment," Sybil said.

"Right."

"You've been saying *entrap-t-ment.* That's incorrect."

"Entrapment."

"Again."

"Entraptment."

Sybil sighed, then reached over piles of documents and went to hand him the brief. Her face tightened, and for a second, turned pale. Cyrus leaned over, placing the papers in Jasper's hand, before trying to examine her shoulder wound. She shooed him away. "I made some notes in the margins."

"I'll have this with me during the hearing?"

"Yes, but you only have thirty minutes. You can't afford to waste time grabbing at loose facts, especially not when the Chief Justice interrupts with questions. Memorize as much as possible."

"Can the other guy do that, too? Object?"

"This is not a trial," Cyrus said, nose deep in some giant legal binder thing he'd hauled from his office. "It is a presentation of facts with case law to support the argument. Their attorney will not object during your allotted time."

"So, he's an actual lawyer. With experience."

"Yes."

"Great."

"If you're worried about appearing inexperienced," Sybil said, "your hair isn't helping."

Jasper had been doing a lot more tucking of strands behind his ears lately. It *was* getting a little out of hand. "You brought scissors, didn't you?"

"I'm always prepared."

"Fine."

"I'll do it," Nora offered.

"After you review the changes," Sybil replied.

And he did, but she kept making more changes, and then making him read them again. Cyrus peppered him with random questions, trying to throw him off his game. It worked most of the time. There were just too many details—too many threads to keep track of. And the case law examples Sybil had dug up to add backbone to their argument were hard to grasp. Jasper was certain that if he walked out of the Supreme Court building alive, he would not be going to law school. But he would be writing to the *Law and Order* directors about peddling a fantasy version of how lawyering actually worked.

By noon, they had made the turn north onto the Potomac. Larkin kept the throttle low and steady—they didn't want to advertise they were in a hurry. Today, they were just some rich people on a small yacht, cruising to the capital. Nothing to see here. Jasper knelt in the cramped bathroom with a towel around his shoulders as Nora unpacked the clipper kit.

"My dad did a three on the side blended to a scissor cut on top. It's basic but professional."

"Anything will be an improvement," Sybil called from the cabin.

Jasper picked up the cheapo plastic insert that had a model sporting some really gelled up style that looked awful. Then he thought about Byron.

"How close can you go?"

"A zero."

"That's what I want. Take it all off."

The vibrating blade felt good against his skin, except for the two times the boat hit a wave and it felt like she'd sliced him. When it was done, he rinsed his head in the small cabin sink and unfogged the mirror to get a good look.

"Whoa." He traced a finger along the indents of his hairline near the scalp. "I don't even recognize myself."

Nora stood behind him, head pressed between his shoulder blades. She held on tight enough to break another rib. "You had to kill Sheldon." She said it like she was settling something in her mind, and maybe in his. "You didn't want to—you had to. That's different."

"That doesn't make it any less awful."

"No. But it's still true. And true things need to be said. They need to be shouted from mountaintops."

Jasper had to work hard to turn around in the cramped space. "I'm sorry you had to break your penance for me."

Eyeliner streaks slipped down one side of Nora's face. "I was thinking that maybe picking up a gun again . . . killing again . . . maybe that's part of my penance. To make up for what I did, I'd have to do it again, but right. For something good."

She clung to Jasper's neck and they swayed with the boat. What was a person supposed to say at a time like this—when this might be it?

Something true.

"When the trial is all over, I was wondering if maybe you'd consider e-cigarettes."

His head smacked into the mirror as her lips found his. Bottles fell off the shelves, and the toilet seat slammed shut. Jasper yelped once when Nora clawed at his busted rib. Sybil cleared her throat right outside the door.

"Lots to do," she said. "It's not as if your life depends on this."

★★★★

Around five thirty, they docked in a tiny estuary. A Middle Eastern man stood by a taxi van and loaded their bags into the trunk. Nora carried the diary. Country roads took them into suburbia, and Jasper saw a sign for Alexandria. His stomach pulled tighter and he turned back to his notes, trying not to imagine the kind of execution the Libertines were planning for him. Would they go old school and hang him? That's probably what Washington would have ordered if Arnold were caught. Seemed fitting. Or maybe they'd pick something more modern, like a firing squad.

"Read," Sybil said, tapping the brief.

The taxi dropped them at Huntington Station. The group ascended a long escalator to the platform where they boarded the Yellow Line, switched to the Orange at L'Enfant Plaza, and finally exited at Capitol South. The sun had dropped below the horizon when they returned to street level. Jasper had been to DC once on a school trip, but he couldn't remember exactly where the Supreme Court building was. He checked his watch and saw they had thirty minutes.

Cyrus led them up 2nd Street, past the Library of Congress. Then past another library, also of Congress. Apparently, there were a few, each named after an early president. The giant US Capitol building loomed ahead of them, and Jasper thought about congresspeople and their staffs doing paperwork and making laws. He wondered if they'd care about Joseph Reed and Benedict Arnold and the feuds that stretched back to the Revolutionary War. They'd probably hold a hearing about it, disagree along party lines, and then get back to reams of paperwork that never did anything. Or go play golf.

Cyrus had warned him, but Jasper didn't even see the car pull up beside them. He was too busy looking at the small crowd around the Supreme Court plaza fountains ahead. They were so close—he'd actually let himself believe they were going to make it to the hearing without any problems.

And then, all of sudden, the white BMW was on the shoulder next to them, the tinted windows lowering in slow-motion, the car braking to match their pace. The world tilted; Jasper knew where this was headed. It's why he'd swapped out his belt holster for a shoulder carrier.

He reached inside his coat and grabbed his weapon as a voice called out, "A word, Counselor."

CHAPTER FORTY-ONE

A DC Metro police SUV cruised by. Jasper relaxed the grip on his gun, but kept his hand tucked in his coat.

The passenger window was half open, and a fat, bald man with acne scars said, "I only want to chat."

"And you are?" Cyrus asked.

"You know who I am." The man checked his watch. "And we both have a meeting to make. So get in. The boy, too."

"No."

"Counselor, if I wanted you dead, you'd already be dead. Believe it or not, war is not in my best interest. So get. In."

Jasper felt around for something else. Found the button. Pushed it, felt it *click*.

"Turn off the car," Cyrus ordered.

"Oh, for Christ's sake." The man opened the door and lifted his arms, flapping his suit jacket to show he wasn't armed. "I'm alone, except for my driver. And he's carrying, just like you."

"The keys," Cyrus said, "and the driver."

The fat man sighed. He jutted his chin at the man behind the wheel, who turned off the car, got out, and walked around the back. "You can kill him if I so much as sneeze," he said to Larkin. He opened the rear door for Cyrus, and then climbed back in himself. Jasper followed.

"Tallmadge," Cyrus said.

"You pronounced it correctly. That's unusual. Good for you."

"What do you want?"

"How is Elsbeth?"

"Alive."

"And singing like a songbird, considering you made it to the Blue Line before we saw you. You gave her the royal treatment, I'm sure."

Cyrus let the silence stretch. Jasper wondered if there was a bomb under the car or if there were more cars waiting just around the corner. This had been a terrible idea.

"Silas was a good man," Tallmadge said. "A snob, but they're all like that. What do you call them? Libertines?" His laugh sounded like a garbage disposal. "Too many bodies, Counselor. Now, everyone is asking questions they shouldn't. Mostly they're blaming you."

"Not for long," Cyrus replied.

Tallmadge shifted his body. The leather seat scrunched. "Wesley—Silas's bodyguard—he had mental health problems. I've got a psychiatric report saying he struggled with dissociative identity disorder. Or that's what it will say."

"What are you offering?"

"Walk away, and I'll make sure Silas's son gets that report. You'll be off the hook for what happened in Philadelphia. Things will return to normal."

Cyrus gestured for Jasper to reply to that one.

He took a page from Nora's playbook: "Go to hell."

There was that laugh again. Tallmadge definitely should see a doctor. "Did you know the Washingtons have hired their family attorney to argue this case? Gabriel Jay. Two decades of experience, half of it as a trial lawyer. I heard they called him the Shark back in the day. Tore through details like chum."

"Are you finished?" Cyrus asked.

"This evidence. You've made copies?"

"Of course."

"And if you lose—which you will—your people will publish the evidence anyway. Slip it to some online journal?"

"They will."

"People deserve to know," Jasper said.

"Why? Because it's true?" Tallmadge adjusted the rearview mirror and stared at Jasper. "Look at these buildings. These monuments. They're true because they're here. Magnificent structures built to honor a magnificent past. You want to dig up the side and show off a hairline crack. I've got news for you, boy: people don't want to see the flaws in their own houses, or their pasts. They want them to stay neat and tidy."

"I didn't build it," Jasper said. "I didn't even break it. I just found it."

"So that's a hard no."

"Yes."

Tallmadge sighed, then shrugged his massive shoulders. "You got balls, kid."

"I've got a list of people who are dead because of you," Jasper said. "And you can choke on it."

CHAPTER FORTY-TWO

Jasper watched the BMW drive ahead, then stop and let Tallmadge out by the fountain. He wondered if anybody else could hear his heart slamming against his chest.

"Not the words I would have chosen," Cyrus said, "but well stated."

Jasper took out the small tape recorder and hit STOP. "How did you know he would be here?"

"People make poor decisions when they're scared." Cyrus pocketed the recorder. "Shall we?"

Jasper guessed there were about fifty people crowded around the fountain. Women in dresses and heels and expensive furs, men in ties and suits and heavy overcoats. Some were stoic, their hands hovering over their coat pockets, glaring at Jasper as he walked to a door under the right side of the expansive staircase. Chief Justice Fletcher waited for them next to a guy that could've been Silas's twin. He had the same large frame and nose, but he was thinner, his hair shorter. As they got closer, Jasper realized he was younger, too. Beside him stood a short, thick man wearing circular frames and holding a briefcase. The Shark.

"Your Honor," Cyrus said with a nod.

"Mr. Barnes." Fletcher motioned to the Silas look-alike. "Virgil Washington, Silas's son."

"I am deeply sorry for your loss," Cyrus said.

Jasper saw the rage and hatred and sorrow flashing across Virgil's face.

"Let's get on with it then," Fletcher said.

He led them up three flights of switchback steps and down a long hallway to a set of large, wooden doors. The library—and it deserved that title, *the* library—was more like a block of wood carved in excruciating detail so somebody could put down carpet and paint the ceiling. A row of chandeliers hung down the center of the reading room and lit up the space like a ballroom. Chairs were arranged in a seating area, with two tables set up to face a third, like a teacher's desk. It was all so beautiful Jasper almost forgot it might be the scene of his death sentence.

"Mr. Jay, on the right," Fletcher said, "Mr. Mansfield, the left." He walked around his table and put on his black robe. Piled in front of him were stacks of folders. "I'll give you a few minutes to get organized."

"That won't be necessary, Your Honor," Jay announced.

"Kiss-ass," Nora muttered.

Jasper set his folder down and took out the brief. The words swam before his eyes. He was breathing harder, but it wasn't really helping him get more air into his lungs, and then he was leaning against the table and Cyrus was helping him into a chair. Jasper's fingers buzzed and his face was on fire.

"Breathe," Cyrus whispered.

"It feels like I'm under water and in the middle of a bonfire at the same time."

Jasper closed his eyes and focused on each breath. Slowly, like when your arm stops tingling from being asleep, he began to feel normal again.

What if that happened during his argument?

"Entrapment," Sybil whispered behind him. "No third *t*."

"Are we ready, then?" Fletcher asked.

"Mr. Chief Justice," Jay said, standing, "may I say what an honor it is to argue in front of you today, in a building filled with such immense history."

"Noted," Fletcher said, putting on his reading glasses. "Each of you will have thirty minutes to present your arguments and answer my questions. I'll give you each a one-minute warning. This is not a trial; there will be no objections." He looked over his glasses at each of them. "Any questions?"

Jasper thought he felt that buzzing sensation starting again. He took three deep breaths through his nose.

"As the petitioner, Mr. Mansfield, you will argue first. It is also your right to reserve time to rebut Mr. Jay when his time has expired. You may begin."

Jasper stood. He glanced at the brief. Notes filled the margins. He tried to swallow, but his throat was closing up. How long had he been standing there? Five seconds? A minute?

"Mr. Mansfield," Fletcher said. "I *said* you may begin."

"Yes, Your Honor." Jasper inhaled deeply. "It's really all about this diary we found."

"Which has already been authenticated by a Smithsonian curator," the Chief Justice said in Jay's general direction, "so you can save yourself time arguing against its authenticity."

Jay coughed.

"In May of 1779," Jasper said, "the Patriot general, Benedict Arnold, started secretly talking with this British spy named John André. After about a year-and-a half of negotiating, Arnold agreed to give up his new post at the military fort, West Point, and the British would give him cash and a new command in their army. But in September of 1780, André got captured, and the plot went public. Arnold ran to the British, got his military appointment, and ended up leading several attacks against the Patriots."

"I do hope you're not going to walk us through the entire Revolution," Fletcher said pointedly.

"No, Your Honor." Jasper found his place on the brief. "What I'm arguing is that Joseph Reed coerced Arnold to switch sides. He had an officer on Arnold's staff named Ira Boswell whisper in Arnold's ear that

225

he should betray America." Jasper said the word in his head. *No third* t. "I'm arguing entrapment."

Jasper fumbled around for the diary copies.

"Exhibit C."

"A," Sybil whispered.

The papers stuck to each other and Jasper spilled the whole pile on the ground. His face went hot. Jay made some noise under his breath.

"Well, which one is it, Mr. Mansfield?" Fletcher asked.

"Uh. Exhibit A, Your Honor. The diary entry from June 13th, 1779, where Ira's wife sees a guy come over to talk with her husband." Jasper fumbled for the next diary entry. "On the 23rd—um . . . Exhibit C— we find out that it's Reed, and the details of the entrapment."

"Which I'm sure Mr. Jay will argue is hearsay," Fletcher said. "Why don't you just clear that up for us now."

Thank God for Sybil. So far, she'd anticipated this thing down to the second.

"Most of what Alice wrote was pretty boring," Jasper said. "Weather. Gossip. Neighbors and when they visited. Other events during the war. A lot of those exact details appear in other journals from the same time period, like the one I included in Exhibit D from Elizabeth Drinker. She was a wealthy Quaker lady in Philadelphia who kept a famous diary."

"So her entries are otherwise reliable," Fletcher said. "Glad that's out of the way. Now, can we get to your use of *Jacobson v. United States?*"

Jasper checked his watch. Eight minutes. He needed to pick up the pace if they wanted to have time to put down their landmine in rebuttal.

"To prove that someone was entrapped by a government agent," Jasper said, "you have to show two things: that he wasn't the type of person to commit treason, and that he did it because of the person who suggested it."

"I went to law school, Mr. Mansfield. I know the case. And you haven't convinced me."

Jasper didn't need his notes for this one—he'd read too many biographies. "Arnold risked his life at a couple big battles during the war. He almost died for America, gave his leg for the Cause. And he fought for years without getting paid. A guy who does that isn't predisposed to commit treason."

"Maybe not. But you have not—and I do not believe you can—prove that he ultimately committed treason because of what Ira Boswell may or may not have 'whispered' to him. As you said, Arnold had started talking with John André about switching sides in May—a full month before this meeting Reed had with Boswell."

"But Arnold cut off communications with André later that year—in October. And . . . the letters . . . Peggy . . ." Jasper could feel the stares on his back, sense the Libertines waiting to haul him off to their gallows. "His wife burned most of his letters and diaries, so we don't actually know what motivated him to change sides, exactly."

Fletcher took off his glasses. "Are you trying to say that you're not sure?"

"No. I'm saying that no proof exists that Ira Boswell's influence wasn't the reason."

"Oh, good God." Fletcher looked past Jasper to Sybil and Cyrus. "Did one of you give him this advice?"

Jasper's face was burning now. "Exhibit F, Your Honor. In July of 1780, Reed wrote his wife a letter asking her to secretly give some money from her fundraising for the soldiers to the Boswells."

"And how, exactly, does that help you prove entrapment?"

"Because Reed was keeping his end of the bargain," Jasper argued. "The deal was money, and so he paid up because Ira had persuaded Arnold to change sides."

"That," Fletcher said, "is a stretch."

"It's also true!" A little too much heat in that response. Jasper could hear Sheldon: *Take it down a notch, diva.*

"Excuse me, young man?"

Jasper floundered for Elsbeth's signed statement. How had the table become a hurricane of papers in ten—no, crap, fourteen—minutes. "Your Honor: why would the Libertines—"

"Who?"

"The True Sons," Jasper said. "Why would they keep trying to kill everybody who got close to Boswell—like, right after you left our meeting in Philly?" He finally found Elsbeth's testimony, and almost shook it at Jay, gloating. "Because they knew he'd been into some shady stuff and wanted to keep it quiet. Elsbeth Reed says exactly that in her statement."

The Chief Justice went quiet. He looked behind Jasper at the crowd of Libertines, maybe worried they might shoot up his library, too. Eventually, he flipped through his brief to the statement. "She also claims to be an operative in a clandestine network called the Culper Ring run by a, uh . . . a Mr. Tallmadge."

Sharp inhales broke the silence, followed by ripples of whispered words. The landmine was planted.

Now Jasper just needed Jay to step on it.

"Tallmadge runs the security for their organization," Jasper said, "but actually he's been doing a lot more. Like trying to keep what Reed did quiet. So the cover-up points to the crime."

Fletcher mumbled something to himself. "What else?"

"I'm gonna save the rest of my time, Your Honor."

"Young man." Fletcher's voice sounded worried. "You haven't yet made your argument clear. Are you certain that you want to reserve the remainder of your time?"

Jasper sat down.

"All right, then. Mr. Jay, the floor is yours."

Jay took about thirty seconds to stand and button his gaudy pinstriped suit jacket. "Your Honor, for the time being, I would like to set aside the character assassination attempted by Mr. Mansfield, as well as his clumsily constructed conspiracy theories. Their purpose is clear:

distraction from a weak argument. I would prefer to, instead, dismantle this ridiculous entrapment defense."

Jay flipped through one legal pad, then another, arranging them on the table like weapons. What was it that Tallmadge had said about him? *He tears through details like chum.*

"Let us assume that Joseph Reed did ask Lieutenant Ira Boswell to encourage Arnold to shift his allegiance to the British. Does any proof exist that Lieutenant Boswell actually followed this directive? No. Reed's payment to Ira proves absolutely nothing. In fact, it further illustrates the greatness of a couple already known to be philanthropic."

"Indulge me, Mr. Jay," Fletcher said. "If Boswell did follow through with Mr. Reed's directive—"

"Hypothetically."

"Yes, *hypothetically*, what reason would you have to contest the entrapment defense?"

"Your Honor, can we seriously believe that Benedict Arnold had no predisposition to commit treason? He *married* the daughter of a Loyalist. His letters are filled with anger over his treatment by the Continental Congress. And the court-martial for his use of military wagons for personal business began months before this supposed meeting between Reed and Boswell. If these are not predispositions, what are?"

Jay smoothed out his suit. "There is no way around it: Arnold is likely to have committed treason without any inducement from Joseph Reed. The entrapment test fails."

Jasper didn't like the way Fletcher's shoulders sank, like he agreed. "And what about this alleged cover up—this Culper Ring run by Mr. Tallmadge."

Jay didn't need to blunder around for his document. He had that paper in hand before Fletcher finished his sentence. "Mr. Tallmadge has also signed a sworn statement refuting Ms. Reed. Yes, she worked for him, but the firm engages in just that: providing protection details for high-ranking members of our organization. Any murder or attempted murder on her part to protect historical secrets—which have not even been proven to be real—were entirely of her own doing."

"Meaning, you'll gladly force me to rule on conflicting testimony."

"Aside from Ms. Reed's word, Your Honor, there is absolutely no evidence."

In his head, Jasper heard the *click* of the landmine arming itself.

Jay had stepped right on it.

"Are you finished, Mr. Jay?" Fletcher asked.

"I am, Your Honor."

"Mr. Mansfield, you have twelve minutes left for your rebuttal."

Jasper turned around to get the recorder from Cyrus, along with the tiny, portable speakers. The exchange was slow, deliberate. Jasper made sure to stare down Tallmadge, who was sitting right next to Virgil Washington.

"Your Honor," Jasper said, "Mr. Jay says there's no evidence to support Mr. Tallmadge's role in this cover up. But there is. I'd like to play an audio file submitted as Exhibit H."

Jay shot up out of his chair. "Your Honor—"

"This is not a trial. You do not get to object."

"But Your Honor—"

"*Silence*, Mr. Jay."

Jay shut up.

"You cannot enter evidence at this stage into the brief, Mr. Mansfield," Fletcher said. "Mr. Jay has not had a chance to hear or prepare statements against it. And neither can we validate the person on it is who you claim him or her to be." Fletcher leaned forward and lowered his voice a little. "This will not help you, son."

Jasper figured when the Chief Justice of United Sates gave you legal advice, you took it. But this wasn't just any evidence.

"I still want to play it," Jasper said.

"I will not give you a second more than your allotted time. Do you understand?"

"Yes, Your Honor."

Fletcher folded his arms over his barrel chest. "Let's hear it."

Jasper hooked the recorder up to the speakers and cranked up the volume. It was a lot of ruffling at first—fabric rubbing against the microphone. Then, Tallmadge's voice echoed across the library.

"Oh, for Christ's sake . . . I'm alone, except for my driver. And he's carrying, just like you."

The conversation from thirty minutes ago in the BMW continued on in all its glorious detail.

Jasper kept his head down, staring at the tabletop because he wasn't sure where else to look. Not at the Chief Justice—he couldn't handle that yet. He'd find out soon enough if this move had had the intended impact. Jay hadn't stirred. Had he been shocked into paralysis? Hopefully. More like obliterated. He was probably wondering how he'd walked right into this.

After the un-Supreme Court like burn of "choke on it," Jasper pressed the STOP button. The silence stretched. His watch said time was up. There was no noise, like the world had paused itself to figure out what to do next.

Jasper turned around just as Virgil threw the punch. It was weirdly formal—a guy in a suit punching another guy in a suit with a bunch of people wearing nice clothes sitting on the sidelines watching. Tallmadge never saw Washington's fist coming, or maybe he just couldn't get out of the way in time. The blow caught him right on the jaw, and he crumpled, taking out four chairs and a couple Libertines on his descent—a walrus hitting the deck.

Somebody screamed and Virgil's bodyguards leapt into action, dragging Tallmadge from the courtroom. Libertines pointed and yelled and exchanged looks of shocked outrage. Fletcher banged his fist on the table and shouted, probably wishing he'd brought his gavel. He'd lost control of the room. His was no longer the main event.

The circus had a better act.

"*I will have order!*" Fletcher shouted.

By the fifth time he hollered the words, they had their intended effect. Or maybe everything had just sunk in enough for the Libertines to quiet down. Virgil righted the chairs Tallmadge had knocked over and walked up to Jay. They spoke quietly for a minute. Jasper felt that same sensation of roasting and freezing.

"Your Honor." Jay cleared his throat. "If it pleases the court, I would like a brief recess to discuss terms with Mr. Mansfield."

"Too bad."

"Your Honor?"

"You wanted this hearing, and now you're going to listen to my ruling."

"We, too, are willing to discuss terms," Cyrus said quickly, joining Jasper at the table.

"I didn't ask what you were willing to do, did I, Mr. Barnes?" Fletcher snapped. "Now, take your seats."

Jasper gripped the table. He'd been so sure it was over.

"If you ask me, all of your ancestors would be ashamed of you. But no one's asking me, are they?" Fletcher huffed and puffed as he stacked the briefs back in their folders. "I do not know if Lieutenant Ira Boswell spoke with Arnold about changing sides or whether such a discussion influenced the general to eventually commit treason. No one can. And I will certainly not conclude that George Washington was in any way involved."

Jasper actually felt himself fall forward. This couldn't be happening. If he ran now, could he make it to the doors before they tackled him? Or would the Libertines just gun him down?

"But this is not a trial on the posthumous guilt or innocence of Benedict Arnold," Fletcher continued. "This hearing is about whether or not this evidence suggests Joseph Reed *may* have entrapped Arnold via Lieutenant Ira Boswell, and on that matter the answer is clear. Alice's diary entry is reliable. I have no reason to believe she lied about what her husband told her. The letter Reed wrote to his wife regarding the payment to Boswell is highly irregular and, thus, highly suspicious. I have every reason to believe that it was, indeed, meant to fulfill the terms of the agreed bribe."

Fletcher stood, and the whole room stood with him. "Therefore, I will gladly fulfill my obligation as intermediary and broker whatever deal you, Mr. Barnes, would like to make."

Nora shouted and Sybil clapped, then grabbed her shoulder, clearly regretting it. Jasper wondered if he was flying—if gravity had actually stopped existing and he'd knock into the chandeliers. Cyrus's granite face cracked into a wide smile that seemed so out of place, it kind of freaked Jasper out—like a statue coming to life. Cyrus shook Jasper's hand, which turned into a brief hug. Behind them, the library had burst into murmuring.

"The terms, then?" Fletcher asked.

Cyrus withdrew documents from his briefcase and handed Fletcher and Jay each a copy. "On behalf of the League Directors, I request a permanent end of all hostilities, including but not limited to: a suspension of the dueling requirement and reprisals for individuals who refuse their challenges. In exchange, we will keep Reed's entrapment a secret."

"What say you to that, Mr. Jay?"

He and Virgil read the document, then did some more whispering. "Those terms are acceptable, Your Honor," Jay finally said.

"Isn't that grand." Fletcher took out a pen and signed the document. Virgil and Cyrus approached the table and added their signatures. "Now, if you would all be so kind as to get the *hell* out of my library. There are actual *constitutional* duties that require my attention in the morning."

The Libertines left first. Not one of them gave Jasper so much as a nasty look—it was all blank stares. They were stunned.

Outside, by the fountain, Virgil stood with a single bodyguard. He said something to the man, who came over and asked Larkin if Jasper would speak with him.

"I am—" Virgil started. Up this close, Jasper could see the red eyes, the sadness mixed with a little bit of shock. On top of his dad dying so suddenly, this kid was having a seriously bad week. "*We* are forever indebted to you for exposing this . . . this treachery within our organization. On behalf of the True Sons of Liberty, I would like to thank you." He swallowed, looking at the ground, clearly trying not to cry. "My father never celebrated the violence, like others. I wish he was here to see its end."

"I actually know exactly how you feel." Jasper extended his hand. Virgil studied it for a second, then shook it. "There's this phrase my dad liked. *Nil desperandum.* It was our family motto. It means—"

"Never despair," Virgil finished.

Libertines knew their Latin, apparently. "It helped me, after he died. It didn't make everything better, but it helped."

Virgil studied the Capitol Building across the street, then took in a deep breath. "Thank you. I hope we meet again someday, under better circumstances."

"I'm pretty sure any circumstances would qualify as better."

Virgil actually smiled. "Yes, I suppose so."

They shook hands again, and then Virgil walked to the street and got into a waiting car.

EPILOGUE

Jasper had already sweated through his shirt when Pastor Bob finished his little sermon. It was June—way hotter than his dad's funeral had been. More crowded, too. There were at least a hundred people at the cemetery: League bigwigs and their families, a handful of students who'd come down after finals. Jasper even spotted Chillingsworth in the back next to Kingsley.

Nora squeezed Jasper's hand. She'd dug out a black sleeveless dress from somebody's closet for the occasion. "You're up," she said.

Jasper walked around his dad's gravestone, past a couple in their fifties. They were short, stocky, and dark-haired. The woman was crying—of course she was crying. It was like Director Forrest had said: loss was a part of membership.

Jasper stopped at the edge of the new plot where they'd just lowered Sheldon's casket. "I want to thank everybody for coming," he said. "I know it was a long drive."

He knew they expected him to say something else—he expected himself to say something else. It had been Jasper's idea to bury Sheldon here; he'd been banned from the Burr plot for obvious reasons. But what, exactly was a person supposed to say at the burial of a traitor? A traitor who was also your friend? Who you'd killed?

Something true.

"Sheldon was my friend," Jasper said. "I miss him every day." There was that familiar burn at the edges of his eyes. "My first day at Juniper Hill, he gave me his bed. His literal bed. He took the one with no heater. He was always doing stuff like that. Helping me. With the research. On the range."

Sheldon's mom whimpered louder. His dad was crying now, too. Tucker was watching from some tree fifty yards away, headphones on, arms folded. Jasper wasn't sure he could keep it together for much longer.

"We all do things we wish we could take back. But those things we do aren't us. They're just pieces. My dad was pretty much all bad pieces."

Where was this even going? Maybe he should've written something down. Or maybe he just needed to dig deep—to speak from the gut. Because hadn't this whole thing come full circle? Wasn't the past just repeating itself?

"My ancestor was a traitor. But he did a lot of incredible stuff before that. Won big battles. Saved a lot of soldiers." Jasper didn't bother looking up at the audience to see how that landed. It didn't really matter. This wasn't about them. It was about Sheldon—about the memory of his friend's life and death and Jasper's role in both. "I guess what I'm trying to say is that nobody is all good or bad. It's not a percentage thing. I get that we remember people for how their life ends, but that's not fair, because it wipes out everything else good they did. We're all just trying to get by, and sometimes we really make a big mess. It doesn't make it any better, but it's still true."

He picked up a handful of fresh dirt and threw it on top of the casket—the killer honoring his victim. His brain still couldn't navigate the complex moral network that allowed him to mourn the person he'd slain. Maybe it never would. He'd carry and remember his friend's life and death forever.

"Thanks again for coming," he said after a while. If he kept talking, he'd be crying worse than Sheldon's mom. "There's going to be some food back at the hotel for anyone staying the night."

The goodbyes and handshakes blurred together. Colton made Jasper swear he'd visit Tennessee, but not in the summer. Apparently, it was hot as hell then. Tucker let Jasper hug him, which was a big step. Lacy was all waterworks and promises—*come visit St. Paul. I'll miss you.* Teachers and Directors milled around until it was just him and Nora staring at a hole in the ground, her arm around his waist.

"That was good," she said.

"I can't believe so many people came. I thought they'd boycott because of what he did."

"They came because of what you did."

A cloud passed overhead, giving them some shade. Jasper patted his pocket for his plane ticket and checked the departure time again. They should probably get going.

"So, it doesn't actually rain all the time in Seattle, right?" he asked. "Because I don't have a raincoat."

"Not in the summer."

"Does it get this hot?"

"Sometimes," Nora said.

"How far are you from where they filmed *Twilight*?"

"I'm seriously reconsidering my invitation."

"I'm just saying that if we're in the area, we should check it out."

"You can take my stepmom on a road trip one day. She's a huge fan." Nora kissed him on the cheek. "Our flight leaves at six."

"We should at least see the beach where they surfed," he called after her. "La Push."

Cyrus walked over from the parking lot, nodding at Nora as he passed her.

"So, do I have to call you Mr. Vice Chairman now?" Jasper asked.

"A mouthful, isn't it."

"You're gonna need new business cards."

Cyrus handed him one. The new embossed title glistened.

"You *would* already have this."

"Between the two of us, I think Sybil had them printed a while ago."

Two cemetery workers drove over in a four-wheeler and started filling the grave.

"Have you given any thought to my offer?" Cyrus asked.

"Not really sure a law internship is for me."

"Take the summer to think about it. Reach out if you change your mind."

"Maybe I'll find myself or something in Seattle."

They watched the two guys shovel for a while.

"Well," Cyrus said.

"Yeah."

"If you are ever in need of advice, you have my number."

Jasper went to shake his hand. Cyrus pulled him into a hug instead.

"You will always wonder if you did the right thing," Cyrus said in his ear. "But you shouldn't wonder, because *you did*."

Tears spilled down Jasper's cheeks. He didn't even try to stop himself—he didn't even care. He hugged Cyrus harder, using the guy's shirt collar as a tissue. The outburst faded, and they pulled away, parting with a handshake.

It was almost three now, and somehow hotter. Mosquitoes feasted on him. The cemetery workers in their overalls had to be miserable.

It seemed like something Jasper should be doing himself—a responsibility.

He didn't ask. He just grabbed the extra shovel from their four-wheeler, took off his tie, rolled up his sleeves, and began digging.

He hadn't asked them to stop, but they must have sensed that he needed to do this on his own—put his friend to rest. Burying Sheldon wouldn't be just empty words he'd trot out in some story recollection in the future. He was a part of this moment, hands dirty as he covered over this chapter of his life.

And there *was* a future, a place he hadn't even let his thoughts wander to before now because it had always seemed too elusive or too horrible to think about. But he was in it now—the rest of the story. Post-epilogue; or was it Chapter One? Whatever came next had to be better because it was exactly that: next.

HISTORICAL DISCLAIMER

This is a work of historical fiction, so I think it would be helpful to clarify where I have intervened into the historical record with fictional ideas.

Joseph Reed did *not* bribe a Continental officer to convince Benedict Arnold to switch sides at the supposed behest of George Washington. Arnold betrayed America all on his own for reasons that are frequently debated. *But*, I think Reed's campaign against Arnold definitely helped him over the cliff.

In the same manner, Lieutenant Ira Boswell did not exist, at least not to my knowledge. I suppose there might be an Ira Boswell, somewhere, and he might be a Lieutenant, but you get the point. I made him up.

Reed's hatred for Arnold, however, was very real, as are the details of other historical persons referenced. Only their descendants who make up the characters of this work are fictional.

Most sadly of all, the descendants of the Founding Fathers have not gathered into ancestral clans or sought to engage in honor duels against those who opposed their ancestors. While I have never met any of these descendants personally, I will assume they are a peaceful bunch. And if this is true, then I must sadly surmise that there probably isn't a league comprised of America's villains—though I think we can all agree that would be really awesome. I sincerely hope one develops (minus the dueling).

Lastly: if I suddenly disappear, consider it a sign that everything above is actually true and I am being interrogated in a basement somewhere by an agent of the new-and-improved Culper Ring. Please contact the FBI. Or Kingsley.

NOTES

Benedict Arnold

Benedict Arnold was an actual person responsible for shocking acts of heroism on behalf of America and the equally shocking act of treason he committed during the Revolutionary War. I have tampered with his life the least, that is to say, everything in this book concerning him (and his historically hot wife, Peggy) *except his interactions with Ira Boswell* are factual.

Joseph Reed

Joseph Reed is, by all accounts, a Founding Father stud; but he was also sort of conniving, and definitely politically savvy. While I made up his cunning provocation of Arnold, I'm not totally certain it would have been outside his character. Nearly all of his actual life and activities in this book are accurate, including his governorship (an office that was then called President of the Executive Council) of Pennsylvania, and his public and private attacks against Arnold. I can only assume that when Arnold did eventually turn, Reed felt burning vindication; I know I would have.

Reed's accomplishments are many, but I'll mention my favorite: as governor, he pushed for and oversaw the abolition of slavery from

Pennsylvania. That's awesome. Go Joseph Reed. Sorry I turned you into a monster.

The Culper Ring

General Washington's cunning use of clandestine operatives as part of the Culper Ring is complete historical fact and did impact the Patriot war effort at various points.

While the Culper Ring is not still active today, I don't think any of us would be surprised if the CIA still used this name as some inside joke that only super awesome agents get.

"Honor Culture" and the *Code Duello*

It is both true and downright hilarious that American culture once allowed (if not *demanded*) men of high social standing to solve their differences by blowing each other away with pistols (and, earlier, stabbing each other with swords). The *Code Duello* was very real and acted as a de facto handbook on these matters. Our Founding Fathers—as *Hamilton* mania has made very popular—lived and died (literally) by this "honor culture" for nearly two centuries. While it is also true that duels were not always fatal because a) dueling pistols were wildly inaccurate, and b) gentlemen often settled their issues beforehand or missed on purpose, fatalities abounded. Just ask Hamilton's family. Or any relative of the men *President* Andrew Jackson killed in duels. (Okay, he wasn't president yet when these duels occurred, but he *was* president when he repeatedly caned a would-be assassin in front of the Capitol Building. You literally cannot make this stuff up. Okay, actually you can, 'cause I made up a whole bunch of stuff for this book, but I'm not making up the story of Jackson beating that guy up.)

ACKNOWLEDGMENTS

Trying to get your first book published is like climbing Mt. Everest (assumes the author, who's watched a couple movies about climbing Mt. Everest). If you do it alone, there's a pretty good chance you'll die of hypothermia or get crushed by an avalanche or fall into some bottomless crevice with a million other people who have bravely/ stupidly gone before you, alone.

What you need is a sherpa to help you summit. Here are some of mine:

Kristy Landis, *the* Woman, who said, "No. Just . . . no," when I was seriously floating the idea of self-publishing this book in 2014 after facing yet another season of agent rejections. This book is for you because *of course* it is for you. Your wisdom reined in my drama that day and led to the Call just three months later. Thank you for believing in me when my drama-queen self despaired basically every five seconds, and for reminding me that writing is something I do, not somebody that I am.

Lauren Galit, World's Bossest Agent, who took a flyer on Jasper when he was just an overly dramatic kid buried in a story with way too many words. She always believed the concept was rock solid, read and edited about a hundred drafts, and got the book into the right hands at Sky Pony and Gotham. I could literally not ask for more in an agent. BOOM. And Caitlen Rubino-Bradway, co-agent at LKG and author in her own right, who suggested critical shifts in portrayals of violence that got to the heart of this novel and made that theme sing like a freaking songbird.

Alison Weiss, Editorial Director of Extreme Awesomeness, who kind of/sort of/definitely made me rewrite this entire book, which was as epically hard as it sounds but also totally necessary. Her ideas during massive brainstorm sessions saved the story from collapsing into giant plot holes and the author from collapsing into even bigger anxiety holes. I am indebted to her relentless work ethic, and often wonder if she is actually a robot. Alison. Rules.

Team Sky Pony, including Bethany Buck, Sammy Yuen, who absolutely slayed this cover; production editor Joshua Barnaby who did typesetting stuff and kept this book on schedule; and the tons of other people doing things behind the scenes to make this book possible.

Dave Connis, the Ultimate Traitor, who knows exactly what he did. He will never be forgiven.

Jayne Pillemer, who helped me streamline an early draft down to the bare essentials. Her advice—to find the story arc and stick to it— was some of the best I got in those early days.

My mom, Mary, who first read my really crappy ramblings in high school and told me that I should keep writing. And my dad, David, whose love of the Revolutionary Era got me hooked at an early age.

And God, who wove this passion for storytelling into my DNA and put the amazing people above in my life that let it become sort of a job.